4

Life's a Witch

Also by Brittany Geragotelis

What the Spell

Life's a Witch

A **LIFE'S A WITCH** BOOK

BRITTANY GERAGOTELIS

SIMON & SCHUSTER BFYR

NEW YORK LONDON TORONTO SYDNEY NEW DELHI

An imprint of Simon & Schuster Children's Publishing Division

1230 Avenue of the Americas, New York, New York 10020

SIMON & SCHUSTER BFYR is a trademark of Simon & Schuster, Inc.

For information about special discounts for bulk purchases, please contact Simon & Schuster Special Sales at 1-866-506-1949 or business@simonandschuster.com.

The Simon & Schuster Speakers Bureau can bring authors to your live event. For more information or to book an event, contact the Simon & Schuster Speakers Bureau at 1-866-248-3049 or visit our website at www.simonspeakers.com.

Book design by Krista Vossen

The text for this book is set in Granjon.

Manufactured in the United States of America

2 4 6 8 10 9 7 5 3 1

Library of Congress Cataloging-in-Publication Data

Geragotelis, Brittany.

Life's a witch / Brittany Geragotelis. — First edition.

pages cm

Life is a witch

Originally self-published as an e-book, 2011.

Summary: Popular high schooler Hadley Bishop, descendant of the first woman executed in the Salem witch trials, must face down an evil, supernatural presence from the past.

ISBN 978-1-4424-6655-5 (hardcover : alk. paper)

ISBN 978-1-4424-6657-9 (ebook) — ISBN 978-1-4424-6656-2 (pbk. : alk. paper)

[1. Witches—Fiction. 2. Supernatural—Fiction. 3. Magic—Fiction.] I. Title.

II. Title: Life is a witch.

PZ7.G29348Li 2013

[Fic]—dc23

2012047851

FIRST EDITION

To all the twitches out there who believed in me when no one else did

June 10, 1692

It was the day Bridget Bishop was sentenced to die and all she could think about was how she would never get the chance to see her daughter marry. She had had three husbands herself. With each marriage she'd learned something different about love and life, and had intended to share these lessons with her only daughter, Christian, so she might save her from some of the mistakes she herself had made.

For instance, make sure your husband-to-be has a strong heart, so people cannot accuse you of bewitching him if he suffers an untimely death, she thought with a sigh.

Then again, maybe the first lesson she should have taught Christian was how to go unnoticed. After all, wasn't it the fact that Bridget was considered a wanton woman that had landed her in the dank basement of the local jail, where she was now shackled? Her friends had warned her about wearing red. That the color seemed to elicit a reaction in the men of Salem Town and, of course, annoy the women whose men drooled after her. Not that she was the only one who donned the attention-drawing color—albeit none of the others also owned taverns. Several taverns actually, which in the 1600s was somewhat unseemly for a God-fearing woman. Men were usually the ones who controlled the flow of ale, and some thought it distasteful for a woman to be around so many inebriated men.

The thought of work made Bridget begin to fret over what was surely happening without her watchful eye on things. No doubt her barmaids were refilling steins for free and allowing the men to gamble. The places were probably in ruins without her. And likely, not nearly as fun.

But she supposed that soon, all of that would no longer be a concern. In the nearly two months since she'd been arrested on suspicions of witchcraft, time had ceased to exist for her. She never knew what hour it was, her cell had no windows and the criminals were all kept separate. But, given the steady flow of visitors she'd had over the past day, she knew that her time must surely be running out.

At least, that's what she'd gathered that morning when the reverend had read Bridget her last rites and asked if she had any confessions before meeting her maker. Bridget's answer had been the same as it had always been: that she'd never done anything in her life to harm another living thing. She'd barely been able to contain her anger as the man of God sighed and shook his head in disbelief before once again leaving her alone in her cell.

She still had no idea how the situation had gotten so out of control.

Before her mind could once again recollect the sequence of events that had brought about the trials, she heard a shuffling of feet and then the sound of a man clearing his throat from just outside the bars of her cell. Although it was rather dark in the room, she knew who her visitor was without seeing him.

"Reverend Samuel Parris," Bridget said evenly. "What brings thou here? I already had my meeting with the church today. . . ."

"You know that is not why I am here, Bridget," Reverend Parris said, walking toward her, the lantern in his hands casting an eerie glow across the cold stony space. He moved forward until his face was just inches away from the bars.

"Come to break me out then, have you?" she asked sarcastically, then snorted.

The reverend didn't answer, but instead looked around the room uncomfortably.

"Oh, come now, Samuel, I know there is aught you can do," Bridget said, her tone turning sad. She looked down at the chains that bound her hands, tugging at them halfheartedly. "I have been trying to get out of these confounded things since they brought me here, but it looks like it will take some serious magic to free me."

It was a rueful pun, but Reverend Parris remained stone-faced. Bridget rolled her eyes and sighed. She had long since accepted her fate.

"'Tis but a folly," she said, trying to catch her friend's eye. When she finally did, he gave her a small smile in return. "How did we get here, Samuel? How did things become such a mess?" She hesitated before asking her next question. It had been weighing on her mind since the whole thing had begun, and she could no longer hold it in. "Samuel, why did they accuse Sarah and Tituba of being witches? How could they have done that knowing . . . knowing what they know?"

"Children will be children, I suppose," he said softly, as if it were a suitable excuse for all that had happened.

"But they're *your* children, Samuel. At least Betty is. And

Abigail, your niece," she said. "And they are part of us! Why would they publicly accuse those in their own coven of casting spells on them? They had to have known that it would create this kind of hysteria."

"I suppose they did."

The reverend slowly bent down until he was eye level with Bridget, placing his right hand on one of the bars for support. At first she thought he might be feeling faint, but another glance revealed something else shining in his eyes. Surely she was seeing things, because she could have sworn there was the tiniest hint of hatred there.

"Oh, Bridget," he said slowly. "Don't look so surprised. I would have thought thou would have figured it all out by now, given your extraordinary ability to perceive the future. But perhaps you are not as powerful as you would have us think?"

Bridget felt as if the wind had been knocked out of her. The truth of what Samuel said hit her harder than even the initial accusation of witchcraft. But she was a proud woman and the last thing she'd do is let anyone see her weaknesses. Let alone her enemy.

"Well, you know better than anyone that what we do isn't exact," Bridget said with a shrug, even though she felt like lashing out at him. "So, why then, Samuel? Why turn your back on your own kind? Your coven? Was it because the Cleri would not elect you its leader?"

The Cleri was Salem's secret troupe of witches—well, they had been a secret until recently at least—and the biggest coven in Massachusetts. When Bridget uttered their name, Samuel let out a laugh, low at first and then hearty as it moved through his body. The sound was unlike anything Bridget had ever heard, and for the first time in the thirty years she'd known the reverend, she realized she never really *knew* him at all. What was worse, since he was a member of the Cleri himself, she'd taught him many of her secrets over the years. Some of which, if in the wrong hands, would prove to be dangerous to everyone around them.

"All you had to do was vote me in," he spat. "No one would have done a better job of leading and shaping the Cleri than I. We could have been the most powerful coven in New England. Possibly even the world. But every time I raised one of my ideas, you overruled me. You treated me as insignificant. As if you cared nothing for me or my plans."

Bridget kept her mouth shut, but her mind was racing, trying desperately to think of a way out of her current predicament. Testing the chains' strength again, she whispered, "Oxum expedis," and put all her energy into trying to free her hands. But a slight tug later, she realized she wasn't going anywhere.

"Ah, yes," Samuel said smugly. "You have no doubt noticed that the chains are difficult—nay, impossible—to break. I suppose I am not as impaired in my spell casting as you may have assumed."

Bridget couldn't believe what she was hearing. The man she'd trusted day in and day out was now saying that she was a prisoner *because* of him. That he was jealous of her power and wanted to run the Cleri. And that was why she would die today.

"I never wanted to dominate the Cleri," she said honestly. "All I wanted to do was oversee my pubs, spend time with my daughter, and perhaps marry once more. That is all."

"I know. And that is most infuriating. Your lack of imagination is *tragic*," he said. "If you had just seen things my way, used your powers for something more than mere small-scale trickery, I would not have had to do any of this." He swept his arms around the room grandly as if he were giving a tour of the dungeon, rather than confessing his sins.

"I told you then and I will tell you now, Samuel. It goes against the witch's oath to use her powers for personal gain or wrongdoing. The line between dark and light is thin and we have all heard what happens to those who confuse the two."

"Indeed," Samuel answered, raising an eyebrow at her mischievously. "Those witches become *infamous*. And so will I once all this is over."

Bridget was getting ready to argue with him when half a dozen guards entered the small corridor outside her chamber and gestured to Samuel that it was time for him to leave. He nodded in assent and then turned back once more to look at her.

She thought he might be remorseful after so many years of working beside her, but she discerned nothing. Which was what Bridget was beginning to feel.

Nothing.

"I truly wish it did not have to end like this, Bridget," he said. To the guards it probably sounded like a good-bye, but she knew better. Samuel meant it as a justification of his despicable actions. And whether he was being genuine or just saying it because they had an audience didn't really matter. The truth was, there was nothing anyone could do for her now. Her time was up.

But things were far from being over. Samuel may have bound her powers, making it impossible for her to get out of her chains, but that didn't mean she didn't have abilities that she could still use.

She needed to reach her daughter.

Bridget had begged Christian to stay home that day so she wouldn't have to witness her own mother's execution. Which meant Bridget couldn't warn her face-to-face about Samuel's plan. Instead, Bridget fell back on one of her oldest skills.

My darling, are you there?

Bridget sent the message from her mind to her daughter's, much like she used to when Christian was a child. She had used this particular gift when trying to teach Christian how to listen to her conscience growing up. But it had promptly back-fired when Christian's friends told her that they didn't *actually* hear the voice of their conscience in *their* heads. When her daughter figured out that it was her, Christian forbade Bridget to use the powers again unless Christian initiated it.

Given the current circumstances, however, Bridget decided that Christian would forgive her this time.

I am here, Mother. Are you all right? What is happening?

Bridget winced at the pain she could feel in her daughter's voice. She knew that her death would weigh heavily on her only child, and now she had to admit that the only family Christian would have left might be working against her. This made Bridget feel even worse about leaving. Bridget tried to clear her mind so none of her anxiety would transfer to her daughter.

Everything is fine, child. I have had several visitors today and some lovely conversation. Her white lies hardly mattered now. *There is something I need to talk to you about and I do not have much time . . .*

Yes, Mama?

There is a traitor among the coven. Reverend Parris is not your friend. He is hungry for power and will do anything to attain it. He is the one who divulged the names of our sister witches. I am not sure whether he will come after you and the rest of the Cleri, but you must get away from him in order to stand any chance of survival.

There was a pause on Christian's end and Bridget could tell

that she was trying to make sense of what her mother had said. Finally, she responded.

I understand. Do I have time to tell the others?

I am not sure who can be trusted. It is probably best if you just leave quietly and without notice.

Okay. I will gather my things right away. Where am I to go? Christian was asking this more to herself than to her mother, but Bridget had an answer.

Do you remember where we spent our summers when you were little? Go there. Nobody knows about the cabin, which means they should not be able to find you. Go there, hide, and be safe, my child.

Bridget could sense the pain her daughter was feeling as if it were her own heart breaking. Perhaps it was just as well that Christian had forbidden her from entering her mind. Sometimes it was simply too overwhelming to feel another's emotions.

"It is time, Goodwife Bishop," one of the guards said, appearing in the doorway after escorting Samuel out of the dungeon and unlocking her cell door. She noticed that he said it as if they were heading out for a walk, not off to her execution.

Bridget nodded and walked over to meet the guard at the door. She held out her hands, hoping they'd take off her shackles and give her one last chance to save herself. But her luck had run out. The man took hold of her arms and began to pull her to the front of the building. She didn't put up a fight. Instead, she spent her last living moments saying her good-byes.

They are calling me now, Christian. It is my wish that you go right away and do everything you can to live a safe and happy life. But promise me this: if they do find you . . . fight them. Fight for me. I love you to eternity, darling. I will always be with you.

I love you, too, Mother. Bridget could sense that her daughter was weeping uncontrollably now, and she had to pull away before Christian could experience what was about to happen to her.

By this time, the guard had already led her outside and through the square to the large wooden structure, standing high above the hundreds of townspeople who'd gathered on Gallows Hill to watch. Bridget kept her head down as she moved through the crowd, being careful not to trip while making her way up the crudely constructed stairs. Bridget knew people hadn't expected that the law would carry out its chosen form of justice so swiftly, but here she was.

A big black X was painted across the boards and she took her place on top of the dark lines. Lifting her bare feet, she examined with curiosity the black marks that now decorated them. When she finally looked up at the audience that had congregated in front of her, she saw a mix of friends and enemies. On some faces there was sadness, even a few tears rolling down dirty cheeks. There were more, though, who looked smug, even pleased, to see her up there.

This is what fear does to people, she thought. Bridget knew these bystanders weren't at fault, not directly anyway. The person responsible for these horrific trials was another witch, same as her. Samuel Parris. All because she wasn't willing to use her magic in the ways he wanted.

The sheriff slipped the noose around Bridget's neck and tightened it until it began to make breathing difficult. Still, she kept her chin up and refused to cry.

"Do you have any final words, Witch Bishop?" he asked her.

Bridget swallowed hard and hoped that her voice would remain strong. "Just that I am as innocent as the child unborn," she addressed the crowd loudly. "I have made no contact with the Devil. I have never seen him before in my life. I am innocent."

Hushed conversations began all around her and she could

hear a few people begin to object, but the hood was already being thrown over her head, blocking out any chance to see who was saying what.

"My allegiance is with my maker and even in death I will always do thy will." The prayer was barely above a whisper, but it filled her with a calmness she hadn't felt since before she'd been arrested. "Goodness will *always* prevail and evil *will* be punished. As God is my witness I will make *sure* of that."

And with those final words, the floor dropped out from beneath her and Bridget Bishop fell to the darkness below.

Chapter One

My body jerked violently as I woke up, just as the woman fell to her death. I was breathing heavily and my hair was matted to my head with sweat. My heart beat as if I'd just run a marathon, even though I'd been asleep for hours.

I looked over at the digital clock on my nightstand and cursed when I saw what time it was. I didn't have to be up for school for another hour at least, but I knew from experience that once I'd had this particular dream, there was no going back to sleep for me.

Great. So I guess I'll be applying extra foundation to cover the bags under my eyes today. I bet no one else has to worry about their beauty sleep being interrupted by the memories of a woman killed during the Salem witch trials.

I sighed and threw back my covers dramatically before hopping out of bed and making my way over to the bathroom. After pulling open the shower curtain, I turned the knobs in the tub until steam filled the room. A quick glance in the mirror showed me what I'd feared: I looked like I'd gotten only four hours of sleep.

That was actually the truth. I'd stayed up extra late, catching up with people on Facebook and adding friends who'd requested me. By the time I'd forced myself to crawl into bed, I'd accepted over twenty-five new people. My count was now at 11,280.

Did I know everyone on my friends list? No. But there was a very good chance they all knew me. I guess I'm what you'd call "popular" at my school. Not to sound snobby, but people seemed to be *drawn* to me. It's always been this way, and after a while, I stopped questioning it. Because who really wants to question popularity? Unless you're on the sucky side of it, of course.

I pulled at the bags under my eyes until they disappeared into my face. When I let them go, the puffiness returned, making me look much older than my seventeen years.

"Gross," I said under my breath, and made a face at my reflection. Knowing what I had to do to rectify the situation, I concentrated on the dark circles and said, "Delemin barrit."

I blinked and they'd disappeared. Smiling, I admired my fresh-looking skin from various angles, and then stepped into the shower and relaxed under the stream. Placing my hands on the wall in front of me, I let my head fall forward so the water was pounding across my neck and shoulders. Whenever I dreamed about Bridget Bishop, I woke up with the worst pain in my upper body. The rational part of me knew it was probably because of the stress, but the magical part of me wondered if my neck hurt because I'd been connected to Bridget when she was hanged in my dream.

An hour later, I was all washed up and heading downstairs to eat and watch CNN. Not many people my age watch the news, but I feel it's important to be knowledgeable on what's going on in the world. I hate being unprepared when people bring up current events. Besides, I think it's important to try to fight the stereotype that pretty girls can't also be smart.

I've been told on several occasions that I'm both.

I pushed the power button on the remote, then took the box of Fruity Pebbles out of the pantry and poured myself a generous bowl. Plopping down in the chair right in front of the TV, I let my legs hang over the armrest and started munching away. Breakfast is the most important meal of the day and I never missed an opportunity to start my day off on the right foot.

I tried to pay attention to what the anchors were saying on the screen, but after a few minutes, my mind wandered back to my dream. It was one I'd had before. Hundreds of times, actually. But it didn't matter how many times I dreamed it, I was always left feeling uneasy. Beyond the fact that it was totally messed up to watch this woman be hanged over and over again, I knew that what I was seeing had *really* happened.

And to top it off, she happened to be related to me.

Okay, so the woman was a few dozen "greats" back, but it was true. I'm a direct descendant of Bridget Bishop. You'd think that'd be a fun fact I could throw out at parties, but people got a bit wigged out when you told them that your great-great-grandmother times twenty was sentenced to death by hanging for being a witch during the Salem witch trials.

Go figure.

And if that wasn't disturbing enough, the fact that I had to watch it happen over and over again . . . well, they don't call them nightmares for nothing.

This time was different, though. I'd never heard the conversation between Bridget and her daughter before. The exchange had left me feeling even more emotionally drained than usual. Not just because of the words they'd shared but because it seemed as if my mom had inherited more than just her good looks from Great-Great-Grandma Bridget. Since I could remember, my mom could always communicate with me telepathically. The only difference between our situation and that of our ancestors' was that I'd learned early on how to block my mom out when I didn't want her in my head.

This new wrinkle gave me something to think about, and I made a mental note to talk to my mom about it later.

When my spoon hit the bottom of my empty bowl, I was brought back to reality. Tossing my dirty dish into the sink, I glanced at the clock on the stove. I had only about a half hour to finish getting ready for school, and even with the little magical touch-up I'd given myself earlier, I still had to figure out what I was going to wear, and do my hair and makeup.

With a glance back at the TV, which was still blaring across the room, I said, "Octo alermo." As I walked away, the screen shut off behind me.

I've always loved the sound that high heels make as I walk. *Click-clack. Click-clack.* Heels make a statement. They convey power, sophistication, and sex with every step. *Click-power. Click-sophistication. Click-sex.* Sure, they're a bit uncomfortable and not very realistic to walk around a high school campus in all day, but the message they send makes the pain totally worth it.

I held my head high and shoulders back and gazed straight ahead as I click-clacked my way across the parking lot, reveling in the fact that I could see the people I was passing but they couldn't see me watching them from behind my superdark sunglasses. Another thing I learned early on was that having an air of mystery about yourself can only work to your advantage. And you should *never* let go of all your secrets.

I spotted my group of friends before any of them saw me, and studied them critically. Bethany, Sofia, and Trish sat huddled on the steps of the school speaking quietly to each other. Probably about the latest gossip or even possibly about me. You never knew with those three. Their collective look was polished from head to toe and so similar that you'd think they'd gotten dressed out of the same closet. Only I knew that the kind of flawless they exuded took over an hour and a half to perfect. And that would be a secret that I'd take to my grave.

Our male counterparts leaned up against the wall behind them, hands in their pockets, looking very runway chic. Dressed in clothes that your typical teen wouldn't even know what to do with, the guys took fashion to a whole new level. Somehow they'd managed to perfect their I-just-rolled-out-of-bed-and-looked-this-perfect-aren't-you-jealous looks at the ripe age of seventeen.

This was the cool crowd. And I was its queen.

Sofia saw me first and scurried to stand as I walked up. She passed me a jumbo-size latte, still warm to the touch. "They were out of sugar-free vanilla today, so I had to get caramel," she said apologetically.

I took a sip and smiled as the liquid warmed me from the inside out. "Good choice," I said genuinely. Though I appreciated her effort, nothing could taste the same as vanilla. Not even something as yummy as caramel. Whispering a spell under my breath, I swirled the cup and took another sip.

Ahh, vanilla. Just the way I like it.

"Thanks, Sof. You have no idea how much I needed this this morning," I said, grinning at her. "But you know you don't have to bring me coffee *every* morning. I can always grab something from the caf."

"I know, but the coffee cart doesn't even make lattes, and

I think what they *do* make might actually be toxic. For real," she said conspiratorially. Then she smiled and took a sip of her own drink.

"Okay, but only if it's not too much of a hassle," I said.

"I'm already getting mine anyway, so it's no biggie," she said sweetly. This might have been true, but I was pretty sure that even if Sofia hated coffee, she'd still pick some up for me. She was sweet like that. Whereas Bethany or Trish never did anything unless they got something in return, Sofia really *was* that nice. This was partly why I'd insisted on pulling her into our little circle. We needed someone pure and good to balance out the rest of us.

"So, what are we talking about this morning?" I asked. As I began to strut across the quad, everyone fell into step behind me.

"Sarah Forrester," Bethany said animatedly. "You know how she was at Peter Frick's party this weekend? You won't believe what she did after you left. I still can't believe you left early, B-T-dubs. It was the party of the year!"

"I'm sure it was," I said with a smile. The thing was, every party was the party of the year to Bethany. She was sort of a party whore, if you know what I mean. She thought she'd just *die* if she missed one. But that's why she was our little gossip queen. And she prided herself on this fact. Her dream was to one day be a host on one of those Hollywood gossip shows. "You know my rule about parties. You make your appearance and then leave people wanting more. Besides, nothing good happens after midnight. Case in point: Sarah. What happened, anyway?"

Bethany hushed her tone to invoke a little drama in her retelling. The girl loved a captive audience. And as much as I tried to stay away from the scandalous side of Astor

High, I had to admit that I was drawn to her little updates. And as president of the senior class, I had to be aware of what was going on at my school—er, AHS. That's just good leadership.

"So, you know how Sarah and Josh broke up last week?" I nodded. "Well, when Sarah showed up at Peter's party, she didn't realize that Josh had already moved on—until she walked in on him and Kara full-on making out in the corner of the living room."

"Uh-oh," I said, already feeling bad for Sarah. She and Josh had been together for over a year, and they hadn't even been broken up five minutes before he jumped on another girl? Nobody deserved that. Especially from someone who'd supposedly loved them.

Ugh. That's the reason I don't date high school boys. Well, that and the fact that none of them could handle me.

"Uh-oh's right. As soon as Sarah saw them, she walked over and poured her beer on them both, causing a major scene. It was like one of those bad shows where the wrestlers all talk smack and stuff, just minus the chair throwing," she said. "Anyway, so after she stopped yelling at him, she disappeared into the kitchen and proceeded to get totally sloshed."

"Poor Sarah," I said, shaking my head sadly. "What does she weigh? Like a buck? A buck five soaking wet? And I don't think I've ever seen her drink, let alone drunk."

"Well, none of us have seen her quite like she was on Friday," Trisha chimed in sarcastically.

"Hey, this is *my* story, thank you very much," Bethany snapped at Trish. The two of them were constantly bickering and I found myself having to be their mediator on a regular basis. Most of the time, it was because Trisha was pushing Bethany's buttons by encroaching on her territory. But that was Trish. She liked to stir things up. This was good when she was on your side, not so great when she wasn't.

Bethany smoothed down her blond hair and regained her composure before she continued, but not before I caught Trish rolling her eyes. "So then a drunkity-drunk-drunk Sarah decided she was going to get back at Josh by doing a little strip-tease dance on a table in the living room, and then she made out with some guy on the baseball team. Lucky for her, Josh left before she threw up in the potted plant."

"It was pretty hilarious." Trish snorted.

A broken heart *and* humiliation? I couldn't see anything funny about that.

"Cut her a little slack," I said, tapping my perfectly mani-cured fingernail on the top of my coffee cup. "We've all done stupid things under the influence of love and alcohol. Or do I need to remind you of that time a few summers ago at the pier, Trish?"

Trish's smile faded into a frown and she instantly looked at the ground. I knew that would shut her up pretty fast. The last thing she'd want was the rest of our crew finding out about her own most embarrassing moment ever. However, we both knew it was an empty threat. I'd never divulge something so humiliating and hurtful about someone.

What she didn't know was that this particular incident had saved our friendship.

Because of her attitude, people at school were quick to think Trisha was an ice queen. And admittedly, I'd thought the same thing at first. I wasn't sure anything could penetrate her bitchy exterior and was wary to have someone like that around me.

But then I found that she could have her heart broken just like the rest of us. And she had. Holding her that day as she bawled her eyes out had reminded me that she actually cared very deeply about people—even if she didn't always show it. Trish looked at her emotions as a weakness when in reality they were an asset. Our feelings remind us that we're alive. That we're human. It's what connects us all.

The silence began to grow uncomfortable, but before I could say anything else, Sofia came to the rescue. "Um, Hadley? Don't tell me that's *another* new outfit. It's totally gorge!" Sofia stopped me in the middle of the hallway to admire the clothes I'd meticulously picked out that morning.

She was always so good at deflection. It was another thing I loved about her. She was like me in that way. In fact, she was a lot like me. Maybe that's why I connected with her so much. She was the only sophomore among us, and if I had to leave the school in someone's hands after I graduated, I'd want it to be someone like me. Fair, commanding, but friendly. Sofia was all of those, which made her a perfect number two.

"What, this?" I asked nonchalantly as I looked down at my outfit and then placed my hands on my hips as if I were posing on the red carpet. The dress I had on was black with slashes of white, as if someone had cut straight through the material and exposed the lining. The top of the dress fell flat across my chest, showing just enough cleavage to leave something to the imagination. My heels matched my bloodred leather jacket, giving my outfit the perfect mix of naughty and nice. To top it off, my lips were stained a beautiful shade of berry, which complimented my ivory skin and dark chocolate-colored locks.

"I *may* have gone shopping this weekend," I said coyly. In reality, I'd simply done a glamour spell that allowed me to make certain outfits take on the look of others. This one was straight off the runway in Milan. Why wear last week's clothes when you could wear them before they were available to the masses?

"I don't think I've ever seen you wear the same outfit twice," Bethany said, narrowing her eyes at me suspiciously. "And I pride myself in memorizing things like that. I can remember just about every outfit a person wears on any given day."

"Oh, yeah? What was I wearing last Tuesday?" Trish challenged.

"Black halter, Seven jeans, ballet flats, and a bomber jacket," Bethany answered without missing a beat.

Trish's eyes grew wide. "That's either incredibly impressive or incredibly creepy."

"It's a gift," Bethany said, looking satisfied.

"Yeah? Then why are you getting a C in American history?" Trish asked.

Bethany shrugged. "It's not interesting to me. Now, if we learned about the designers that people wore when we invaded other countries or which leaders had extramarital affairs while in government, then I'd own that class. But the stuff they teach us is totally boring. What Hadley wears on a daily basis is way more my speed."

"Well, I wear the same stuff all the time," I said, turning on my heel and walking away. The truth was, Bethany was right about my revolving wardrobe, but there was no way I could let *her* know that. Barring having rich parents, no one my age could afford as many style changes as I'd made in the last year, and telling the truth was out of the question. What was I supposed to say? I have a new outfit every day because I've put a charm on my wardrobe. Ask me how?

Yeah, right.

"I seriously can't remember the last time you sported a rerun," Bethany insisted as she struggled to keep up with my click-clacking footsteps.

"Of *course* I wear clothes more than once." I could feel the power coursing through my words as I said them. It wasn't like I was brainwashing them or anything. I simply had a way of convincing people of things I wanted them to believe. This was *my* gift, as Bethany had put it just a minute ago. It's probably why no one ever wanted to go up against me in debate class. "Hello? I wear this jacket nearly every single day."

"Well, yeah, I guess so . . . ," Bethany said reluctantly, but giving up the fight.

"New or old, the girl looks *hot*," Trish said. There was the tiniest hint of jealousy in her voice, making me wonder if it was a compliment or just an observation. She took out a compact and checked her own reflection as she walked. The exact opposite of me in the looks department, Trish knew that she always came in second on the "Hottest Girls at Astor High" list. She acted like it didn't bother her, but every year her hair got a little blonder, her skirts got a little shorter, and her cup size got a little larger.

I personally couldn't care less what anyone thought of me here at Astor, as long as I was still the most influential girl around. In the end, looks didn't matter all that much to me. Although of course, they didn't hurt. All in all, I was fully comfortable with the skin I was in.

"Okay, new subject. Are we on schedule for the class meeting after school?" I asked, maneuvering myself around a group of guys who were either reenacting a scene from an action movie or break-dancing in the hallway. "We're supposed to come up with a theme for homecoming and decide what charity the proceeds will benefit this year. And, Sofia, can we make sure that everyone's there on time today? I have an appointment at five that I can't be late for."

"A *date* kind of appointment?" Bethany teased.

I rolled my eyes at her. "You know I don't date high school

boys, B. And besides, when am I supposed to have time for a relationship when I'm busy running this school, cheering on our athletes, and keeping my 4.0 GPA intact so I can graduate at the top of our class and get into the Ivies?"

"Yeah, but part of having it all is *having it all*. And that includes a man," Bethany said.

"Or men," Trish chimed in with a devilish smile. "You know you could have any guy here. Probably a few of the girls, too."

She may have been right, but romance was the last thing on my mind. I'd watched too many girls get derailed by a cute guy with a cool car. It would take more than that to catch my eye. I needed a challenge, someone who could make it worth my while and wasn't intimidated by strong women. And as far as I'd seen, the guys at our school just didn't fit the bill.

"Ah, but I have you guys and that's all the fun I need," I said jokingly, bumping my hip into Sofia's. She returned the bump and giggled at me.

The bell rang and I looked around as people began to scurry to their first classes. Bethany and Trish gave us a wave and headed back in the direction we'd just come from, promising to see us at lunch. I turned and looked at Sofia before continuing toward our respective classrooms.

"I'll make sure that the word gets out about the meeting today," Sofia said, hugging her books tightly to her chest. "Is your appointment after school anything I can help you with? Need a shopping partner or a copilot?"

I smiled at my mini-me. "Nah, I've just got to go and see some old friends of the family, that's all," I said. "But I promise, next time I need a wingwoman, you've got shotgun."

She beamed and hopped a little before disappearing into the computer lab. I wouldn't have minded having Sofia along for the drive, especially since it was going to take nearly an hour for me to get to the meeting spot. But then she wouldn't be able to come inside once we got there, and I didn't think it'd be fair to make her sit outside until the meeting was over just so I could have some company along the way.

Nope. I'd be making this trip alone once again.

Chapter Two

"Whooooa, caught in a bad romance," I sang at the top of my lungs along with Lady Gaga. I was in my car, jamming to the megamix playlist of the over-the-top pop singer that I'd created just for this trip. It was the perfect music to get a person in the mood for some spell casting.

After all, I'd known Gaga back when she was just plain Stefani Germanotta, a gangly teenager who liked to play the piano and put on productions of musicals at coven gatherings. It wasn't until she'd fully embraced her magical side that she really hit it big in the entertainment world. I mean, why else would people be okay with a young woman running around in the crazy outfits she wore?

Still, you gotta love a girl who uses her God-given talents.

The song ended as I pulled into the Hobbses' driveway, parking behind at least three other cars that were already lined up in a row.

Looks like I'm the last one here. Again.

I hated being late to anything, and according to the clock, I still had a minute until the meeting would start. Turning off the ignition, I swung the car door closed behind me and bounded up the front steps. Ringing the doorbell, I smoothed down my dress, ran a hand through my hair, and waited for someone to answer.

"Well, hello, Hadley!" Mrs. Hobbs said when she opened the door. She was pretty, in her early forties, maybe, and was dressed in a pair of jeans and a black sweater. At first glance, she looked like your typical suburban mom. However, I knew better.

"Hi, Mrs. Hobbs!" I said politely, waiting for her to invite me in. When she stepped to the side, I joined her in the foyer.

"Everyone's already downstairs. Why don't you grab something to drink on your way? You know where everything is," she said before disappearing into the living room, where the TV was blaring.

"Thanks!" I shouted, rushing to the stairs and taking each step as fast as I could in my four-inch heels. When I'd made it down to the bottom safe and sound, I pushed open the door to the basement den and burst inside.

"I'm here! I'm here!" I yelled, scurrying to my usual spot on the windowsill.

"You heard the girl, let's get this party started!" said Fallon, sitting on a beanbag chair in the corner. I narrowed my eyes at him and made a face. He was kind of dorky-looking and his body was a bit too puny for his head. But it was his out-of-control hair that really labeled him a grade-A nerd. If I didn't know Fallon personally, I'd probably gloss right over him walking down the hallway. But I did, and he was a total thorn in my side.

"Nice to see you, too, Fallon," I said, glancing around the

room at the other dozen or so kids. A quick search showed me that I was, indeed, the last to show. Did I mention that I *hate* being late? Even if it's just by a few minutes, my stomach starts to feel queasy. All the research I've done on influential people has said that it's actually *good* to make people wait for you. It's supposed to subconsciously make them think that your time is more valuable than theirs. Still, I'd always thought it just made a person seem irresponsible and rude. And I couldn't help but feel like everyone else in the coven felt the same way. They wouldn't say it, of course—well, maybe Fallon would—but I think it just gave them more of a reason to shy away from me.

I may have commanded my school, but here I wasn't exactly the center of attention. Maybe it was because I wasn't the only extraordinary one in the room. Or because spell casting came easily to me, which meant I didn't have to work quite as hard as the others and didn't need to attend as many of our magic meetings to pass our spell tests. This gave the others more time to bond and left me sort of on the outside looking in. But I was too busy with all my commitments at school to hang around witch classes just to watch others try to catch up to where I was. And as of yet, I hadn't been able to find a spell that allowed me to be in two places at once. Until then, I'd just have to be okay with having the best of one world.

This didn't mean I didn't try to get along with the others, though. I looked over at Jackson with an apologetic smile. He was parked at the front of the room where he always stood, arms crossed over his chest. I could tell he wasn't exactly annoyed that I was the last one to show. In fact, he seemed more amused to hear my excuses than anything. This was probably because I was a lot like him when he was my age. The first couple of years that I'd gone to Cleri magic lessons, Jackson had been there, too, only he'd been in high school at the time. I remember thinking that he had everything together: He'd been incredibly driven and excelled at everything he'd done. He'd gone on to become president of his fraternity in college and then went to work for an advertising firm after graduation.

That's why it wasn't surprising when he'd been appointed the new leader of our witching lessons when our old one retired. He could show us how to lead a balanced life as a witch in this world.

In other words, he'd managed to do what I couldn't: dominate in both his personal life and the responsibilities of his coven. Even so, I think he understood my desire to have a life outside the magical realm. This is where the others and I differed. They'd all chosen to focus more on their magical sides. Me, I thought there was more to life than just practicing spells in someone's basement. Jackson understood both and worked hard to try to get us to meet in the middle.

"I had a student government meeting after school," I explained. "We were picking a theme for homecoming and it ran a little longer than expected."

"What did you decide on?" Sascha asked. She might have been the only ally I had in the group and I knew she was genuinely curious to hear the answer. I had a feeling Sascha lived vicariously through me. Like, she knew she'd never be able to have a big social life, so she settled for hearing about mine. I'd tried on several occasions to give her tips on how she could rule her own school, but she insisted it wouldn't work. And like they say, if you think you can't, you're right. A person had to be confident to live the kind of life I lived.

"Our theme is: Something Wicked This Way Comes," I announced proudly.

"Wow, and it took you *two whole hours* to figure that one

out?" Fallon asked, snorting as he cracked up at his own joke.

I bit back a nasty response. No one could get on my last nerve quite like Fallon. I knew I shouldn't be bothered by a kid who was several years younger than me, but he irked me every chance he got.

We fought like brother and sister, which in a messed-up way, we kind of were. Not through blood of course, but through the bonds of the coven. It was a connection that went back hundreds of years, to the original Cleri members. To Bridget and the witch trials. This wasn't what made us bristle with antagonism toward each other though. No, Fallon was the only one who challenged me every chance he got. And I was of the mind-set that you should respect those more powerful than you.

"I think it sounds cool," Sascha said, still stuck on the theme of the dance.

"Hell, if we had themes like that, I might actually attend school functions," Jasmine said, picking at her black nail polish. Jasmine was the kind of girl people automatically assumed practiced witchcraft, based on her appearance alone. To say she was a fan of the color black was an understatement. Her makeup was a little on the theatrical side and she had a tendency to frown more than she smiled, but that was who she was. With Jasmine, what you saw was what you got. In a way, she was the only one of us who was being 100 percent herself, 100 percent of the time.

She didn't even hide her magical abilities. Of course, people just thought she was weird. Goes to show you how clueless the nonmagical community can be. She also didn't sugarcoat the fact that she thought things like dances were beneath her. According to Jasmine, being witches made us superior to civilians, and typical teenage things like attending parties had no place in our world. She'd rather spend her time perfecting her spells. Needless to say, this might have been the reason we weren't exactly best friends. Still, it wasn't like we were enemies, either.

"As much as I'd love to talk dance themes—and my school had a few doozies—we need to get started on today's lesson," Jackson said, walking to the middle of the room. He motioned for us to stand up.

I nearly groaned but knew it wouldn't go over so well with this crowd. It wasn't that I didn't *like* talking magic. Like I said, it sort of came naturally to me and I used spells for just about everything in my daily life. But our bimonthly lessons tended to be about things that didn't affect me personally. Most of the spells I used on a daily basis I'd either taught myself or created out of necessity. The stuff Jackson taught us had been passed down from generation to generation, and to be honest, seemed a bit *old*. Sometimes we talked so much about the past that I couldn't see how it had anything to do with the present.

Jackson said it was like high school in that way: it may seem like we won't use anything we learn, but eventually it will come in handy. I wasn't so sure, but until I turned eighteen, I had no choice. At least according to my parents. They said that if witch lessons were good enough for our ancestors, they were good enough for me.

So I kept my thoughts to myself as we gathered around him.

"Does anyone know what our greatest asset is when it comes to our magic?" Jackson asked.

"Knowledge?" Peter, the youngest in the group, said.

"Intelligence?" Sascha guessed.

"Our ability to trick our opponents!" Fallon shouted, as if we weren't all standing within a few feet of him. I covered my right ear, which was now ringing, and prepared to answer.

"Power." There was no doubt in my mind that this was my greatest asset when it came to performing spells.

"All of those are good answers, and in a way, you're all correct," Jackson answered, shoving his hands into the pockets of his fitted jeans. The charcoal color of his sweater made his blue eyes stand out even more than usual. I could see why he'd been such a catch as a teenager. If he weren't so old now—almost twenty-five—we might've made a great power couple. Alas, I'd never understood the whole teacher/student attraction. Not for me, thanks.

Jackson continued his lecture. "Good guesses, but there's one very small, very simple thing you're each overlooking."

We looked around at each other quizzically. I still thought my answer was right, but I was willing to see where he was going with this. After all, he *was* our teacher, and this was his lesson.

"Fallon, come on over here a minute," Jackson said, motioning for my nemesis to stand beside him. We all took a step back to watch. "Okay. Now try to hit me with a spell. Doesn't matter which one. Surprise me and put everything you've got into it."

A devilish smile grew on Fallon's face as he was given permission to do his worst. I couldn't remember the last time we were given free rein to go crazy with our magic during a lesson. I could tell Fallon was going to enjoy this, and I had to be honest: part of me wished I could switch places with him.

Jackson steadied his stance and rolled his neck in a circle as if he were warming up for a five-mile run. See, it's important for a witch to be as calm and loose as possible in order to sustain an attack from another witch. If you're too tense, it's easier for the magic to work its way into you.

Besides, when your mind and heart are clear, you can respond a lot more quickly to things.

Right before Fallon spoke the words to his spell, I caught Jackson mumbling something under his breath. Everyone else was focused on Fallon, waiting to see what spell he'd choose. Instead, his eyes grew wide as no sound came from his lips. Fallon opened and closed his mouth like a fish out of water, but still, nothing happened. When he began to claw at his throat, Jackson said, "Muflix sertikin," and carefully put his hands on Fallon's shoulders.

"What the hell was *that?*" Fallon yelled, gasping, when he was finally able to speak again, sending a nasty look Jackson's way. He was shaken—and it was more than just embarrassment over failing to one-up our teacher.

"Calm down and let me explain," Jackson said evenly. "Did everyone just see what happened here?"

"Fallon couldn't get his magic to work," I said, snickering a little at the implication.

"True. But any idea why?" This time nobody answered. Finally, Jackson told us. "I took away his ability to speak."

A few people still looked confused, but I had a feeling I knew what Jackson was getting at. "No voice, no spell," I said, already admiring the cunning behind his simple counterattack.

"Exactly, Hadley. Very few witches have the power of thought alone to pull off a spell. Take away a person's voice, and you take away their ability to use that power," said Jackson.

"Excellent," Jasmine said, smiling.

"It's cheating, if you ask me," Fallon mumbled, not enjoying the fact that he'd been the butt of a joke, even if it *was* to prove Jackson's point.

"Oh, come on, Fallon. You had *no chance* from the very beginning," Jackson said, trying to smooth things over with him. "There's nothing a person can do when their voice is taken away. What we're going to learn today is how to perform the mumming spell on our enemies, and of course, how to deflect them so we're not caught in such a vulnerable position. Now, split up into groups of two and start practicing."

For the next hour, we took turns performing the spells on each other. I teamed up with Sascha, who's usually good at casting spells but isn't very aggressive with her magic. This meant that after the first few times I deflected her mumming spells with no problem, I stopped trying to avert them in order to give her a chance. Nobody likes a show-off.

Fallon obviously didn't know this, and I watched as he refused to allow Peter to bewitch him. As much as I hated to admit it, Fallon was probably the most powerful kid in the coven besides me. Peter, however, was only eleven and hadn't really found his voice yet, which made him an easy target. Because of this, I couldn't help but feel protective of him. Maybe if *I'd* gone up against Fallon, I could've kept him from running his mouth for the rest of the night.

Ahh, there's always next time.

When Jackson felt we'd had a sufficient chance to put the new spell into practice, and most of us seemed comfortable with it, he had us gather around for the history portion of the night.

We met only twice a month since our members lived across several neighboring towns—not like in the olden days when covens were determined by location. After the trials, the original Cleri members who were left felt it would be safer if they spread themselves out. So those who escaped Salem Town moved far away and then tried to separate themselves so as not to draw unwanted attention.

Because we had to travel a ways to get to each meeting— the location of which rotated—Jackson had to try and cram as much into our lessons as possible. The truth was, with the state of the world being what it was, our parents didn't have the time they used to to devote to our daily lessons. So most of our group depended on our magic classes to learn about our powers and the Cleri heritage.

I got to do both. My parents both used magic pretty regularly and had always encouraged me to develop mine. And as much as I loved to take advantage of the practical side of magic, I felt like I knew all I needed to about our history.

Maybe too much, I thought, recalling that morning's dream. *Why relive such a gruesome part of our past over and over again? We're not masochists.*

"Now, can anyone tell me when this spell was first used and who created it?" Jackson asked as he paced across the floor. My hand remained by my side, even though he was looking straight at me as he said it. I wasn't sure why, as I never knew the answers to these types of questions. "No guesses?" We remained silent. "Well, Hadley, it would do you some good to do a little research into your family's past. Given your lineage, many of our lessons stem from your relatives. This one in particular was thought up by your great-great-great-aunt Trixie Bishop."

"Ah yes, Great-Aunt Trixie," I mumbled, already bored. "I believe she's referred to as Crazy Aunt Trixie in our house. Not the finest example of the Bishop bloodline apparently."

Jackson chose to ignore this comment and instead moved on. "And can anyone tell me why Trixie cooked up the mumming spell?"

This time, several hands flew up all around me. Seemed like my classmates had actually listened when Jackson suggested that reading material a few months back. They must not have had a school to run, a squad to lead, a reputation to uphold . . . Even so, I hated that they knew something I didn't, and I began to rethink my position on studying magical history.

"Jinx?" Jackson asked, calling on the pretty brunette sitting in the corner. Looking at her now, I thought about how the name didn't match her at all. The girl in front of me was mild-mannered and quiet and came from a really great family—you'd never know it but her parents were very well-off. She got good grades and was liked by everyone as far as I could tell. Despite her name, she was the last person you'd ever consider to be bad luck.

"It's said that Trixie came up with most of her spells as a way to fight off future attacks from Samuel Parris's coven," Jinx answered, placing her manicured hands demurely in her lap.

"A lot of good it did her against the Parrishables," I said, just loud enough for people to hear me.

"That's correct, Jinx. And, Hadley, you know that's not the proper name of the coven," Jackson said with a sigh.

This was true. After Samuel broke off from the Cleri, he'd started his own coven, which he'd named the Parish. But almost from the start, people had called them the Parrishables, because of their ability to wipe out so many other witches. I still wasn't clear why we even bothered to learn about the original name, though, considering it seemed to have died along with Samuel.

"Oh, come on. This isn't Harry Potter. We can call them whatever we want. Parrishables. Barbarians. *Murderers*. It's all the same if you ask me."

"Hadley," he warned. I could tell he was starting to get annoyed, but I was sick of constantly having this same conversation.

"I just think it's sort of a waste of time," I said, raising my eyes to his. "It's not like anyone's seen or heard from the

Parrishables in like forever, right? I've read enough of *Magic Through the Ages* to know that. I think we've all got better things to do than gear up for a battle that isn't likely to happen."

"And if it did, what then?" Jackson asked slowly. "What if the Parrishables were to come back and try to finish what they started?" A dangerous tone had crept into his voice. I was always pushing the boundaries with him. Usually I knew when to stop before I took things too far. Right now, though, I was teetering on the edge—and wasn't ready to stop.

"In that case, shouldn't the question be, why are we sitting around waiting for them to come after us?"

Chapter Three

"Please tell me you didn't say that, Had," my mom said as she put a plate down in front of me. "Jackson's an elder and deserves your respect. He could mean the difference between your tapping in to your heritage or letting your craft fizzle out. And besides, what he's teaching you could actually save your butt one day."

We were sitting at the kitchen table, a pepperoni-and-onion pizza between us, the cheese hot and gooey. I'd been so fired up about what had happened at the meeting that I'd made the mistake of participating in some mother/daughter share time before dinner. You'd think I'd have learned by now: when in doubt, fill your mouth with cheese so you can't get yourself into trouble with your mom.

"But, Mom, he asked me a question and all I did was answer. I wasn't being disrespectful . . . I was just being *honest*," I said between bites. "And isn't it you who always says that honesty's the best policy?"

Mom tilted her head at me, not at all amused with my ability to argue about anything. In this case, however, I didn't have the power to convince her to see things my way. I wasn't sure if it was the familial lineage or that her magical skills were simply stronger than mine, but what usually worked to my advantage on others fell flat whenever she was around. It was a minor setback that I was constantly working to rectify. In the meantime, it was just plain annoying.

"Hadley Anne Bishop, you know that's not what I meant. Yes, you *should* tell the truth, but not if it means being rude," she said. "I've seen you around your friends and classmates and you'd never talk to them that way. If one of your friends was having a bad hair day, you wouldn't say they looked like they'd been hit with the ugly stick, would you?"

"There's an ugly stick?" I asked, suddenly interested in where this conversation was going.

Mom's eyebrows knit together in frustration. My face fell as I realized there was no magic wand out there that granted or took away beauty.

But what if there were . . .

"Don't even think about it, Hadley," she warned. My mouth dropped open, a piece of pepperoni falling to my plate. She'd managed to read my mind again.

I have to stop letting her sneak in like that.

"I don't understand why you're so amicable with your friends, but when it comes to the rest of us—your family and coven—you're so . . . *combative.*"

"I'm not combative," I mumbled. But I knew it was true. For some reason when it came to other witches, I simply didn't hold back. Why was that? Maybe because they knew all my secrets? There was definitely something a little scary about someone really *knowing* you. And the truth was, the kids at school—even my good girlfriends—didn't really know me. Well, not the whole me, at least.

"Case in point," my mom said. "And in this case, you're *wrong.*"

"I'm just thinking *rationally.* Look, Mom, you know I don't believe in this whole prepare-to-die, epic good-versus-evil battle stuff. I know you and Dad and the other elders want me to think the same way as you, but I'm sorry, I just don't. I stopped believing in the boogeyman a long time ago, and as far as I'm concerned, the Parrishables are just one big boogey-man. They don't exist. And until I have proof that they do, I'd rather be worrying about something else," I said.

My mom closed her eyes and tried to control her breathing. "For a girl who's usually so smart, you're incredibly naive sometimes, Hadley," she said.

The comment caught me by surprise and my blood began to boil with anger.

"I'm not the naive one here. You are," I spat. "Look, I agree that what the Parrishables did to our family and others over the past three hundred years sucks. At one point, they were a real threat, and if I'd been alive back then I would have taken them all out. But living our lives always looking over our shoulders when there's not even any proof they're still a threat? I just think there are better things I could be doing with my time. Things that *actually* matter."

"And you don't think that what Bridget Bishop went through matters?" she asked, her voice raising an octave.

"Of *course* it matters," I answered, thinking about the dream I'd had the night before, and the feeling of the rope around Bridget's neck. I swallowed hard to clear the lump that had suddenly formed in my throat. "But that was then and this is now. And news flash: we're alive *now.* I believe in living my life to the fullest instead of focusing on the maybes and the what-ifs."

My mom paused and looked at me suspiciously.

"You've been dreaming about her again, haven't you?" she asked me. "That's not good, Hadley."

"Geez, Mom! Get out of my head!" I growled, and started to stomp out of the room in frustration. I was halfway to the door before I whirled around on my red heels and stared hard at her, feeling slightly unhinged. "If you guys want to live in fear, be my guest. But don't drag me down with you. As far as I'm concerned, you guys are just as crazy as the Parrishables were."

I heard my mom gasp at the words, but I was already turning and heading out the door.

I was having a really great dream. A great dream about a boy. No, not a boy; he was an almost-man. I think he was in college or something. But those details didn't really matter. What mattered was that he was *hot*. Way hotter than that kid in those Twilight movies (and my dream guy was definitely not a vampire; although I'm pretty sure I wouldn't have stopped him if he'd tried to bite me). And he was into me, too.

In the dream, my dark-haired hottie was walking through a crowd of people, his eyes trained on me. I could tell he wanted me by the fact that he wasn't even looking at any of the other girls he was passing by. At one point, he even walked by Trish, and I could see the disappointment on her face as he ignored her. Not that I was happy that she felt bad . . . it's just nice when your dream crush actually goes for you instead of your friends.

So, Dreamy McYummykins was making his way toward me, and even though in the back of my mind I knew he was a stranger, I was oddly drawn to him. I also knew with absolute certainty that he was going to kiss me.

And I was going to let him.

I lightly licked my lips in anticipation and prepared for him to take me in his arms and . . .

"Hadley, let's get to it," he said, placing his hands firmly on my arm.

"Huh?" I asked, confused. I'd been ready to kiss the guy, but a line like that was the last thing I'd expected to come out of his mouth.

Then he started to shake me, lightly at first, and more firmly when I didn't do what he said.

"Had, it's time," he said again, though the voice sounded farther away from me now.

My eyes fluttered open and suddenly I was no longer looking at my hot, young man-boy.

Nope, I was looking straight into the eyes of . . . my dad.

"Hey, little girl, it's time to get up," he whispered to me in the darkened room. "If we want to get that workout in before I have to leave, we need to start in fifteen. You still want to go?"

Shaking the image of my nighttime rendezvous out of my head, I pulled myself up so I was resting on my elbows. "No, yeah, I'll get up. Just give me a few minutes?"

I watched as my dad padded out of my room, leaving the door open as he left. There was just enough of a glow from the night-light in the hallway for me to see the workout clothes I'd laid out on my chair the night before. I crawled to the foot of my bed and retrieved them, looking back at the clock as I pulled on my sports bra, a pair of shorts, and my sneakers.

Six a.m.

Ugh. If my dad weren't leaving for three weeks, there's no way I'd willingly be getting up at this ungodly hour. But it was hard to score time with him as it was, since he was always working late or traveling for business, so I'd take the father-daughter bonding any way I could.

I couldn't exactly be mad at him for not being around though. My dad runs a nonprofit organization called Empower, which helps battered and abused women get support and restart their lives. Because it's nonprofit, it means that most of the year he travels from state to state to try to convince various Fortune 500 companies to donate to the cause. My dad's also a witch, although the other employees at Empower aren't exactly hip to this fact. But to put it simply, that's why the company's so successful. See, Dad shares my powers of persuasion—that's where I get it from; some people have their parent's nose or eyes, but my genes are of the magical variety—which comes in handy when you're asking multibillion-dollar companies to spare a couple hundred grand for a good cause.

Let's just say he's *very* good at what he does.

But this also means that he's gone more often than he's home, which brings me back to the reason I was walking through the living room like a zombie at the butt crack of dawn that morning. Working out wasn't usually a part of my a.m. routine, but when my dad asked, I said yes. Even if my body was screaming, "Go back to bed, you idiot!"

"What torture are you putting us through today?" I yawned as I dragged myself over to where my dad was stretching near the couch. Taking his cue, I grabbed onto my right foot and pulled it behind me until it was resting against my butt. I let out a little groan as I felt the muscles in my thigh stretch like a rubber band.

"I thought we'd start off doing two miles to warm up and then head back for some kickboxing and a cooldown. We'll be done in just a little over an hour," he said, looking down at his watch. It was black and plastic and had a stopwatch and heart-rate monitor embedded in it. I'd given it to him as a present when I was nine, and he never took it off. It was a really sweet gesture, but even I knew that it clashed with the suits he wore to meet with potential clients. Yet I think someone would've had to pry it off him if they wanted him to change it up. "Don't worry, Had. We'll be done in plenty of time for you to get to school."

"No worries, Daddy," I said, although part of me *was* wondering whether I'd be able to perform my usual morning routine and perfect my look before I headed off to class. I didn't have time to worry about it now though, because Dad was already headed out the front door.

Outside, it was just cool enough to need a light jacket, and the grass and leaves were all dewy, leaving sprinkles of wetness on the backs of my legs as I sprinted off across the lawn. I took a deep breath. There was nothing like the smell of morning. Everything was fresh and clean. For some reason, it was always easier to breathe at this hour. You know, before the heaviness of the day started piling up on you.

I followed behind my dad as he led us out of the neighborhood and onto a trail through the woods at the end of the next block. There were several different paths to get lost on, but he chose the one that would lead us just inside the fold of the trees. Neither of us spoke as we jogged along, enjoying the company and quiet the blanketed woods provided.

Twenty minutes later, we turned onto our block and headed toward home. I surveyed the houses of our neighbors as we ran by, wondering if anyone was awake inside yet. As we passed a brown-and-white house off to our left, I noticed movement out of the corner of my eye. The front door opened soundlessly and a guy walked out and started down the driveway.

He was my age, I guessed, but walked with an ease that

most teenagers our age didn't have. His hair was jet-black, messy, and came to a point at the top of his head in a fading faux-hawk. As my gaze drifted to his face, I was startled by what I saw. His eyes were the color of the sky after a storm and his lips . . .

I became so distracted that my foot caught on an uneven part of the road and I stumbled slightly before resuming my original gait. The guy chuckled quietly before raising his hand and giving me a wave. The gesture was so simple, yet it caught me off guard. I was used to guys keeping their distance. My friends said it was because they were intimidated. The fact that this guy had the balls to act like we were old friends was new territory for me.

"You know him?" my dad asked, raising an eyebrow at me.

I tore my eyes away from the cute guy and focused instead on the pavement where my feet were currently pounding. But even once I'd looked away, I could still picture him.

"Nope," I answered.

"Must be Ms. Abbott's nephew," he said. "Mom mentioned he moved in a few weeks ago."

"What's he doing here?" I asked, curious to learn more about our mysterious neighbor.

"No clue," he said. "You're lucky I even remembered that. Sometimes when your mom talks about neighborhood gossip I can't help but tune out. Don't tell her, though."

I laughed. We were always teasing Mom behind her back, but it was all in good fun. Only this time I saw the truth in his words. "Your secret's safe with me."

"Speaking of Mom," he said as we lumbered up to our house. "She told me all about your conversation last night."

I collapsed onto the lawn and breathed in deeply. My lungs felt like they were on fire and my legs had officially turned to Jell-O.

"Let's be honest," I said between gasps. "It wasn't a conversation. It was a full-blown witch hunt."

Dad joined me on the grass and began to stretch. "Poor choice of words, Had."

"Well, if the broom fits," I muttered.

Dad gave me a warning look. I refrained from continuing and instead kept my mouth shut. We'd been having such a great morning and I didn't want to ruin it with something so stupid.

Taking my silence as a momentary peace offering, Dad got to his feet and helped me to mine. We headed inside and straight down to the gym in the basement. He tossed me my red boxing gloves and began to pull his own on. Once mine were secure around my wrists, I punched them together a few times like the professionals always did in the ring.

"Now remember, keep your arms up near your face and never stop moving," he said, throwing a half-speed jab at me. I easily blocked the hit and then threw a few of my own, too fast for my dad to avoid. Speed had always been one of my biggest assets when it came to hand-to-hand combat. That and being able to intuit what my opponent's next move would be. Not that I got into fistfights often, but after more than five years of karate, self-defense, and boxing, I'd managed to learn a thing or two.

My parents had said it was so I could defend myself against the Parrishables or any other coven-on-coven attack that might happen. I agreed to participate because I thought, as a female especially, I should know how to take care of myself. It was a practical skill to have, and it made me feel powerful. Like no one could touch me. And now they couldn't.

Jab, jab, right hook. Jab, jab, uppercut.

But this thought brought me back to the argument I'd had

with Mom and I became instantly annoyed all over again. Part of me didn't want to bring it up, but I knew my dad was more rational than Mom was and wouldn't likely blow up on me. "I just don't understand why everyone thinks the Parrishables are still around," I said, slightly out of breath.

"Hadley, you know that many of our ancestors were killed by the coven," Dad said. "Nana used to tell your mom what it was like losing her grandmother at the hands of Samuel's brood. It was devastating to her. So Mom's vowed never to let you feel the same grief over losing someone you love. And between you and me, neither of us could handle losing you. So, please, just do whatever she asks, even if you *do* think it's a waste of time. Humor your old man, will ya?"

"Do you really think they'll come back, though?" I asked, throwing a particularly powerful punch his way. "I mean, really, Dad. You've got to know this is silly. I think you're *really* only teaching me this stuff to fend off the college boys. I'm onto you."

"Don't even joke about college boys, Hadley Anne," he said seriously, dropping his hands to his sides. "And just because you don't see the Parrishables doesn't mean they don't exist. An intelligent man is wise enough to expect the unexpected."

"Woman," I corrected. "An intelligent *woman* is wise enough to expect the unexpected."

Then I moved forward, closing the space between us within a second, and threw three punches in a row. He wasn't prepared for the first but managed to block the others.

"I would say I've got that covered, wouldn't you?" I said gleefully before walking over to the counter where he'd placed an ice-cold bottle of water. I pulled off my gloves, then twisted off the top and gulped down the contents in under a minute.

I definitely earned a Krispy Kreme this morning.

"Look, sweetie, we just want you to be prepared for *anything*," he said. "As much as I wish I could be around my two girls twenty-four hours a day, seven days a week, to protect you, we both know I can't. And it would just make *me* worry a lot less if you knew all the ways to defend yourself. Your mom feels the same. So do me a favor and just grin and bear it?"

I moaned to exaggerate the pain it was going to cause me to do as he wished. "Fine! I'll try and lay off her for a bit. But I'm not going to be happy about it. . . ."

"Deal," he said, reaching out and shaking my hand. Then he paused briefly as he looked at me sideways. "You *were* joking about the college boys, right?"

Chapter Four

"One last time and then we're out of here," I shouted to the rest of the cheerleaders, before turning and taking my place front and center. Someone cued the music and it quickly filled the practice room for the hundredth time. We'd been at the routine for over an hour and were so close to perfecting it that I almost didn't want to let everyone leave. I also knew that Coach, who was letting me run practice today, was expecting us to rock our routine at the game next week. Even so, I'd learned long ago not to burn the team out. Better to leave on a high note and pick things up next practice.

As Bon Jovi belted out "Livin' on a Prayer," we began to perform the choreographed dance moves in unison. With a pop of my hip, I moved toward the back of the mat and prepared to do my signature tumbling run: a front tuck, round-off back handspring full-twisting layout. As I landed, a series of stunts went off behind me, and then I joined the rest of my team in time for the big finish. We each struck a pose as the music faded, and soon the only noise I could hear was our labored breathing.

"Nice job, guys! That would've gotten us to Nationals in March, easy," I said, walking over to where I'd left my water bottle. "But first, the game next week. Bring that energy then and we'll kill it out there. Let's show them why we're number one!"

Nobody dared groan even though I knew they all secretly wanted to. Instead, most of the squad collected their stuff and headed toward the locker rooms. I stayed behind to put away the equipment, satisfied with how well practice had gone. Following my lead, Trish, Sofia, and Bethany stuck around too, rolling up the mats and placing the crash pads and poms in our storage closet.

"You run a tough practice, Captain," Trish said, wiping the sweat off her forehead with the bottom of her tank top.

"Oh, come on. That was nothing. Come Nationals, we're going to be doing it full-out, three times in a row," I said. "You'll be lucky if you don't throw up when we're done."

Trish made a face in distaste and smoothed her blond hair off her forehead. "Seriously gross, Had."

"It wasn't *that* bad," Bethany cut in. One look at the gossip queen, though, and I could see she'd broken a sweat too. Her skin was dewy and her cheeks were pink with heat. I knew she was hurting just as badly as the rest of us, but she'd do anything to show up Trish. "In fact, I could totally go for a cheeseburger right now."

She looked over at Trish, who'd turned a light shade of green at this, and smiled devilishly. "Doesn't that sound good? A big, fat, juicy cheeseburger with bacon and onion rings and a ton of barbecue sauce slathered all over it. And french fries. I think I definitely burned enough calories for all that. Anyone else in? We could go to Sloppy Joe's and see what's going on there?"

Trish convulsed slightly and her hand darted to her mouth.

"Think you're on your own this time, B," I said, trying save Trish by changing the subject. "I gotta go and help my mom down at the shop. Thursdays are her busiest days. That's when all the new ingredients come in for the perfumes. . . ."

My voice trailed off as I realized I would have rather gone to eat with the girls. Even though I'd told my dad I'd go easy on Mom, I hadn't gotten over our argument from the other night. I knew that if I was stuck in the store alone with her for hours, she'd find some way of revisiting it. And then it would be a lot harder to keep my promise to my dad.

I looked at the girls, hoping they'd offer to help me out and give me a mom buffer. But they avoided my eyes as we headed across the room.

"Sorry, Had. My stomach's calling," said Bethany, patting her flat stomach.

"And I have a date with my DVR," Trish answered, ignoring Bethany's mention of food and not even bothering to get creative with her excuse as to why she couldn't come.

"I'll go with you," Sofia offered, shrugging. "I've got some homework to do, but I guess it can wait."

"Thanks, Sof. You're the *best*," I said, gushing at my faithful sidekick. "We'll go get fro-yo afterward with as many toppings as you want."

"Well, you know me. I'm not going to turn down frozen yogurt."

We disappeared into the locker rooms and changed before taking off for Mom's store, Scents and Sensibility. Mom had opened up the perfume shop a few years before I was born, and according to everyone who knew her, it had been a dream of hers ever since she was a teenager. She'd barely been old enough to wear perfume before she'd started mixing scents in with her spells, and the result was magically infused fragrances. Now when people came into the store, my mom created a perfume unique to each individual and her needs. She even made cologne for men.

As we walked through the front door, the sound of chirping birds filled the room, and once again I was reminded of how much I liked the sound that alerted my mom to customers. It was like stepping into a whole new world. One filled with an almost tangible energy. The smell of lavender, vanilla, and gardenia hit my senses and I was instantly put at ease. The scents were so familiar to me that anytime I smelled them, I felt like I was home. I sighed with delight, my anxiety and stress almost melting away.

Almost.

"I've always loved this store," Sofia said, echoing my thoughts exactly. "The stuff your mom comes up with is so much better than anything you'd ever find in a department store. The perfume she made for me just genuinely makes me feel better whenever I wear it. Is that weird?"

"Not at all." She was right, though I couldn't tell her why. Mom had told me a little while back that the blend she'd created for Sofia had a mixture of fearlessness and self-confidence. That and a dash of clear thinking, and the concoction pretty much described my friend. Not that it changed who Sofia was deep down. Mom's perfumes just enhanced the true essence of a person. Sort of like makeup for the soul.

As we walked to the back of the store, I could see Mom was finishing up with a customer. I watched as she quickly picked bits and pieces from thirty to forty different bowls scattered across the white counter that stood in the middle of the room.

The surface was lit from below and glowed brightly, giving the table an ethereal feel. My mom's face scrunched up in concentration as she moved swiftly, her hands reaching in and out of bowls so fast that I could barely keep up with what she was grabbing. She began to slow down and then shifted her focus once more onto the customer standing quietly in front of her. The middle-aged woman stood there looking a bit nervous, like she wasn't quite sure what she was supposed to be doing.

First timer.

Mom raised an eyebrow before reaching out her hand one last time and coming back with the final ingredient. "A little cinnamon, for mystery," she explained.

She mashed up the contents in the mortar with a pestle, like waiters did to guacamole in Mexican restaurants. Then she carefully placed some of the mixture into a little vial of liquid. Shaking it up like a snow globe, she closed her eyes and muttered a few words to herself. The customer probably didn't think anything of it, but I knew better. She was infusing the perfume with a spell.

The customer's face changed from nervous to giddy and she happily handed over a fistful of bills to Mom and then left clutching the tiny pink bag to her chest as if it were filled with gold. Little did she know that Mom's products were as good as that.

My mom watched the woman leave and then finally turned her attention to us. "Hi, girls. How was practice?" Her voice sounded friendly, but I could tell she was keeping things light because Sofia was there with us.

"It was okay," I said noncommittally, picking at a bowl of sage.

Mom blew right over my comment and continued as if things between us weren't strained. "And what brings you here,

Sofia? You couldn't have finished your perfume already . . ."

"I've still got plenty left, Mrs. Bishop," she answered politely. "I'm just here to help out."

"Well, aren't you the sweetest!" Mom exclaimed as she moved around the table to give her a hug. I looked away in case she was thinking of hugging me next. "I'm so happy Hadley has such great friends."

I rolled my eyes and waited for her to let go of Sofia. When she finally did, I took a few steps away and started to shrug off my fitted black leather jacket. The sooner we got started, the sooner I could go home and take care of everything else that needed my attention. I had cookies to bake for a squad fund-raiser, math homework to do, and I still had to write my column for the school newspaper. This week's subject was going to be about replacing the junk-food vending machines with the kind that offered healthy options like fruit and granola bars. You'd be amazed at how many overweight teens are walking around my school, candy bars and chips in hand. It's just plain difficult to watch sometimes. Obviously not everyone has my willpower and of course I'm happy to do my part to end teen stress-eating.

"Where should we start?" I asked Mom.

"Um, well, all the herbs need to be separated and restocked along that wall," she said, pointing to her left. "And then the spice jars should be filled to the top over there. When that's all done, I've got some plants in the back that need to be watered and trimmed. You guys know where everything is, right?"

We nodded and got to work. Sofia had helped out at the store a few times before, so I didn't need to give her much direction before she started restocking. Since I'd been around this stuff for as long as I could remember, I stuck with replenishing the herbs and plants. I took six jars to the back room, where all the supplies were, and began to fill them up. As I pulled bins off the shelves, I ran through the uses of each ingredient in my head before placing it away.

Horsetail fern. Helps give the wearer a more polished look. Perfect for interviews, first dates, or any appointment where you want to impress.

Arnica. Used to soothe both bruised egos and bruised bodies. I took baths with this after particularly hard nights at cheer practice.

Wormwood. This one's great if you have a friend or frenemy who's dragging you down. It removes internal parasites of all kinds; totally worth the side effect of indigestion.

"You're out of sage!" I yelled, looking into an empty jar before plopping it back onto the table. When Mom didn't respond, I started to walk from the back room into the main part of the store. "Do you want me to order more?"

"Yes. I can be there in an hour," Mom said quietly into her cell phone just a few feet away from where I stood. "I can't believe this is happening, Julia. Poor Peter. How's he holding up? Uh-huh? That's horrible. Okay, I just need to close up the shop and I'll be there as soon as I can. Keep the coven together until I get there and try not to panic."

I'd never heard my mom use the C-word in public before and looked around to see if Sofia was within listening distance. I spotted her working on the shelves at the opposite end of the room, satisfied that she hadn't heard what my mom said. Turning back around, I leaned over the counter and stared at my mom as she finished her conversation and hung up the phone. Without explanation, she started to rush around the store absentmindedly, as if she didn't know where she was going or what she was looking for. When she disappeared into the back, I followed her.

"What's going on?" I asked. I was still annoyed with her, but at the moment my curiosity was stronger than my resentment. "Who was that?"

She looked up at me, startled, as if she'd forgotten I was still in the store. "What? Oh, honey, you're still here," she said, distracted.

"Yep. Still here," I said, wanting to add, "thanks for noticing," but thought better of it. Instead, I walked over to her and put my hands on her shoulders to stop her from moving around. "Mom. What's going on?"

She looked me in the eyes, but I could tell that her mind was far away. "Something's happened to the Glovers," she said.

"Are they okay?"

She shook her head. "It doesn't look good, sweetie. Peter came home from school today and his parents weren't there, and the place was a mess like there was a struggle. Nobody knows where they are or what happened."

"Maybe they're just out? I mean, it's only been a few hours, right?" I suggested, though I wasn't sure I believed it myself. "Anyone try calling them on their cells?"

"Of *course* they called them," Mom snapped at me. Realizing what she'd done, she softened her face and took a deep breath and tried again. "Had, they found blood, but no bodies. They didn't just go out for coffee or something."

Blood?

"Oh," I said, feeling uneasy.

"I have to go and meet with the others. We're having an emergency meeting to discuss our options. But first, I have to close down the store."

"Where are you going? I'll come with you," I said, forgetting for the time being that I was still mad at her. The threat of danger can do that to you.

"No, Hadley. You stay here," she said forcefully. "No need to bring you kids into this too."

I wanted to argue with her, but she was already turning to leave. So I sighed and snagged her purse and coat off the chair and handed them to her. "Here. Go. I'll close up."

She looked at me, eyes wide with surprise before they softened into gratitude. "Thank you, Hadley." I could tell she meant it.

She stood there a few seconds longer like she was debating what to do next. Then she took her things from my hands and started toward the door. "Don't forget to lock up the back and turn off all the lights. Oh, and you know the alarm code. Just remember to use it on your way out," she said, visibly scattered. I followed her to the door and before she reached it, she turned back and hugged me tightly. She planted a kiss on my cheek before pulling away. "Grab some money out of the tip jar and order something for dinner. And, Hadley, please be careful. Something's going on here and I need to know that you're going to be safe."

Her eyes pleaded with me, and I got the feeling this was about more than just a typical case of overprotection. "I'll be fine, Mom. Promise."

"I love you, Hadley."

The vibe was getting a little too serious for me, so I laughed nervously. "Back atcha. Now go! And wake me when you get home? I want to hear what happened."

She gave me a little smile and a wave before disappearing out the door. I watched as it swung closed and stared at the wood for a few minutes afterward. But the door didn't open again.

"Where was your mom going?" Sofia asked, still filling up jars. "Seemed like she was in a hurry or something."

"Family emergency," I said quietly. After a moment I turned to face my friend and forced a smile onto my face. No use in having her suspect anything was going on. And I certainly couldn't tell her that trouble seemed to be a-brewing in the good old coven. "What do you say we hurry up and finish so we can go home?"

"Sure," Sofia said, nodding. Then she gave me a sympathetic smile and took a step toward me. "You gonna be okay?"

"I'm not sure yet," I said truthfully, turning away before she could see the worry reflected on my face.

Chapter Five

I dropped Sofia off at her house, and then headed back to mine. I knew I had things to do, but I couldn't concentrate after what had happened back at the shop. Hell, I was surprised I was even able to make it home without running off the road, considering how fast my mind was spinning.

I slipped in the front door, locking it behind me. The house was silent except for the sound of my heels hitting the hardwood floor. The comfort I usually found in that familiar click-clacking didn't do anything to make me feel better. With Mom out and Dad away on business, I was in for a quiet night.

Too quiet.

I listened for any foreign noises but didn't hear anything. One thing was sure, hearing that all they'd found of the Glovers in their home was drops of blood had definitely put me on edge. Suddenly everything around me seemed creepy.

Way to jump on the paranoia train, Hadley.

Shaking my head, I took the stairs two at a time and didn't

stop until I was safely behind the door of my room. I hung my bag on the back of my chair and grabbed my laptop from where I'd left it on my desk. Flopping down onto my bed, I pried it open and waited for the screen to go from black to blue.

"Come on, come on," I muttered to the computer, willing it to start. Finally it complied and I keyed in my password and then logged on to IM. A quick scan of my friends list showed what I'd hoped. I double clicked on user P-Diddy13 and then hit connect on the video chat.

A few agonizing seconds later, I was looking at a slightly blurry shot of Peter in what I could only guess was his bedroom. Behind him were posters of Harry Potter and Iron Man, exactly the kind of decorations you'd expect in the room of an eleven-year-old male witch. The funny thing was that Peter *did* sort of resemble a young Daniel Radcliffe, only minus the accent.

"Peter," I said, letting out the breath I hadn't realized I'd been holding. "I just heard. Are you okay?"

What I really wanted to ask was "What's going on?" but I didn't want to be callous, so I swallowed my desire for answers for the time being and focused on the young boy on my screen. Upon closer inspection, I could now see that his eyes were rimmed with red as if he'd been crying.

"Hadley. I've been waiting for someone to come online all afternoon! Everyone's been MIA for hours," he exclaimed, sounding even younger than usual. Peter had never been particularly loud or gregarious, but at this moment he looked *fragile*. I instantly felt horrible for the kid and gave him a strained smile.

"Sorry, Pete, but I only just got home. My mom rushed out of Scents and Sensibility like her hair was on fire and barely told me what was going on. I had to lock up so I only just got back," I said, all in one breath. I tried to bite my tongue, but I couldn't hold it any longer. "Peter . . . what the heck happened?"

His eyes started to well up, and just when I thought they were going to spill over, he swallowed his tears bravely. "I don't know," he managed to get out before looking up at the ceiling. Maybe video chat hadn't been the best idea after all.

"Mom said that when you got home, your parents were gone and it looked like someone else had been there?" I asked him softly, not wanting to push but desperately needing to hear it from him.

"Some of the furniture was turned over and there was water boiling on the stove. And there was blood," he said in a whisper. My heart ached as a tear rolled down his cheek. He was trying so hard to be strong, but he was clearly terrified. He sniffed and then continued. "It wasn't a lot, but it was definitely blood. Do you think they're okay, Hadley? I mean, they *could* still be okay, right?"

I wanted so badly to reassure him, but I had a feeling we both knew the truth. That this could be serious and chances were his parents *weren't* okay. But if he needed to hear a lie to get through the next few hours, I was going to give it to him. "I'm sure they're fine, Peter," I said, feeling incredibly helpless. "Besides, the rest of the coven is on top of it. If anyone can figure this whole thing out it's the elders."

I tried to put all my energy into helping him believe that what I was saying was true, and as my words crossed the web to him, I saw his face relax just a tiny bit. "Thanks, Hadley."

"No problem, kid. You got someone there with you for the night?"

"My uncle's on his way over and my neighbors are here

now," he said, looking over his shoulder and offscreen. I could hear another voice but couldn't make out what the person was saying. When Peter turned back to me, he gave me a little smile. "I gotta go, but thanks for this. I feel a little better now."

We said our good-byes and I waited until he'd closed the window and signed out to do the same. The stimulation of the past few hours was finally catching up with me and I was suddenly exhausted. Placing my computer beside me, I snuggled deeper into my pillows and closed my eyes as I went over the events of the afternoon.

Nothing like this had ever happened to anyone I knew. Not that I even *knew* what *this* was exactly. It was still possible that Peter's mom had accidentally cut herself while chopping vegetables and his dad had rushed her to the hospital because she needed stitches.

And in their haste to get out of the house, they'd flipped over the furniture. . . .

And didn't bother calling Peter to tell him where they were. . . .

And still weren't back yet.

I know. Even I didn't believe it.

But what was the alternative? That something bad had happened to Peter's parents? That maybe we weren't as safe in our own homes as we thought? That despite their magical abilities, Peter's parents hadn't been able to defend themselves against whoever had been waiting for them?

I opened my eyes and looked over at my door, which was still cracked open from when I'd come in earlier. "Noxum clasitor," I said with a wave of my finger. Within seconds, the door had closed and locked from the inside.

Just in case.

• • •

The sound of my cell playing "Defying Gravity," from my favorite Broadway show, *Wicked*, interrupted the dream I'd been having. I was confused at first, and glanced down at myself to see that I was still wearing my clothes from the night before. I jolted out of bed and looked frantically around my room. If anyone had been in here with me, they would've been able to hear my heart pounding in my chest, it was beating so hard. But after a thorough inspection of every corner of my room, I collapsed back onto my pillows.

I was alone.

I reached over and hit the snooze button on my phone. My alarm meant that it was 6:30 a.m. and that my mom would likely be pounding on my door any minute to make sure I was up for school. Before she could give me a second wake-up call, I rolled out of bed and padded into the adjoining bathroom to brush my teeth as I waited for the water in the shower to warm up. I turned on the radio before jumping in and allowed myself to sing along to one of Ke$ha's songs, even though I wouldn't be caught dead doing so in public.

I had a reputation to maintain, after all. And singing was one of the few things I wasn't good at.

An hour later, I unlocked my bedroom door and peeked my head out, listening for the familiar sounds of my mom getting ready for work. I was met with silence, but headed down the hall anyway, glancing in her room along the way.

Empty.

The bed was made, which wasn't unusual, since she always made the bed as soon as she got out of it. This didn't mean that it had been slept in, though. My suspicions grew as I entered the deserted kitchen. One look at the cold coffeepot told me with certainty that she hadn't been home the night before.

I opened up my mind fully, attempting to channel my mom,

but I was getting nothing. Then I tried her cell. It rang, and when her recording picked up, I left a message asking her to call me as soon as possible.

My chest grew tight with nerves. Was she okay? Did something happen? Should I call the cops and tell them that my mother, who was a grown adult, hadn't been there when I'd woken up this morning and hadn't checked in yet? If I did that, I was pretty sure they wouldn't take me too seriously. But there was someone who wouldn't think I was silly.

I keyed in my dad's speed dial and brought the cell up to my ear. I stood at the counter and stared out the window into the backyard as the phone rang and rang. Four times, then six. On the eighth ring, Dad's voice mail clicked on and he was telling me to leave a message.

"Hey, Dad, it's Had. I was just calling because I was wondering if you'd heard from Mom? Something happened at the Glovers' last night and I don't think she came home," I said, trying to keep my voice under control. No need to get hysterical. Yet anyway. "Um, I was just kind of worried. I'm going to try her on her cell again, but can you call me back when you get this? Thanks, Daddy. Love you."

I hung up and swallowed the lump in my throat. Then, to head off my hysteria, I busied myself with making breakfast, trying to appreciate the comfort that my morning routine brought me. I poured myself a bowl of cereal and then flipped on the TV, expecting my friends from the *Today* show to give me a distraction.

Instead, I saw something I wasn't expecting. My hand stopped halfway to my mouth as I realized what I was watching on the screen in front of me.

"This quiet neighborhood was shocked and saddened yesterday when it was discovered that a young couple had disappeared from their home in what appears to be a violent kidnapping," the newscaster said solemnly. It felt like she was talking to me, her eyes boring into mine.

Please don't be talking about what I think you're talking about.

"Those close to Mr. and Mrs. Glover say the couple is friendly and outgoing, and can't imagine why anyone would want to hurt them," the anchorwoman continued. "The couple has an eleven-year-old son who is beside himself with worry and grief and just wants his parents back safe and sound. If you know anything on the whereabouts of the missing Glenndale couple, please contact the number at the bottom of your screen."

I dropped my spoon back into the bowl. I was finished eating. My stomach felt sick as the newscaster talked about the family I knew so well. Something about it being covered on television made it that much more real. And it meant that the coven hadn't learned *anything* during their meeting.

That at least made me feel the tiniest bit better, because now I knew why my mom hadn't come home. She and the rest of the Cleri were probably still working on the mystery behind the Glovers' disappearance. That *had* to be where she was.

Suddenly, for the first time since I'd heard the news, I felt a wave of relief rush through me. Finally I could get on with my day without worrying. Good thing, too, because I had a quiz in science that morning and hadn't studied for it.

And somehow I knew that the excuse of "Members of my coven were kidnapped last night and we're waiting for the ransom—so I didn't have time to go over the chapter" wouldn't garner me much sympathy. In fact, it might actually get me a one-way ticket to the insane asylum. And maybe Kate Moss could pull off the straitjacket look, but I knew I couldn't. Unless it's custom-made in red.

I grabbed my bag and car keys off the counter and rushed

out the door, determined to make it to school with enough time to cram in a study session before the first-period bell rang. As the car warmed up, I texted Sofia to bring my coffee straight to the library. I had a feeling I was going to need it.

By the time I'd made it through my first few classes, I'd pretty much forgotten all about what was going on at home. My science quiz had kept my mind locked on something other than the fate of the Glovers. School always had a way of doing that to me. It was the one place where I felt 100 percent in control of things. As class president, I made decisions based on what would be best for my classmates. I told everyone what to vote for and what they should care about, and I set the standards of what a good role model should be. When people went against my wishes, like by bullying other students or not holding up their side of a group project, I persuaded them to see the errors of their ways.

With magic, of course.

This was when I was at my best, you could say. And I reveled in my role. Especially when life got crazy like today, and I was able to get lost in my duties. Like, for instance, I'd already handled an issue that had come up regarding where the homecoming dance would be held as well as diffused a meltdown that Trish was having over a freshman girl who was wearing the same outfit as her to school that day yet refused to change into her gym clothes to rectify the problem. And this was all before lunch.

It was a great escape for me.

At least it was before something brought me crashing back to reality.

"Did you hear about those people who went missing a few towns over?" Bethany asked as we sat down at a table outside in the quad. It was lunchtime and I was famished on account of not having finished my breakfast and going to sleep without eating dinner the night before. I'd just settled down to a chopped salad, loaded to the lid with veggies and protein. However, given the topic change, I was afraid I was about to lose my appetite again. I forced myself to take a bite because I knew I wouldn't have enough energy to make it through the day if I didn't get something in my stomach.

Besides, it would totally mess up my metabolism if I started skipping meals on a regular basis, and that would just make me even more stressed out. And no one likes a stress pooch.

"My mom is freaking out over it, and she's forced the family into lockdown for the foreseeable future," Bethany continued, rolling her eyes. "I reminded her that if the kidnappers were looking for targets who they could get big ransoms for, it wouldn't be us. She didn't find that very funny."

Oh, geez.

"So, on account of the fact that my mom has clearly gone insane, I can't make it to our weekly today," she finished, looking more bummed than apologetic. Bethany was talking about our regular excursion to the nail salon—and knowing how she felt about gossip, I knew it was killing her to opt out of a prime opportunity to gab. She'd probably begged and pleaded with her mom to change her mind to no avail.

Watching her try to choke out the words, I decided to put her out of her misery. "It's no biggie, B. I was gonna cancel this week, anyway. I've got some stuff I have to take care of at home. I have cookies to bake, reading to do . . ."

And moms to track down.

I still hadn't heard from Mom, but she knew about the "no phone calls at school" policy and insisted on following the rules. The sooner I found out she was okay, the sooner I could get on with my regularly scheduled life.

"Guess we'll all wait until next week, then?" Trish asked, not bothering to acknowledge the fact that Sofia hadn't canceled. But if her feelings were hurt, Sof didn't show it.

Bethany looked relieved to hear that she wouldn't be missing out on the dish after all. She smiled at me and I returned the gesture, happy she was happy, but wishing I felt the same.

Chapter Six

Mom wasn't at home waiting for me when I got there and she still wasn't answering her cell. She hadn't shown up by the time I started dinner, but I cooked for the both of us anyway, and eventually sat down to eat by myself. Desperately needing a distraction, I flipped through the channels until I found a movie starring one of those goofy guys from *Superbad* and forced myself to watch it. Ever try watching a comedy when you're just not in the mood to laugh? Apparently, it has the opposite effect, or so I found out when I started to feel even more on edge than I'd been before.

Putting the leftovers in the fridge for Mom, I practically jumped out of my skin when my phone went off. My heart hammering in my chest, I flipped open my phone without even looking at the caller ID.

"Mom?" I asked. I hadn't intended for my voice to sound so hopeful, but I couldn't help it.

Unfortunately, it wasn't her on the other end.

"Hadley?" It took me a few seconds to place the voice.

"Jinx?"

"Yeah," she said meekly. I could feel the fear coming through the phone as clearly as if she'd expressed it out loud. It was more than just the hesitation in her voice, though. Right now it was as if I was feeling what she was feeling. And her emotions were overwhelming. For a second, this threw me off, because for as long as I'd known Jinx, she'd always been in control. She was never over-the-top; she was even-keeled. Calm and collected. Prim and proper, without being a total Stepford. Her easygoing attitude made it so that she got along with pretty much everyone. There wasn't a person who didn't like her—including me. So the fact that she was now acting a little unhinged set off alarms in my head.

"What's wrong, Jinx?" I asked.

"Have you seen my parents? They left last night—said they were going to meet your mom and the rest of the Cleri for something—and, well, see . . ."

Her voice trailed off and I was left waiting on the line for a few seconds. I wanted to tell her to spit it out, but forced myself to take a deep breath before talking. "What happened, Jinx?"

"They never came home," she finally said. And with those words, my heart sank. It wasn't just my mom. "I tried calling Jackson first, but couldn't get ahold of him. So I thought maybe you'd heard from your mom and knew where they were? That you could tell me that they're okay? Are you still there?"

I'd only had a few conversations with Jinx before, and none of them had been outside of witch classes, yet here she was asking me to give her answers. Sure, I'd been the second person she'd contacted, but she obviously thought I could help. And I wanted so badly to do that.

After all, she'd always been kind to me—on the rare occasions that we'd said more than a few words to each other, at least. And despite the fact that Jinx had experienced a much more luxurious upbringing than I had, she'd never treated me or anyone else like we were below her. We might've even been friends if we'd gone to the same school and I'd been able to devote the kind of time that went into a friendship.

I wished I could shed some light on the situation that was clearly stressing her out. Unfortunately, I was just as in the dark as she was.

I must have gone momentarily catatonic because Jinx had to say my name a few more times before I responded.

"I'm here," I said finally. "I'm sorry, Jinx. The truth is, I haven't heard from my mom since last night either."

The line buzzed with white noise as neither of us said what we were both thinking. So I broke the silence. "Listen, I'm going to give the others a call and see if anyone else has heard from our parents, and then I'll call you back, okay?"

I knew this wasn't what Jinx wanted to hear, but the wheels in my head were already spinning and I didn't have time to console her. I had to find out what was going on. Still, I felt bad about leaving her feeling so helpless.

"We're going to figure this out. I promise," I said before hanging up and heading to my room to find the others' numbers.

First I called Sascha. And then Jasmine. When I'd gone through my entire witchy address book, I finally dialed Fallon's number, not even bothering with pleasantries. As I hung up, I collapsed back onto my bed, eyes wide and feeling eerily numb. If I hadn't been positive that I was awake, I would've thought I was having a nightmare. But there was no doubt this was really happening.

No one had heard from any of our parents in over a day, and the sinking feeling was steadily growing in the pit of my stomach.

I stared up at the ceiling, noticing for the first time that there was a discoloration right above my head in the shape of a turkey. Like the kind of turkey you made in first grade by outlining your hand. How had I never noticed that before?

I blinked. I had to snap out of it.

Picking up the phone again, I dialed the only number I hadn't called yet. And I didn't have to wait long for someone to answer.

"It's bad, isn't it?" Peter said before I could even say hello.

"Something's definitely going on," I answered, unwilling to confirm what I thought he was saying. Before I went overboard with conspiracy theories, I had to assess things for myself. And Peter might be the only one who had the clues I needed. "The Cleri held an emergency meeting last night. You know anything about it?"

"Your mom was over here for a little bit with a few of the others, and they were talking about getting the group together. They thought I wasn't listening, but I was," he said, sounding slightly guilty.

"That's *great*, Peter," I said, encouragingly. "Did you hear where they were going?"

My pulse was racing. If Peter didn't know this, we really had no leads. And my fear was that time was already running out for our parents.

"They said something about trees or bushes," he said.

"They met in a park?" I asked, confused.

"No, it was like a type of tree, I think," he said slowly. "Name some trees and maybe something will sound familiar."

Thank God I aced my environmental science class

freshman year. "Fir. Maple. Spruce. Evergreen. Elm. Pine—"

"Elm! It was the Elm. Or maybe Elm Street. No, it was definitely the Elm. They didn't say where it was exactly, but it seemed like it was kind of close to here."

I pumped my arms in the air in victory. Then I remembered that I was alone in my room, and I let them drop back down to my sides. I could celebrate later, when I'd found our parents. The important thing was that we had a name of the last place the Cleri was before . . . well, before they never came home.

But I couldn't think about that right now. I had to keep my focus on the job at hand. "Peter, you're amazing," I said happily. "And if you weren't total jailbait, I'd definitely kiss you for this."

I hopped off the bed and scurried over to my computer, quickly typing in "The Elm" and the city Peter lived in as well as the surrounding areas. I had no idea what I was looking for: a restaurant, a hotel, a church. It could be just about anything.

My heart sank when only a few listings popped up. One was for a dance club about an hour away. The second for a diner right off Highway 64. And the last appeared to be a warehouse that stored construction equipment. None of them sounded like places where the Cleri would meet.

But this was the only lead we had.

So we had to narrow it down. No way were a bunch of old people hanging out in a club, so I crossed that one off the list. And when I called the diner to find out the hours, an answering machine message told me that it had closed earlier that year. So that left only the warehouse.

Once again I dialed Peter's number and waited for him to answer. When he did, I started right in. "Give your aunt and uncle an excuse so you can get out of the house. We'll pick you up in an hour."

• • •

It ended up taking longer than I thought to round everyone up, and I didn't pull up to Peter's until an hour and a half later. By that time, my stomach was upset over the fact that I was running so late. It had already grown dark and I could barely see Peter standing in front of some bushes just out of eyeshot of the house, behind him. I hadn't even come to a full stop when he pulled open the back door and jumped inside.

"Whoa, Speed Racer, what's the rush?" Jasmine asked Peter sarcastically before I sped off down the street.

"My aunt thinks I left forty-five minutes ago to work on a school project," he explained, throwing back the hood of his sweatshirt. "They'd freak if they saw me get into a car full of kids."

"But we're not just kids, we're *twitches*," Sascha said from the passenger seat.

Peter looked at her like he had no idea what she was talking about.

"She means teen witches. Twitches," I said.

"Ohhhh," he said, nodding. I saw Jasmine roll her eyes and then look out her window, already bored with the conversation. Her requisite black ensemble made her nearly disappear into the darkness of the backseat.

"Well, *twitches* or not, they'd freak if they knew what we were doing," Peter said, settling back into his seat. "Ever since my parents . . ." His words trailed off as if he didn't know how to finish the sentence.

I instantly felt awful about what Peter must be going through. Here we all were, freaking out over having not heard from our parents in less than a day when Peter's family had been gone for twice as long. And in the Glovers' case, there was proof of a struggle. A struggle that had ended badly. At least the rest of us still had hope that our parents were just holed up somewhere.

I knew it was a long shot, but it was better than the alternative.

"It's all right, Peter. We get it. They're a little overprotective right now because of everything going on," I said.

He just nodded from his place in the back.

"Not to change the subject or anything, but do we know where we're going?" Sascha asked, chomping on her gum. I'd picked her up first and she hadn't shut up since she got in the car. If it were anyone else, I'd think it was simply nervous energy, but Sascha was a bit of a chatterbox to begin with. I'd just never been stuck in a car with her for a half hour before. Still, a nonstop monologue was better than silence. My mind tended to wander to dark places when it wasn't occupied. Sascha usually kept things light—her favorite topics of conversation were celebrities, boys, or celebrity boys. I typically thought this was endearing. But tonight I couldn't help but feel there were more important things going on than Taylor Swift's latest relationship.

"We're headed to the Elm warehouse over on one-nineteenth," I answered for the third time that night. The GPS said we'd be arriving at our destination in nine minutes, but it wasn't fast enough for me. Not when I had no idea what was happening to our parents.

"I think what Glinda here means is, why are we going to some random warehouse?" Jasmine chimed in. I waited for Sascha to make a noise like she was offended by Jasmine's comment, but it never came. I guess I was still getting used to Jasmine's sense of humor. Or total lack of a filter. But the others seemed to accept her—probably because they all hung out together pretty frequently—so I was going to try too.

I locked eyes with Peter in the mirror and at first neither of us said anything. When it became clear he wasn't going to explain, I cleared my throat.

"We're pretty sure that's where the elders went last night. And that means it was the last place we know they were."

"But why a *warehouse*?" Sascha asked, wrinkling up her forehead. I'd been wondering the same thing since I'd decided that this was the only possible place they could've gone. We drove in silence as the question hung in the air.

"Ohhhhh!" Jinx said finally, surprising us all. "I *totally* get it now."

She'd been silent since I picked her up, and I had to admit, I'd forgotten that she was even in the car. When she didn't elaborate, I shot her a look in the mirror, urging her with my mind to clue the rest of us in.

"I think I get the warehouse thing. Remember Phil Clinton? He graduated from Putnam a few years ago? Well, our families used to summer together in the Hamptons while we were growing up," Jinx explained. "Anyways, they own a construction company, so his dad has a ton of equipment warehouses scattered around. I bet that's where we're going."

I faintly remembered Phil. He was four years older than me and had graduated from high school before I'd gotten there, so we hadn't exactly run in the same groups. Apparently, he'd headed off to college on a basketball scholarship. Either Dartmouth or Berkeley or something like that.

People said he'd refused to go to Cleri classes. Claimed that he was too busy spending his dad's money to care about advancing his powers. It was hard to imagine that he and Jinx were from the same world. I hadn't known his dad, but the connection made sense. Members of the Cleri were still active even if their kids weren't attending classes anymore.

"In three hundred feet, turn right onto Fitzgerald Street. Continue to 10128 Fitzgerald Street, on left," said Jane, otherwise known as the voice of my GPS. Not long after my parents gave the tech toy to me, I'd taken to calling her Jane. The computer-generated voice had the tiniest hint of a British accent, and I imagined the owner of the voice to be about twenty-five years old, sophisticated, and super-intelligent. Jane was most likely single—but it was by choice, not because guys weren't into her. In other words, I sort of pictured her as being an older version of myself, but with a way cooler accent.

"Arriving at 10128 Fitzgerald Street," Jane said.

As she said it, the five of us looked out our windows expecting to see acres of flat, indiscriminant buildings. But there was nothing there.

"What are we looking at?" Peter asked.

"I have no idea," I muttered, straining my eyes to see in the dark. I pulled the car over and turned off the engine. Getting out, I let the door slam behind me, not even waiting for the others to follow. The street was empty as I crossed it, and all I could hear was the sound of crickets as they chirped in the night, followed by the echo of my heels hitting the pavement.

As I made my way to the other side of the road, I started to get a nervous feeling in my stomach, which always told me when something bad was about to happen. My fear threatened to turn into panic and my breath caught in my throat as I stepped up onto the sidewalk. I didn't even realize that my hands had covered my mouth to stifle a scream. But the scream came anyway, a shrill cry in the quiet night. Only it wasn't me; it came from one of the other girls just behind me.

Funny, I hadn't even heard them come up.

I tried to speak, but for some reason I couldn't. My mind had shut down and the rest of the world was quickly slipping away.

Because in front of me, on that chilly, dark evening, I was standing out on the sidewalk and looking at the last place my mom was known to be.

And the whole thing was burned to the ground.

Chapter Seven

I don't remember the drive home. At some point I must have told Jasmine to call an emergency meeting with the other twitches. Someone tried reaching Jackson again, but only succeeded in getting his voice mail. Either he'd been with the rest of the elders, which was highly possible, or he was out there and unable to connect with us. Whichever it was, it became clear at that point that we were on our own.

By now, I would've done just about anything to get away from the wreckage that used to be the construction warehouse. Even if it meant going home and telling the others what I feared had happened.

There had been so much wreckage.

As soon as I had realized exactly what it was I was looking at, I'd gone numb with fear. The place was a charred mess. Everything was burned to the ground, and what wasn't completely incinerated was covered in black soot, masking any evidence of what had once been standing in its spot. One look at the steaming acre of burned wood and steel and I knew nothing had survived.

And no one.

Before I knew what I was doing, I began to stagger forward, stepping onto the brittle remains of the grounds, not realizing until I'd already walked a few feet that the remnants were hot enough to melt the bottoms of my shoes.

That's when I knew I was officially out of it. I was aware that my brand-new Jimmy Choos were being destroyed and I didn't stop walking. I just didn't care. I kept moving forward, even as I slipped on the loose pieces of debris below my feet. I slowed down only when something caught my eye among the sea of black.

It was shiny and small.

I veered over to see what had been reflecting the light of the moon, approaching where I thought the glint was coming from. The ground wasn't as hot here and I crouched down, hoping to see a little better.

There it was again. Just a tiny hint of gold among the darkness.

I got down on my hands and knees and began to pick through the ashes and toss burned-up objects behind me. Clawing through the debris, I briefly wondered if I'd been seeing things, and then my hand hit something warm and smooth in the dust. Carefully withdrawing my hand from the mess, I knew from the feel of it that it had a chain. Either a necklace or a medal, maybe. Pulling the scarf out of my hair, I spit on the object and begin to polish it. A thought came to mind about how disgusted my girlfriends would be to see me crawling around in the dirt and spit-shining trash, and I found I didn't care.

All I cared about was trying to figure out what the hell had happened here. And whether our worst fears had actually come true.

When I was sure I'd gotten the object in my hands as clean as I could without taking it to my jeweler, I tossed my scarf aside and held it up in front of me—and gasped.

It was a gold necklace, thin and delicate, with a pendant about an inch in size attached. The medallion read, "Be the change you wish to see in the world," and it hung from a fourteen-inch chain. The piece was beautiful and obviously handmade.

And completely familiar to me.

It was the same necklace my mom had worn as far back as I could remember. My dad and I had both bought her other jewelry over the years—some expensive, some one-of-a-kind, one piece was even priceless—but she never took off the necklace engraved with the quote from Gandhi.

Except she wasn't wearing it now, because it was here in my hand, covered in soot and still warm from the fire. As I thought about what that meant, my head drooped to my chest, defeated.

That was when I officially checked out.

After that I somehow made it back to the car. The others filed in after me, everyone dealing with their grief in different ways. Without my suggesting it, Jasmine told the rest of the coven to meet at my house ASAP. Her usually sarcastic tone had been replaced with one that was softer, kinder. The last thing I wanted was a bunch of kids running around my house—my parents' house—but I didn't have the energy to argue. I was having a hard enough time keeping us on the road because my eyes kept blurring with tears.

"Throw your stuff wherever," I mumbled as we walked inside. The monotone voice that came out didn't sound like my own and I had to look around to confirm that I'd actually spoken. I locked eyes with the four of them for the first time since we'd left the Elm, and froze. I had no idea what to say. So I said what my mom would have if she'd been there.

"There's food in the kitchen. Help yourselves. I have to . . ." I looked around for an excuse to leave the room but was having trouble forming complete sentences, let alone being creative. ". . . go somewhere," I finished lamely. Not even waiting for a response, I turned away from my coven and trudged over to the stairs, climbing them slowly. I felt like I was moving through quicksand and by the time I'd reached the top, I was exhausted. And I was usually *always* energetic. A few kids had even nicknamed me the Energizer Bunny back in freshman year.

But now just *existing* felt hard.

My room was exactly how I'd left it a few hours before and I felt minor relief as soon as I saw all my stuff. I needed to feel the familiar. See things that gave me even a tiny bit of comfort. But before I could fully enjoy the homecoming, I heard someone follow me into my room.

"Hadley?" said a quiet voice. I recognized it as Sascha's. She sounded much less peppy than usual and for this I was thankful. "I'm sorry to bug you but, um, everyone's downstairs and we're not sure what to do or where anything is."

I looked at her blankly. I guess in my haste to get upstairs, I'd completely forgotten to show them where things were. I forced myself to concentrate on what she was asking and tried to be a better hostess. "There are pillows and blankets in the closet down the hall. People can either find a room or a chair to sleep in. The couch downstairs pulls out into a bed. It's been a long day . . . let's just regroup tomorrow."

I turned around and walked over to my bed and collapsed face-first onto it. With minimal movement, I kicked my destroyed Choos onto the floor and buried my head in one of the pillows.

Sascha didn't say anything else as she watched me retreat to my mattress, and after a few seconds I heard the shuffling of feet and then the door close.

I was finally alone.

I wasn't sure exactly what woke me, but once my eyes sprang open, I lay in bed listening for what it might have been. But it was quiet. Well, except for the white noise ringing in my ears, which was almost more frightening than if I'd heard something go bump in the night. I wasn't used to the stillness.

I stared up at the ceiling, willing myself back to sleep, but finally stopped trying when I heard a noise. It sounded like the scraping of a chair across the kitchen floor, followed by glass clanging against tile. Someone was in the kitchen.

I groaned. The banging continued and so I weighed my options. I could stay in bed and most likely run over the events of the night or I could head downstairs to see what was happening. Sighing, I threw my legs over the side of the bed and yawned as I pushed my feet into my slippers. The sooner I got them to cut out the noise the sooner I could get back to bed and try to forget that this whole sucky day had ever happened.

I walked quietly down the stairs and peeked around the corner into the kitchen, expecting to see Sascha or Peter, or even annoying Fallon. But when my eyes adjusted, I saw the back of a woman as she worked her way around the cabinets. I stood frozen as she pulled out a box of cookies and then moved over to a steaming mug that was waiting for her on the counter.

As my eyes adjusted to the dim light, I watched her pull out a bag of chamomile-and-peppermint tea. My heart immediately started to race as recognition hit me.

It couldn't be.

I lurched forward, stumbling over my own feet as I tried to close the space between us.

"Mom?"

She turned around at the sound of my voice and I couldn't even describe the joy I felt at seeing her face. I fell into her arms and buried myself in her hair before starting to cry. As I blubbered, I thought about all the questions I had for her.

Where were you? What happened? Are you okay? What's going on? What happened at the Elm? Where are the others?

But none of that came out of my mouth. "I'm sorry, Mom" was all I could manage before squeezing her even tighter. All my other questions could wait. The important thing was that she was there with me. What I'd thought had happened in that burned-down mess had just been a big misunderstanding. She was okay. We were okay.

"Aw, sweetie, I know," she replied, rubbing my back soothingly. "Me too."

"I love you and I'll do whatever you want me to," I told her. "I'll train. I won't argue with Jackson anymore. I promise. I'll be better."

"That's good, baby," she answered softly. "Because I'm going to need you to be strong. I need to know you'll do whatever it takes. That you'll fight."

"I will," I promised, pulling away from her and looking straight into her eyes. I still couldn't quite believe she was standing there in the kitchen with me. "If anything happens, I'll be ready."

"You don't know how happy it makes me to hear that," Mom said. But the look on her face was more like relief than happiness. I cocked my head to the side as I tried to read her mind. Unfortunately, my mom had had a lot more practice at reading my thoughts than vice versa and I couldn't get anything from her.

"What's going on, Mom?"

"Hadley, sweetie, something bad's happened," she said quietly.

"I know. Peter's parents were kidnapped," I responded. "And no one knows where their parents are. We went to the Elm and it was a mess. And then I found your necklace and I was so worried . . ."

My words trailed off as I saw her wince at this. I opened my mouth to keep talking, but then promptly closed it. Something was really wrong. I was starting to feel sick to my stomach again.

"You have to be strong. For me and for the others," she said finally, reaching her hand out toward me.

"What are you talking about?" I asked, my bottom lip starting to tremble.

"I'm so sorry, sweetie. I didn't know this was going to happen. We were just trying to fix things, but they knew where we were. They surprised us," she said, swallowing hard. "I tried to stop them, but we didn't have a chance. There were too many of them and not enough of us."

"Why are you saying all of this?" I asked, confused. My chest was feeling heavy and I was having trouble breathing. "You're here. You're fine."

"I'm not," she said bluntly.

I flinched as if I'd been slapped. "You are," I whispered, my eyes tearing up again. "You're fine! Stop lying!"

I was screaming now, and couldn't care less if anyone heard. I was so confused and hurt and tired, I just wanted to figure out what was going on so we could go back to our regular lives.

"I'm telling you the truth, Hadley." She said this sadly, a

tear rolling down her cheek. "We were at the Elm and Parris's coven knew we were there. I'm not sure how they knew, but they did. Our powers wouldn't work for some reason, and before we could get out . . . the flames spread so quickly, we were gone before we even realized what was happening."

"No," I whimpered. "No, no, no, no, *no!*"

She took my face in her hands, kissing my wet cheeks. Even though I was upset, I let her do this, mostly because it was better than trying to make sense of what she was saying.

"Listen to me. I know this is going to be hard on you and I wish you didn't have to go through this, but you've *got* to be strong. You're going to be sad, and that's okay, but I don't want you to be sad forever," my mom said gently. "Because all those kids in there? They need you."

"What about what I need? I need *you*, Mom. I need you. Here. With me."

"You have me, Hadley. I'm here, watching over you always. But I can't do what needs to be done next," she said. "You are stronger than anyone else I've ever known—more powerful as well. You're the only one who can stop the Parrishables."

"I thought you didn't want me to call them that," I said, sniffling.

She smiled at me. "That's my girl. Always arguing," she said. "That's good. You're going to need that fight in you for what's ahead. They're strong, and none of you are prepared for their darkness yet. It's up to you to teach the coven. You're the only hope of keeping the Cleri alive."

"But I don't know what to do," I said, looking down at my hands, suddenly more unsure of myself than I'd ever been before.

"Yes you do. Trust your instincts, Hadley, and you'll be just fine."

"I can't do this alone, Mom," I said, hating to admit I wasn't fully capable of handling any situation that came my way. But in this case, I was terrified at what she was suggesting. I wasn't sure I could be the one everyone was counting on. Hell, if I could barely even get out of bed, how was I supposed to save anyone from an ancient, evil witch coven?

"You *can* do this, Hadley. In fact, you're the *only* one who can do this. And you won't be alone. You'll have the power of your ancestors behind you," she said.

It was hard for me to believe that I was our coven's only hope. That I was somehow strong enough to do what our parents couldn't. I mean, sure, I could convince my friends and classmates to do what I wanted, but when it came to outsmarting deranged witches and stopping their mission of total witch-world domination, how was I supposed to be anything but a well-dressed teenager who was uniquely skilled in the art of persuasion?

Could I be more than that? Was I more than that?

"What am I supposed to do?" I asked, my voice shaky. I still wasn't sure that what my mom was saying was true, but since this might be the last time I talked to her, I wasn't going to argue. I'd done that enough when she was alive and look where it got me.

"First, you need to get the coven out of town. Somewhere the Parrishables won't be able to find you. Our summer cabin, maybe? It's plenty big for all of you and no one but us knows about it. Then you need to take over training. They're going to be resistant at first, but you have to convince them that they need to get prepared. If not, you'll all be in danger."

I nodded, recognizing how surreal this conversation was, but agreeing nonetheless. "And then what?"

"Then you wait for them to find you, and you fight like hell."

Chapter Eight

A knock pulled me from my dream and I shot up in bed, reaching out for my mom, who was no longer there. I looked over at my door for some sort of evidence that it hadn't actually been a dream, but saw that I still had on the same clothes from earlier and realized the truth.

She was really gone.

The loss began to hit me in waves, slow and dull at first, and then increasing to an almost crippling pain that grew from my chest up to my throat and finally to my eyes. Just as I was about to let my grief brim over, there was another knock at my door.

Go away!

I wanted to scream at whoever was on the other side, but I collapsed back onto the bed and buried my head under my pillow instead. My guest must have taken my silence as an invitation to come in though, and I heard the muffled sound of the knob turning and the squeak of the door swinging open.

Oh, for the love of . . .

"Hadley?" It was Jasmine. "We need to talk about what happened."

It was getting hard to breathe with my face pressed into my sheets, but I didn't want to turn around and look Jasmine in the eyes. I just wanted to be left alone with the memories of my mom. I could tell she was waiting for me to say something though, so I sighed in frustration before answering.

"Don't you get it, Jasmine? We're on our own now," I said. "What's there to talk about?"

The room grew silent and for a few seconds I thought I'd succeeded in driving her away too. I was wrong. Before I could react, the pillow was ripped away from my head and hit the wall opposite us. I jerked around to shout at Jasmine but stopped when I saw her face. "Stop being such a witch and snap out of it already," she growled.

Her usual indifference to everything and everyone had turned into a laser-like focus I hadn't seen before. For the first time, I saw what most people outside of our coven probably saw: Jasmine looked scary. Like crazy scary. Her black hair shot up in all different directions and her eyes were fiery. She adjusted her stance like she was about to attack and I couldn't help but back up on my bed.

I opened my mouth to speak, but she wasn't done yet.

"Look, I know you're used to being little miss Teen Queen and that your witch duties usually come in second place, but you seriously need to rearrange your priorities," she said. "We let you come and go before, because it didn't really affect us, but now it does. And I have no idea why, but you are more powerful than any of us. So we need you to step your homecoming-court, rah-rah ass up to the plate and start swinging."

Something inside me clicked. Commanding crowds at school came so easily to me, and it shouldn't be any different with this particular group of twitches. Hadn't my mom basi-cally said this to me in my dream? That I needed to take con-trol of the situation?

In my heart, I knew she was right. I *was* stronger than the others, and given my natural abilities, I was likely the only one who could lead this group. But how could I possibly do that when I felt seconds away from falling apart?

Jasmine relaxed a little as she watched me process what she'd said. When I didn't respond, she took her time walking away. She placed her hand on the door, but instead of leaving she looked back at me. I could tell the fight that had been in her was now gone.

"I know this sucks—it's hard on all of us. And you're not the only one whose parents are gone. But bottom line, we really need everyone to rally now, including you."

Jasmine walked out of the room without a backward glance, closing the door behind her. I blinked back my tears and stood up, walking slowly over to my bathroom. Inside, I splashed water on my face and paused to study myself in the mirror. Only this time it wasn't for beauty reasons. I was trying to see what the others saw in me.

My mom had said I was their only hope.

"Well, I guess we're about to find out," I said out loud.

Before doing anything else, I tried to get ahold of my dad again since he still hadn't called me back. On the one hand, I wanted to know that he was okay and hear him tell me that I would be okay too. But at the same time, I dreaded having to tell him what had happened to Mom. How do you tell some-one that the love of his life won't be coming home? I almost threw up just thinking about it.

The call went to voice mail and my worries turned from breaking the news to Dad to dealing with the fact that he might be in trouble too. As I dialed the number to the hotel he was staying at, I started to wonder if I was really ready to know the truth. Someone answered and I nearly froze, unsure of what I was supposed to say next.

"This is the Meadowland Hotel; my name is Darcey. How may I assist you today?" a woman asked. She sounded nice. Like she really wanted to help.

Can you tell me if my dad's still alive?

"Hi. I need to be connected to the room of Drew Bishop," I said instead, pacing around my room. "He should be a guest there?"

There was a pause as Darcey clicked away on her computer keys. Finally, after what seemed like forever, she cleared her throat. "I'm sorry, ma'am, but Drew Bishop is not staying with us right now."

The blood drained from my face. "But he was supposed to be there," I said, helplessly.

"I do have a record of his reservation, but it appears he never checked in," Darcey said. "Could he have made alternate arrangements and forgotten to cancel these?"

"No," I said, defeated.

"I'm sorry about that, sweetheart," Darcey said. Then she paused uncomfortably before saying, "Is there anything else I can help you with?"

Sure. Can you fix my life that's currently imploding, Darcey?

"Um, can you tell him to call home if he does get there?" I asked.

"Sure thing, hon." Darcey sounded like she felt bad for me. She had no idea how bad I felt, though.

This new development made me begin to think the worst, but I shook it off. I couldn't let myself go there right now. There were other things to do. Like, tell the rest of the coven what had happened.

But instead of heading straight for the living room, I went to the kitchen first, hoping I might be able to pull some strength from my mom for what I was about to do. I'd half hoped to see her standing there at the sink like before, or cooking up a storm. It was what she would have been doing had she been there. Weekends had always been our time. During the week, we never had a chance to eat breakfast together, because I was usually running late for school and she was trying to get to the shop on time. And since Dad was always traveling, Saturdays were our time to slow down and catch up, just the two of us. She'd make waffles or pancakes and top the plate off with some eggs and bacon. If Mom was in a particularly good mood, she'd surprise me with smiley face pancakes with chocolate chips for eyes and a mouth.

Though I never would've admitted it to her before, I'd looked forward to it all week long. And when I saw that the kitchen was indeed empty, my heart felt like I was on a roller coaster racing down the tracks at a hundred miles an hour.

I walked over to the sink and placed my hands where my mom's had been, taking a moment to miss her. I'm not sure how long I stood there, but eventually I heard someone cough behind me.

"See anything out there?" a voice asked. I turned quickly to see Fallon standing there and almost groaned.

Great. The last person on earth I wanted to see was standing in my kitchen, arms folded over his chest and looking at me with a smirk on his face.

But when he saw my expression, his softened, and then his arms dropped to his sides. Surprisingly, he walked over to the table and took a seat, motioning for me to sit, too. I swiped at my face in an attempt to make myself look like less of a mess. I sighed because I knew it was futile and crossed the room to join him.

"What do you want, Fallon?" The words came out sounding harsher than I'd intended.

I braced myself for a sarcastic retort, but instead, he just looked at me with this weird expression on his face. If I hadn't known him so well, I might've said he looked sorry for me. But that wasn't possible. This was *Fallon* we were talking about.

"You okay?" he asked, his voice surprisingly quiet. Almost caring, even. I nearly snorted at him for mocking me, but something told me he was being serious. It threw me off so much that he had to repeat himself just for me to believe he'd said it.

I wanted to tell him to mind his own business, but I didn't have the energy to be mean to him. Not tonight. Besides, it seemed wrong somehow, to start something up when he appeared to be waving the white flag on our frenemy war.

"Honestly? Not really," I answered finally. I looked down at my hands to avoid his eyes, because how do you tell someone something like this? That my mom was dead and his parents were too? How could my mom and Jasmine have actually thought that I'd be able to do this, not once, but over a dozen times?

"Look, Fallon, something serious is going on and it's heavier than anything I've ever dealt with before. I have to tell you guys something, but I really don't know how. I don't think . . ." I got choked up and had to stop talking in order to swallow the lump that had formed in my throat. "I don't think I'm strong enough to do this."

I had no idea why I was being so open with him. He was my least favorite person, pretty much ever, and it went against everything I believed to show weakness to anyone, let alone an enemy. But hard as I tried, I couldn't hold it together. I knew there was a chance that Fallon would use our private conversation against me. But I just couldn't shoulder all the responsibility alone anymore, and Fallon was asking to be let in.

"So what do I do?" I asked, staring down at the table.

He was silent for a minute and I resisted the urge to look up at him. "Use the Band-Aid approach," he finally said.

"Huh?"

He rolled his eyes at me, but it wasn't malicious for once. "You know. If you pull a Band-Aid off slowly, then you feel every single hair rip out of your body. And it hurts like crazy. But if you pull it off nice and quick"—he made a quick tugging motion at an imaginary wound—"it's over fast and it hurts a lot less."

I crinkled my eyebrows.

"Oh, come on. This is sort of common knowledge, Hadley," he said, teasing me now. "Where have you been?"

"I don't rip off my Band-Aids. I use magic to make them disappear," I said simply. "Why would you *willingly* rip off a Band-Aid? Unless you're a glutton for punishment, and in that case . . ." I let the sentence trail off as I raised my eyebrows at him.

"Fine, fine, whatever, but you get my point, right? Tell us quickly. It'll hurt less that way. Don't think about it, just do it," he said. Then he looked straight into my eyes and said it again, more as a command this time rather than a suggestion. "Just do it."

I took a deep breath and did as he said. "There was a fire where our parents met last night and they were caught inside," I blurted out, not able to look at him as I said it. "Fallon . . . I don't think anyone survived."

There was total silence, and after about thirty seconds I dared to peek at this boy whose life I'd just turned upside down. I felt awful about being the one to break the news because I knew exactly what he was feeling. He was realizing that the life he'd once had was over. That it would be a long time before he felt safe again.

When I finally looked at Fallon, he was staring out the window behind me, his body as still as if he were frozen in place. His mouth was pulled tight in a straight line, but other than that, I had no idea what he was thinking. I was almost scared to find out but knew I had to check if he was okay. After all, I'd done this to him.

I reached out my hand and placed it on his arm, hoping to give him some solace. But almost as soon as I'd touched him, he pulled away and turned his gaze back at me. "So," he said, taking a deep breath, "what do we do now?"

It wasn't what I'd been expecting him to say, but I was glad I wasn't going to have to get all touchy-feely with him. He wasn't my favorite person, and the truth was, I had no clue how I was supposed to help him with his emotions when I hadn't been handling my own all that well.

"Well, first I think we need to tell everyone else," I said, still hating this part of the plan. I had a feeling not everyone would react like Fallon had.

"Then what?" he asked.

"Then we get out of here. Go someplace the Parrishables won't come looking for us."

"Any ideas on where that might be?" he asked.

Remembering my mom's suggestion of our family's cabin, I nodded. "Yeah. I think I do."

"Okay," Fallon said, getting up from his chair. "Let's do this, then."

"Rip it off like a Band-Aid?" I asked.

"Just like a Band-Aid."

Chapter Nine

It felt like the longest day of my life.

And the most exhausting. I knew it would be difficult telling everyone what had happened to our parents, but I had no idea it would be like this. In a way, I should have known it wasn't going to be a quick fix. After all, how long had it taken *me* to simply become coherent again after figuring out what had gone down at the Elm?

After my talk with Fallon, we'd gathered the Cleri members who'd been at the Elm and discussed what we were going to do next. I told them about the dream I'd had of Mom and shared my suspicions that the Parrishables were, indeed, back. Given the circumstances, they couldn't argue with this fact and quickly agreed. But identifying our enemies didn't help to make us feel any better.

"I know this is beyond painful, but we've got to be strong for the others," I said quietly. I studied each of the five faces that sat around the table in my kitchen. "They're going to be devastated and scared. Some are going to fall apart. But we have to pick them up. I think our lives depend on it."

A few people nodded, others sniffled, still trying to get a handle on their emotions. Jasmine, who'd been so strong just a while before, had mascara lines running down her face. I doubted she'd cried in front of anyone else, but it was evidence that she was hurting just like the rest of us. Sascha, who was usually so bubbly, had clammed up and wasn't talking to anyone, and Jinx had her arms wrapped around herself, like the action was the only thing keeping her from crawling out of her skin. Peter seemed to be in shock.

And me, I felt uncomfortable, sad, and helpless. I had no idea how to make any of them feel better, and we'd just agreed that I would be the one to tell the rest of the Cleri—which meant I was about to double the grief in the house.

Once we'd all pulled ourselves together the best we could, we joined the others in the living room. Some had no idea what was going on, while others started crying as soon as they saw us. I choked back my own tears, remembering that the more I held it together, the better off we'd all be.

Then I commenced to give them the worst news they'd probably ever get in their lives. It dawned on me that from here on out, whenever they thought about the day that their worlds came crashing down, they'd be reminded of me. It wasn't exactly the way I wanted to be remembered. But it was too late to worry about that.

Taking Fallon's advice, I told them quickly, sparing them the more graphic details; no reason to give them nightmares on top of their nightmares. They were going to have a difficult time sleeping as it was. I used my powers of persuasion to try to fill the atmosphere with soothing vibes, willing them to feel comfort and a sense of calm as I explained that our parents wouldn't be coming home and neither would we—for a while at least.

"I know that this is hard to hear, but we're all here for you," I said softly. "We're each other's family now. And that means we watch after one another and have each other's backs. I want you to know that I *will* take care of you. The next couple of days aren't going to be easy and you might want to give up, but just remember, we can get through anything as long as we're together."

As I finished up my speech, I could already feel that my persuasion had managed to help at least a tiny bit. There was still that cloud of sadness hanging over all of us, but it could've been so much worse. I found a bit of solace in the fact that I could be helpful in even the smallest of ways.

In the end, I offered myself up to anyone who needed to talk. A few had questions I didn't have the answers to. Why did this happen? What's going to happen to us now? How long will we feel this way? All I could do was try to answer them honestly, but I worried that I was leaving them with more questions than before. Many people snuck off to separate sections of the house, wanting to deal with the news on their own and crying themselves to sleep.

By the time things began to die down, it was around one in the morning and I felt like I was sleepwalking. Covering up those who'd already passed out and giving blankets and pillows to the rest, we tried to get some sleep. But even after I returned to my bed and closed my eyes, my mind wouldn't shut down.

I'd felt the weight of the coven on my shoulders as I'd stood before them earlier. They were all waiting for me to tell them what to do next. It was clear on their faces. And all I had was the next phase in our plan: to get everyone away from danger. Mom had said it in my dream, and I knew we had to disappear. Go somewhere the Parrishables couldn't find us.

And I knew just where to take them.

• • •

I'd been in and out of sleep all night, and as soon as I saw the first rays of the sun coming out, I got up and started preparing for our departure. The more I'd thought about it, the more I'd realized just how dangerous it probably was for us to be at the house. Every minute that we stayed put us closer to the possibility of running into the same people who'd gone after our parents. And we weren't ready to deal with that yet.

One by one, I woke everyone up and told them we were leaving. Three of us had licenses and we quickly divided everyone up into cars. With thirteen kids rounding out what was left of our coven, everyone had to keep an eye on each other. Peter was one of the youngest and I was the oldest, with ages ranging in between.

Between my powers of persuasion and the threat of the Parrishables fresh on everyone's minds, we packed up everything we could fit in the cars—blankets, food, and anything else we might need—and were ready to go within a half hour of waking. I took as many of my clothes as I could, knowing that I could always change them later with a spell.

Once everyone was outside, I sat down on the couch and looked around the house that I'd lived in since birth. Even though I'd been home alone dozens of times, it had never felt so empty before. My eyes fell on a framed family picture sitting on a side table. It was from six years before, and I was positioned between my parents and we were all wearing white. We'd been at the beach on vacation that particular weekend, and my parents had forced me off the sand and into my sundress in order to take the photo. I had made it quite clear that I was *very* unhappy to be taken away from the surf and the new friends I'd made. Kicking and screaming as they carried me up the stairs to our beach house, they forced me into the shower and then pulled my dress over my head.

By the time they'd gotten me outside and seated on the wall that separated the boardwalk from the beach, I'd stopped fighting them. But it wasn't because I'd tired myself out; when I was younger, I had lungs that would make any scream queen from a slasher flick jealous. No, it was because another plan was forming in my mind.

Since we were at the beach by ourselves my dad had to set the timer on the camera in order to take the picture. So he lined us up in the camera's window and then pressed the button. Shuffling back to us, he slid into place on the other side of me. I was front and center now, staring straight into the camera lens.

When the warning light went off, letting us know the picture was about to be taken, I crossed my eyes and stuck out my tongue. As soon as I heard the click, I let my face relax and turned back to my parents.

"Can I go back to my friends now?" I asked.

"Sure. See, that wasn't so hard, was it?" my mom asked me as I ran off toward the house to change back into my swimsuit.

Before I made it to the door I heard my dad say, "That's going to be the best family picture yet."

I snickered as I thought about the surprise he'd get when he developed the film a few weeks later. My dad didn't like to use digital cameras and insisted on taking our pictures old-school, which meant that there was no screen to review the images after taking them.

In a way, my dad was right. That picture turned out to be my favorite family portrait. And although they rolled their eyes every time they looked at it, I knew that it had eventually become their favorite too.

I think that was when my parents first realized that I had a mind of my own and would do just about anything to get my way.

A tear rolled down my cheek and fell onto my hand.

There would be no more family pictures. That realization nearly knocked the wind out of me, and I had to force myself to take deep breaths. I reached out and ran my thumb over my mom first and then my dad.

Dad.

I had no proof that he was alive or dead at this point. Part of me knew that if the Parrishables had managed to find the rest of the coven at a random warehouse, they'd probably be able to find him, too.

But just in case, I ripped out a piece of paper from my notebook and began to write.

Dear Dad,

I'm not sure if you'll get this—in fact, I don't know if anyone will ever read this—but just in case you *are* reading this, I want you to know that I'm okay. Some pretty messed-up things have happened since you left and . . . well, I had to leave. We all had to leave.

But you don't have to worry about me. I have a plan. If you *do* get this and want to come looking for me, we're going to the place where you first taught me how to ride my bike. I figure we'll be safest there.

Speaking of safe . . . none of us are. I think you were right—they are back and out to get us all. But don't worry, I *remember what we talked about and will keep my promise.*

Please be careful and know that I love you!

*Love always,
Hadley*

When I was finished writing the note, I folded it up until it fit in the palm of my hand. Then I went through the kitchen to the back door and stepped outside. My eyes landed on a rock sitting next to the door. It was painted yellow and green and read "Welcome" in big, bubbly letters. I'd decorated it when I was just six years old and my parents had refused to let me get rid of it.

Picking up the rock, I turned it over to the flat side and ran my fingers over the smooth, hard surface. Closing my eyes, I quickly said, "Hiddemus opendum." As soon as I'd said it, a hole appeared where the bottom of the rock used to be. When I was younger, this was our family's way of hiding our house key. But almost from the beginning, my dad had also taken to hiding little notes for me in there. He'd leave me funny jokes or inspirational messages. Sometimes he'd just say he loved me. It was sort of our special thing. I used to leave him notes too, but as I got older and then entered high school, I started to carry my own house key and the messages just kind of stopped.

Still, I had to believe that he'd find it if he was looking for it. If he came home at all. My eyes started to tear up again and I shoved the letter into the rock, sealing it back up with a spell before I had a chance to break down.

Placing the rock back in its spot, I shook my head and blinked back tears.

"Hadley! We're ready to go," Sascha called out from the front of the house.

I went inside and locked the back door behind me. "Coming!" I walked through the living room, picking up the picture frame along the way and hugging it to my chest.

Something to remind me of home, just in case I never make it back.

I threw my bags over my shoulder and then made my way outside to meet up with the rest of the coven. As I locked up, I turned to look around my neighborhood for what might be the last time. Everything about it felt comfortable to me. After seventeen years of playing hide-and-seek and games of tag, and eventually sneaking around and finding secret spots to kiss boys, I knew everything about this place. I could navigate these streets with my eyes closed.

I sighed and started to walk toward my car. Everyone was waiting for me and I climbed in and started the engine. As I pulled out of the driveway, I looked in my rearview mirror once more. And as I did so, I saw something I wasn't expecting. Squinting to make out what it was, I saw the guy my dad and I had seen the last time we'd gone jogging. Even though I was more than twenty feet away by now, I could have sworn he was looking straight at me. I felt a momentary sadness that I wouldn't get to learn more about him and then felt guilty over the selfishness of the thought. The boy cocked his head to the side as he watched us drive away and I let the image of him fade as I turned the corner and focused on the road in front of me.

Right now, the most important thing was getting everyone to the cabin safely. I could worry about boys with piercing eyes later.

Chapter Ten

It shouldn't have taken us more than an hour and a half to drive up to the cabin, but between the three cars and thirteen people, we had to stop practically every twenty minutes for either food, gas, or bathroom breaks. I had no idea what small bladders everyone had until I was forced into a road trip with them.

It's called holding it, people!

The one positive thing about the drive was that it allowed us all to leave the horror behind us to an extent. We began to think more about what we were heading to, instead of what we'd lost. Our parents weren't far from our thoughts, but the trip was a good distraction for everyone.

By the time we arrived at our destination I was so happy that we wouldn't be making any more stops that I nearly jumped out of the car before I'd even pulled the emergency brake, and kissed the dirty ground we'd been driving on. Of course, I didn't actually do that—I mean, what sort of message would that send to the rest of the coven?

No one respects dirt kissers.

Instead, I rolled down the windows and took in the fresh air that came along with being at this altitude. And then I saw our refuge. The cabin was smaller than I remembered it. But that was to be expected, I suppose, since the last time I'd been there I was still a kid. And everything looks huge when you're only four feet tall. Still, even though it wasn't exactly the mansion I'd been picturing on our way up here, it wasn't small by anyone's standards. Good thing, too, because we were about to have a full house.

I pulled the car up to the garage but didn't have the remote to open the door, so I parked right there, turning off the engine and enjoying the relative silence. I didn't bother waiting for everyone else before getting out of the car, and threw my arms over my head to stretch after such a long and painful drive.

There were only so many road trip games a person could take before freaking out, and apparently I was horribly slow when it came to identifying VW bugs. That, coupled with the fact that I wasn't exactly in a game-playing kind of mood, and I was pretty sure I would never be playing slug bug again.

But even *that* couldn't spoil my mood now that I was here. The air was crisp, but not cold, and I felt like I could just breathe easier. Lord knows we were all going to need a little bit of fresh air over the next couple of days. I couldn't help but smile, thinking about my parents, as I looked around at the place where I'd spent most of my childhood summers.

Over to my right, just behind the garage, was the shed that one summer, I'd insisted was my own mini-cabin. I'd somehow managed to convince my parents to let me clean out the storage space (and by clean out, I mean that I took all my dad's tools and piled them up in the garage next to the cars) and made the area into my own personal getaway. Armed with an old cot, my comforter and pillows, my entire stash of stuffed animals, a few picture frames, a stack of magazines, a handful of books, and my battery-operated CD player, I decorated my new place in true tweenage fashion.

I bragged for hours about how I was going to spend the rest of my summer in the practically windowless shed and how amazing it was to finally have a house all to myself. It didn't even cross my mind that a place as small as that was nothing to be proud of. Yet after I officially moved in, I posted a sign that asked visitors to please "knock before entering" (which, let's face it, just meant my parents) and then spent the next couple of hours listening to CDs, reading magazines, and lounging on my new bed.

As the lights outside began to dim and the shed got steadily darker, I got my first inkling that Operation Freedom might not be as perfect a plan as I'd thought. For one, at the rate the sun was setting, I'd be heading to bed a few hours earlier than my regular bedtime, simply because I didn't have electricity in the shed and hadn't thought to bring a flashlight with me. And there was also the fact that I'd left my secret stash of Pop-Tarts and Funyuns up in my old room. Finally, when my bladder started to fill up, I knew that my fantasy of having my own place at the age of nine was over. No way was I peeing in the woods just to get a little privacy.

And so I'd thrown all my stuff into the middle of my comforter and dragged it back to the house. They never said it, but I think my parents had always known I'd end up back home, and that's why they hadn't fought me when I'd "moved out." It used to annoy the hell out of me that they'd always seemed to be one step ahead of me.

Now I would have welcomed a fight with them if it meant having them around again.

My smile faded and I shoved my hands deep into the pockets

of my cashmere pants. I'd seen a model wearing them in *Cosmo* a few weeks back and thought they managed to look dressy while still being incredibly comfortable. Besides, they made my ass look great. Not that I was trying to impress anyone here. But I was a firm believer that dressing nice when you felt like crap did wonders for your self-esteem. As Blair Waldorf would say, "Just because you feel like shit, doesn't mean you have to look like shit."

"Hadley, your cabin is freaking incredible," Sascha said, passing me and walking toward the summer home to get a closer look.

"Yeah," added Fallon. "The place is a chick magnet."

"You do realize that you'd have to get the girls to actually *agree* to go anywhere with you first, Fallon?" I asked.

He stopped scoping out the grounds long enough to look back and glare at me.

Whoops. So much for our cease-fire.

"It really is amazing," Jinx said, talking just loudly enough for me to hear, which didn't take much effort since she'd managed to sneak up behind me while I'd been daydreaming about my short-lived stint in the shed.

"Yeah, it's pretty cool," I agreed. Too bad everything in this place reminded me of my parents and the fact that I wouldn't be making any more memories with them. My face fell as I fought the direction my mind was heading.

Shaking my head as if to clear it, I looked at the others and then forced a smile. "Let's grab the stuff and get inside," I said, making myself think about what we were here to do and not the circumstances behind the fact.

I went to the car to retrieve my duffel bag full of essentials—clothes; makeup; hair products; the popular girl's bible, *Cosmopolitan*; and a few odds and ends. My thinking was that if

I could bring some sort of normalcy to our lives then we might not slip into utter depression. Maybe it was denial, but focusing on something else for the meantime made me feel better.

As I walked back toward the house, I noticed that everyone was lined up outside the front door like it was a run-through at the beginning of a football game. Except no one would be cheering for me.

God, I missed cheer.

Especially because the squad was performing the routine we'd been practicing for weeks at the upcoming game. During one of our many stops along the way, I'd called my coach to let them know there'd been a family emergency and I'd be out for a while.

Knowing that I was letting down my squad made me feel horrible. But given the situation, I couldn't see any way around it. It's not like I could put my life, and the lives of the rest of the coven, in jeopardy just so I could cheer on our starting lineup. I texted Trish, Bethany, and Sofia to let them know as well, and kept things just as vague. Beth and Sofia asked if I was okay, while Trish asked if she could fill in for me as captain. I agreed, although it hurt to give up my position.

But I was clear with Trisha: my hiatus wouldn't last forever.

"Lead the way," Sascha said, motioning to the door in front of us. Her arms were full of bags, pillows, blankets, and food— all things we'd picked up along the way. I decided it was a bad idea to go back to everyone's houses to get their things, so we'd gone on an impromptu shopping spree at a Target after safely fleeing town. There was no telling how long we'd be gone and people needed the basic necessities. We used the credit card my parents had given me for emergencies, since I figured they would've agreed that this was one. As Jasmine shifted under the weight of her bags, I shuffled forward to let us inside.

"Hand me the keys and I'll open her up," Fallon said, stepping in front of me and holding out his hand.

"I don't have keys," I said.

"Are you kidding me? Then why did we come here?" he asked me with a sneer. Then he got an evil look in his eyes and said excitedly, "Do we get to break some windows?"

"No, dunce. We don't need keys to get in," I said, placing my hand up in front of me, fingertips just inches away from the door.

For as long as I'd been coming here, our doors had never been locked in the traditional sense. No lock. No key. No worries. My parents explained to me that the cabin's inhabitants had always had a unique way of coming and going. We used our own magical distinctiveness to gain access to the house.

See, a person's magic has its own kind of identity. Sort of like magical DNA. And our cabin was effectively *closed* to those who didn't share our lineage. In a way it was nice. I never had to worry about losing my keys.

I closed my eyes and concentrated on letting my powers flow through my fingertips and penetrate the invisible barrier that was surrounding the house. Within seconds, I could feel it disappear, and then I reached out and turned the knob.

"Home sweet home," I said as I stepped inside, smelling the familiar scent of my family's cabin.

I wandered into the living room just off to my left. Everyone else piled in after me, going off to explore the house. "You can take any room except for the one at the end of the hall upstairs," I said, still checking to see if anything had changed since I'd last been there.

"The princess doesn't want the peasants staying in her room?" Fallon asked sarcastically from the hallway behind me.

"That room was my parents'," I said, shooting him a look. That was all I had to say to shut him up, and I appreciated the silence that followed. "Like I said, you can have any room except for that one. Linens and blankets are in the closet near the bathroom and the couch pulls out into a bed. "

I walked around the living room, running my hand across various objects as I rediscovered my family's old vacation house. The sofa had the same soft feel I always loved as a kid. Now I realized that the microfiber was a pretty common fabric, but back then, I used to call it "the marshmallow couch" because it was so soft.

Then I made my way over to the fireplace, where we used to pile up on the floor on chilly nights. When I was old enough to carry in the firewood, it became my job to add logs before the embers burned out. I took the responsibility very seriously and never once let the fire get too low. It wasn't exactly cool enough outside to need additional heat yet, but old habits die hard and I found myself with the urge to gather up wood before the sun went down.

Instead, I headed upstairs, passing by kids as I went. A few of the older ones were arguing over who was staying in which of the three other rooms, but I was too focused on what I was doing to get involved.

When I arrived at my parents' door, I placed my hand on the cool surface. I almost knocked before I remembered that I didn't need permission to go inside because it was empty. Pushing the door open, I stepped across the threshold, almost expecting to see my parents, unpacking and having the little private conversations they had whenever they thought they were alone. But the room was silent. So silent that I could hear the air flowing into my ears, which was incredibly unnerving. Needing to fill the empty space with something other than my thoughts, I picked up the remote control and pressed the power button.

Flipping through the channels, I eventually landed on an old movie that had been one of my mom's favorites. I just couldn't seem to get away from the memory of her, so I gave in and snuggled back onto the pillows on my parents' bed. I watched as kids were chased down by a family of bad guys while searching for hidden treasure. In the movie, the misfits managed to avert booby traps and close calls until they foiled the evildoers and saved the day at the end.

I allowed myself to get swept up in the drama and thought about how we weren't much different from the kids on the screen. We were on the run from people who wanted to hurt us, and things were likely to get worse before they got better.

As they cut to a commercial break, my mind was brought back to reality and I got up to go to the closet where my parents kept the bed stuff. I grabbed some sheets and pillowcases and started to make the bed. When I was done, I lay back down and breathed in the scent of the pillows deeply. The strong odor of detergent filled my nose, but underneath was the hint of something else. My parents. I could smell the tangy citrus of my mom's perfume and the muskiness of my dad's cologne. After so many years the aroma had faded but not completely. Still, I would recognize it anywhere and it made me feel like they were there with me.

I began to cry, lightly at first and then harder, until my body shook like an earthquake. Thank God I'd closed the door, because I didn't want the others to see me like this. Weak and tired and broken. It was important that I kept up appearances and at least *looked* like I had it together. Even if I didn't feel that way on the inside.

The movie started back up again and I forced myself to

pay attention. Any escape from reality was sorely needed right now. Wiping tears from my now blotchy face, I watched as one of the boys gave his friends an inspirational speech to keep them going. My mom had told me once why she loved the movie so much. She explained that the kids were all unlikely heroes. People who took on challenges much bigger than they were and never gave up, even when winning the fight seemed impossible.

Mom had said that those were the qualities she'd always tried to instill in me.

I sat up straight on the bed and took a deep breath, feeling as if there were no coincidences in this world. This movie was a reminder of what I needed to do.

Was I completely justified in my feelings? Of course. Did my mom's death make me ache like a vital part of me had been ripped from my body? Definitely. But should I let it destroy me and everything I'd ever worked for? Hell no. A hero never bowed down to challenge.

And it was what my mom would have wanted.

I was done crying, alone and hopeless in my room. It was time to take my position as leader of this group. I needed to take my power back. Not just for me but for the rest of the Cleri. Because the shit was about to hit the fan and I wasn't about to be covered in it.

Chapter Eleven

When I made it back downstairs, I noticed a group of about five sitting in the corner and became curious. A girl named Emory was in the middle of it all and she had the other kids listening to her with rapt attention. I had to admit, I didn't know Emory very well at all. I think she went to even fewer meetings than I did and seemed to almost blend into her surroundings. Not to say she wasn't pretty, though; with a full head of wavy red hair and eyes that appeared thoughtful, she was your average girl next door.

What I *had* noticed about her was that she wore a lot of flowery clothes: shirts with daisies on them, lilac-adorned jumpers, ballet flats topped with roses. She looked fresh off *Little House on the Prairie.* That is, if the prairie were run by witches, of course.

In the past, she'd seemed more of a listener than a talker, but here she was, commanding a small audience. Because of this, I decided it was about time I got to know her and some of the others a little better. After all, we were going to be squished together in this cabin for an indeterminate amount of time. And it was best to know all my allies.

I watched from a distance as Emory talked quietly to the others. Intrigued by what it was she could be saying, I eventually wandered over to where she sat.

"What we fail to remember in times like these is that the dead aren't ever truly gone," she was saying in a soft, soothing voice. "They're around us all the time. Watching. Keeping us safe. Guiding us to the next right action. So see, in that respect, this isn't the end. We just need to be open to hearing the messages they have for us and keeping their memories alive. Because it is by tapping in to their power that we honor them."

I was surprised by what she was saying, but not because I didn't believe her; I knew from my own dream of my mom that our parents weren't completely gone. What took me aback was the fact that it was coming from *this* particular girl. Hers was more than just a faith in life after death. There was no doubt in my mind that Emory was speaking from experience.

"Is my dad here now? Can you see him?" a young girl asked. The hope in her voice was palpable and I had to slow my breathing to keep from getting upset.

Emory nodded. "Of course he's here," she said with a smile. The girl returned the grin and I could tell that it had been enough to make her feel better.

"Does he have a message for me?" she asked, her voice squeaking as she squirmed in her seat.

"He loves you and is very proud of you," Emory answered, a faraway look on her face. "He wants you to be careful and says it's important that you listen to everything Hadley says. She knows what she's doing and she will get us through this."

"Can you tell him I will? And that I love him?" the girl said in a voice barely above a whisper. She paused then, as if she was debating saying something else. Before she could finish though, Emory cut in.

"He knows that you're sorry, Anna," Emory said gently. "And he's sorry too. He doesn't want you to be sad about this. You're his greatest creation."

A single tear dropped down Anna's face. I thought maybe her heart was breaking at first, but then I realized that what I was witnessing was a healing moment. Letting out a little sniffle, Anna got up and gave Emory a big hug and then headed out of the room and into the sunny yard beyond the door.

"Why don't you guys go and get something to eat, head outside, and take it easy for a bit?" Emory suggested to the kids captivated in front of her.

I watched as the group dispersed, all looking a lot better off than they had since we'd broken the news to them. I felt major respect for this girl I barely knew, and vowed to take our time at the cabin to get to know the rest of my coven. I was starting to learn that nothing—or no one—was what they seemed.

"Emory, hey. That was amazing," I said to her once the others were out of earshot. "You are *so* great with those kids; I think you really made them feel better. How did you do that?"

Emory gave me a shy smile before casting her eyes downward and starting to play with the bracelet adorning her wrist. A string of baby's breath, from the looks of it. I couldn't be sure, but the flowers might have been real. "I don't know. I've always sort of been able to do that. I just figured it might help them deal if they knew their parents were okay. Was I wrong?"

She was clearly worried that I might be upset, but that was the last thing on my mind. I was impressed with her maturity and intrigued with these natural powers she seemed to have. "Of course not!" I said soothingly. "In fact, if I'd known you could do that, I would've let *you* break the news to everyone."

Emory looked up at me, relief washing across her face. I took her by the hand and led her over to the couch. We sat down, folding our legs underneath us like old girlfriends. "Can I ask you something?" She nodded. "Were you telling the truth back there? Can you see them? Our parents, I mean—are they really here?"

Her eyes got big and she looked around to see if the others were listening to our conversation. "Yeah. But I can't see them in the same way that I can see you guys. It's like the shadow of them. Like they're on the periphery, you know?"

"And they talk to you?" I asked, amazed by what I was hearing. It made me think back to my conversation with my mom. I'd been so confused by the encounter and felt totally drained the next morning. I couldn't imagine doing that on a daily basis. At the same time, how incredible would it be to be able to communicate with the dead on a regular basis? And with those other than your relatives?

"Sort of. They're not as loud as you and I; it's more like they're whispering to me most of the time," she explained, her face scrunching up as she tried to convey what she was thinking. "I have to really concentrate in order to get what they're trying to say."

"Does anyone else know you can do this?" I asked.

"Just my parents and a few of the elder Cleri," Emory said. "Or they did, at least. People sort of start to look at you weird when you tell them that you see dead people. It's not nearly as cool as they make it out to be on TV. It's like a one-way ticket to the loony bin."

I rolled my eyes at her. "Think of who you're talking to. If anyone would understand having abilities that no one else can wrap their head around, it would be me," I said with an easy smile. "This is amazing, Emory. It's what makes you special, and whether or not others see it that way, it's an incredible power. I have to admit, I'm a little jealous."

The expression on Emory's face bloomed into pride. It made me think back to the first time I divulged to another magically inclined person—in my case, my parents—about my additional powers of persuasion. When I realized I wasn't going to be judged for it, it was like the hole in my heart, which had always been full of fear, was filled up with confidence and acceptance. In other words, the experience had changed my life.

And now, in a way, I was giving that gift to Emory.

"Would you mind if I sent some of the other kids to talk to you if they need to?" I asked. "I have a feeling you might be able to help them in a way that none of the rest of us can."

I could feel gratitude emanating from her as if it were my own. Who knows, it may have been a combination of what we were both feeling. But it didn't really matter. What mattered was that our coven had someone who could be a conduit for the other side. And that was an invaluable resource, now that we no longer had access to the elders.

I got up from the couch and smoothed down my cashmere pants, while balancing on some dangerously high wedges. Seeing Emory's powers in action had kind of boggled my mind, and I needed to think about how this could factor into what we'd be doing here at the cabin. I started to walk away, but Emory called me back.

"Hadley? There's one more thing," she said, looking me straight in the eyes. "Your mom's here too, and she's being really loud about something. She says it's important that you know this."

My heart started to race and I looked around as if I would suddenly be able to see her standing with her hands on her hips, waiting for me to pay attention. I hadn't expected any more messages from my mom, since I'd had the dream the day before. I figured she'd said all she needed to then.

Or maybe I just hadn't been listening well enough.

"She says that we have to start training. That we're not ready for what's coming," Emory said seriously. Her eyes shifted to a place just over my right shoulder, which caused me to look back too. All I saw was a wall full of family photos surrounding the words painted in gold: "Breathe. Relax. Live." It had been one of my dad's favorite sayings.

I turned back to Emory, fully believing that my mom was in the cabin with us. My eyes began to well, but I forced the tears down. I could cry later.

"Hadley, she says that you can't trust everyone. That there are people you'll think are good, but they aren't. She says sometimes you have to listen to your head and *not* to your heart. Never underestimate your enemies, she says. It will be our downfall."

"Wait, who can't I trust?" I asked her, whispering now in case others walked in. If members of our coven had ulterior motives, I couldn't risk having them know we knew about them.

Emory squinted and then began to wildly look all around us. Finally she settled back on my face. "I'm sorry. She's gone."

The depth of my sadness upon hearing this surprised me. It wasn't like I was even talking to her or seeing her myself, but just knowing that she'd been there and then was gone was like losing her all over again.

Emory gave me a second to collect myself and then spoke gently. "Hadley? What did she mean? Is there an enemy among the Cleri?"

I shook my head slowly, chilled to the bone. "I'm not sure," I said, my head swimming and my fears giving way to anger. "But God help them if there is."

Chapter Twelve

It took me a few days to recover from my conversation with Emory. The more I thought about the possibility of a traitor living under the same roof as us, the more freaked out I got. And of course, Fallon had gone back to being his regular annoying self, which made me wonder if he really *was* evil. Twice, I found him going through the stuff in my parents' room. He said he was looking for extra blankets, but I didn't buy it. He was under my bed, for God's sake. And then when I'd found him showing a bunch of the other boys embarrassing photos of me as a kid, I thought about using magic to knock him out so I wouldn't have to worry about him causing any more trouble.

It wasn't just Fallon I was suspicious of, though. In fact, I found myself starting to question the motives of everyone around me to the point where it was difficult to be around anyone without my mind running wild with conspiracy theories. But I couldn't exactly barricade myself in my parents' bedroom and stay there for the rest of my life. Not only was it unrealistic, but being around the others was the only way I was going to find out who wasn't really who they claimed to be. And if I didn't figure that out, we'd most likely lose this battle.

And "loser" was *not* in my vocabulary.

So instead I forced myself to leave the safety of my room and wandered through the house, looking for something that might be able to distract me from our impending doom. I thought about making lunch for everyone, but when I got to the kitchen I saw that people had taken my instructions at face value; they'd been helping themselves to any food they could find. I picked up an empty can of Chef Boyardee and tossed it into the trash behind me. There were two half-eaten bags of chips on the counter and a turned-over box of cream-filled cakes lying across the table.

We had food with us when we arrived, but it would last us only so long—especially with a group as large as this—and eventually we'd have to go into town for more. The spread in front of me was proof that maybe the younger twitches shouldn't be the ones picking out the meals. Where were the vegetables? The fruit? Did they think that Skittles counted as a food group? Unwrapping a little cake, I popped half of it into my mouth and chewed thoughtfully.

"*There* you are," Sascha said, appearing behind me. Jasmine and Jinx were in tow. Sascha walked over to the counter and pulled herself up until she was sitting on top, her legs swinging through the air in front of her. Jasmine plopped down at the table, bringing one knee up to her chest and pulling at a loose string on her black jeans, while Jinx snatched a cake of her own and began to unwrap it.

"What's up, guys?" I asked, trying to sound as normal as possible.

"We're bored," Sascha said.

"And some of the others are getting on my nerves," Jasmine added.

I looked over at Jinx, waiting for her to complain about something too.

"I'm just hungry," she said, shrugging before sticking her finger into the middle of the spongy cake to retrieve the frosting.

"Well, I think I can help you out with most of those," I said to them. "We're going to start training tomorrow, so you better be ready to work hard."

I leaned back in my seat and placed my feet on the kitchen table. If my mom were here, she would've lectured me about appropriate etiquette or said something along the lines of, "When you grow up and get a place of your own, you can put your feet up on the furniture all you want. But until then, feet on the floor." Thinking of my mom out of the blue like this made me sad and I slowly brought my feet down off the table out of respect for her memory.

"Finally. That's the most sane thing I've heard you say since this whole thing started. I've been itching to cast something," said Jasmine, wiggling her fingers excitedly.

"Good. Make sure you get some sleep tonight," I warned. "And tell the others to do the same, because tomorrow's going to be a long day. Everyone's going to need their energy for what we'll be doing."

As they left, I thought about how much I wished I could take my own advice and rest up. Instead, I turned back to the now deserted kitchen and placed my forehead on top of the table. The surface was cool against my face and I knew that if I closed my eyes now, I'd be out within seconds.

But there was still too much to do and I'd be lucky if I got any sleep at all that night. Sitting back up, I picked up the note-pad I'd been doodling on earlier and began to make a list of all the spells we'd be going over the following day. Two hours and three pages (front and back) later, I had what I thought was a good beginning. And although there were enough spells to keep us busy for months, I had a sinking feeling that it still wasn't going to be enough time to prepare for whatever was coming.

"Okay, everyone, let's do it again," I said, looking around at the exhausted faces around me. We'd been at it for hours now. Going over spell after spell, every last one Jackson had taught us since I'd started attending magic classes. They ranged from basic everyday stuff like protection from harm to deflection spells. Most knew them already, but there were a few the younger members hadn't learned yet.

Jackson had always insisted there should be an order to our learning process and that some of the spells were too intense for the younger witches, but seeing as how we were now faced with a potential danger beyond anything we'd thought was possible, I figured people were going to have to grow up a little bit faster. Besides, if the Parrishables came looking for us, I wasn't going to be able to hold anyone's hand; chances were that the rest of the twitches were going to have to fend for themselves.

So, one by one, we attempted to perfect everything we'd been taught. This proved to be excessively time-consuming, though, as not everyone was catching on as quickly as I'd hoped.

"Everyone get ready!" I yelled out. I watched as each group of two slowly faced each other, standing a few feet apart. As I paced across the backyard, I noticed Fallon mocking me when he thought I couldn't see. Ignoring him for the time being, I went back to the matter at hand. "People on the defensive, relax your body and get ready for the attack. Spell casters, quiet your mind and focus on what you're about to do. Remember, if there's no power behind your words, the magic itself won't be powerful."

I counted down and watched them go.

"Aeromus une cyclenae!"

Immediately, groups all around me gave the spell their best shot. A few came close to having the desired result. Jasmine was the first to perfect it, sending the wind-whipping spell to Sascha. Before Sascha could react, she was immediately caught up in a twister of air, making it impossible for her to see. Once the wind died down again, the look on her face was priceless. To say Sascha was unhappy to be a magical guinea pig was an understatement.

"Do you have any idea how long it took me to get my hair to lie flat this morning?" she screeched through clenched teeth.

"You're kidding, right?" Jasmine asked, a smirk on her face.

"Hadley?" Sascha asked, looking to me to back her up. And to be honest, under normal circumstances I would have. You don't mess with a girl's hair. But this might've been the only time and place where fashion couldn't be our first priority.

"Sorry, Sascha," I said. "Jazzy's right."

"It's Jasmine," the dark-haired girl chimed in.

"You knew we were training, Sascha. Best to ponytail it up in the future."

Sascha's mouth closed into a tight line and she turned away from me angrily. My pulse raced slightly as I wondered if I was making an enemy out of her. I still wasn't used to people not just blindly following me. At school everyone liked me.

Even Trish, who I knew secretly wanted to take my throne, would've done anything I asked her to and would respect me for it. Here, with the rest of the Cleri, I was still proving myself to them. And right now it felt like I was failing.

I took a deep breath and continued. "Okay, so Jasmine was the only one to execute her spell properly that time, which means the rest of you need more practice," I said, growing frustrated. It had never been very difficult for me to pick up on our lessons. Maybe it was because I'd grown up creating my own spells or maybe it just came naturally to me, but the others paled in comparison. Ordinarily, I would've tried to be more understanding, but we didn't have the luxury of time right now. Somebody needed to push them to their limits.

"Switch partners and try it again," I yelled, not giving them time to recover.

They did as they were told and I called for them to begin. A few seconds later, I was enveloped in a rush of air. I tried to cry out, but it was difficult to breathe with the wind forcing its way down my throat and up my nose. It lasted only about ten seconds but it was long enough.

When I was able to see again, I looked around for the culprit. I heard snickers, which led me to Fallon, who was facing my way and looking smug. There was no doubt he'd done it. And the thing was, he wasn't even trying to hide it.

"Whoops," he said, shrugging innocently. "Guess my aim is off."

"Or not," I said, my body beginning to buzz with anger. I closed my eyes and let the fire that was building inside slowly fizzle out. It would be pointless to waste my energy on Fallon and it wouldn't set a very good example for the others. When I'd calmed down, I opened my eyes and stared straight at Fallon. "Let's try it again!" I shouted.

"Had, we're all tired," Jinx said lightly, arms hanging limply by her sides. Sweat had matted down her usually pristine bangs, and her chest was heaving. "Can we take a break? Maybe get water and something to eat?"

"Yeah. I think some of the little ones might need a chance to catch their breath," Emory said, motioning to a few twelve-year-olds who were sprawled across the ground.

"Come on, you guys! We've barely gotten through the first few charms and there are still people who don't have it down perfectly yet," I said, placing my hands on my hips. I tapped my black sequined booties on the ground impatiently. I was running this training session the way I would run cheer practice—and I wasn't even making them do flips or stunts. If you asked me, they were getting off easy.

"Look, I really need you guys to rally so that you'll be armed and ready for whatever's coming next. Because the fact is, they're coming. Whether we're ready or not."

We all knew I was talking about the Parrishables, but none of us wanted to say it out loud. That would make it all too real.

That prompted a few people to sigh as they stood back up to get into place. The others groaned and followed suit. Then they all stood there silently, waiting for me to tell them what to do next. I called for them to go back to the disarming spell, which was meant to take away an object from our enemies. I watched as Jasmine knocked a book out of Sascha's hands. It flew with such force that it fell apart at the binding as it hit the side of the house.

"Great job, Jazzy—sorry, *Jasmine*. Now if you could just rein in your power a little you won't have to worry about knocking anyone else out at the same time. Unless of course you want to, in which case, let it fly," I said, nodding.

As I turned away, something else flew past my head,

narrowly missing the tip of my nose. "What the hell!" I yelled, jerking my head back in Jasmine's direction. But she was just as clueless as me and shrugged in response.

"I must be off today," Fallon said, a hint of a smile on his face. "Or maybe I'm just too powerful for my own good."

My face grew hot with anger. I should've known. After all, our little truce couldn't have lasted forever. "I don't remember mentioning that I wanted a nose job," I said to him nastily.

"Really? With a schnoz like that? My bad." He said it as if he hadn't just tried to take my head off.

"How about you try to control yourself a bit, huh? I'd hate for your magic to fizzle out prematurely," I said. "I mean, imagine how embarrassing *that* would be for you."

The smile remained on his face, but I saw his lip twitch just a tiny bit, letting me know that what I'd said had gotten to him. I smiled back. In the end, Fallon was still just a little boy trying to show off in front of his friends. *Go ahead and give me your worst,* I challenged him silently. There's nothing he could throw at me that I couldn't handle.

"Do it again," I dared.

He studied me and then looked around at the others, who were all waiting to see what was going to happen next. I knew I'd backed him into a corner and wondered if it had been a wise decision.

"Screw this."

And with one last look, he thrust his hands into the pockets of his hoodie and started to walk away.

"Where are you going?" I asked, my eyes boring into his back. The rest of the coven had begun to look at each other questioningly.

"I'm done," he said. "You're not the only one here that can cast, you know. So why are you the only one standing around?"

"Because *somebody* has to lead this group."

"And that automatically means it should be you?" he challenged.

"Right now, yeah," I bit back. I was through being Ms. Nice Witch.

"Well, I didn't sign up for that," he answered.

All activity in the yard had stopped, and the rest of the coven had become so quiet that I'd almost forgotten they were even there. Now they were looking back and forth between the two of us like they were witnessing a shootout in an old Wild West movie. And in a way they were. Only, both of us were waiting for the other to back down or draw our guns.

In the end I won.

Fallon rolled his eyes before walking inside the house. "Whatever," he muttered before disappearing completely. I knew he was pissed and things had certainly gone too far, but there was too much to deal with right now without adding Fallon's overactive ego to the list.

"Why don't we all take a fifteen-minute break and then we'll get started on counterspells?" I asked, forcing a smile. The vibe in the group was still uneasy and I needed a chance to cool down before trying to work any more spells. Wouldn't want a bewitching incantation to go awry because my emotions were all jumbled.

Unless of course it ended up hitting Fallon, in which case, a little anger behind my spells might do him a bit of good.

Chapter Thirteen

I tried to get us through as many spells as I could over the rest of the afternoon, but everyone's attention had left after the confrontation with Fallon. Reluctantly I called it a day and headed straight for the shower to try to wash away my stress. I had no idea it would be so hard to keep a bunch of teenagers in line.

And Fallon. I never should've let the twerp get to me like that.

I wasn't sure why he was constantly challenging me . . . unless he was trying to destroy the Cleri from the inside, a fact that I hadn't yet ruled out.

I placed my face right into the spray of the water and let the echo drown out my thoughts for a while. When I came up for air, I had to admit that no matter what Fallon's motives were, this feud had to end. We needed to come together as a group and our constant bickering was affecting the others, too. I decided I had to find Fallon and institute a truce with him for real this time.

As I dried off and put on a black lace jumper and some over-size costume jewelry that I'd replicated from Tori Spelling's vintage collection, I thought about what I'd say. But when I went looking for him, I couldn't find him anywhere.

Asking around yielded even less information at first, and when I looked in the room he was staying in and saw that a bunch of his stuff was gone, I started to get a sinking feeling in my stomach. Something wasn't right.

"How could he have just left?" I asked, shaking my head. Sascha, Jasmine, Jinx, Emory, and I had retreated to my parents' room after I'd discovered that Fallon was gone.

"Well, he *did* seem pretty mad," Sascha said, in a much better mood now that she'd taken a shower and eaten something. "Emotions were definitely running high." It felt almost like an apology for her outburst earlier and I appreciated the gesture.

"We all got a little out of hand," I said, letting her know how bad I felt about it too. "All that matters now is getting him back home safely. He may be able to pull out a lot of spells, but he won't be a match for what's out there."

"What a little brat!" Jasmine said, annoyed.

I shook my head, even though I was angry too. "It's my fault. If I hadn't reacted like that, he wouldn't have felt the need to walk out. Besides, he's right. He doesn't have to listen to me at all."

"So what are we going to do?" Jinx asked, twirling a strand of her hair.

"I'm going to go after him."

Their eyes widened with shock.

"Hadley, you can't," Sascha said. "*They're* out there."

I sighed, knowing what I was suggesting. "As stupid as it was for him to do this, I don't see any other options."

"We could leave him out there," Jasmine said jokingly.

"You know we can't do that," I said, without giving myself time to consider it.

"How are you even going to find him?" Jinx asked thoughtfully.

I started to answer and then realized I didn't know.

"I guess I'll start by driving around?" I said, grasping at straws. "He couldn't have gotten very far. He left on foot, after all."

"Unless he hopped a ride with someone," Jasmine said. We all thought about what this would mean. "It's what I would've done."

"I'm gonna kill him," I said, imagining him hitchhiking his way into town. Fallon was putting us all at risk by taking off and I wasn't exactly happy about it. Even with the power of my lineage behind me, I knew it was going to be dangerous to go looking for him.

"I think I can help you find him," Emory said suddenly. She slid off the bed and ran out the door, returning a few minutes later with a blue blanket and a watch. "Once, our next-door neighbor disappeared from the park near our house. She was only four years old and had managed to slip away while her mom was talking to another parent. My mom used this spell to find her."

I was beginning to realize that Emory was full of surprises and I leaned forward, eager to learn the new spell. "What's that stuff for?" I asked.

"We need an object with the person's essence on it. Typically it's something that the person owned, but the blanket from his bed should work," Emory said, sitting down across from me. "The watch acts as a compass, showing us where to find him. It's basically like a magical GPS."

"Cool," Sascha let out.

"And you think it'll work?" I asked her hopefully.

"It should," she said.

They all looked at me for confirmation as I weighed our options.

"Fine. Do it," I said.

We all moved off the bed to give Emory room to cast the spell. She placed the blanket on the surface and then put the watch on top. Then she pushed her red hair out of her face and smoothed down her tulip-decorated dress. Finally, she settled and closed her eyes, muttering something I couldn't quite understand.

Then she began.

> *Take this token of that which is lost*
> *I pray thou find it whatever the cost.*
> *Whether taken, misplaced, or kept at bay*
> *The veil that blocks is now cast away.*
> *Time is short and there is nowhere to hide*
> *So take us now to where it doth reside.*

The watch began to glow and then lifted up off the bed. Leaning in even closer, I could see that the arms of the time-piece were moving quickly in a clockwise motion. After several laps around the face, the tiny shards of metal stopped abruptly and pointed in the direction behind us. I glanced backward and realized it was pointing directly at the door.

"Emory, you're a genius," I said in awe.

"Why was the spell so wordy?" Sascha asked, confused.

"It was created by my great-great-grandmother," Emory said. "Back then they took their time with magic."

"Jackson mentioned it in one of our classes," Jinx added. "He said as time has passed, witches have gotten more impatient and began to shorten the wording."

We all paused at the mention of Jackson. We never had heard from him. Without saying it out loud, I knew we all presumed he'd suffered the same fate as our parents.

All of a sudden, Sascha broke through our thoughts. "Like

texting for the witching age!" she said as if she'd just figured out the winning *Jeopardy!* response.

Emory giggled at the comment while Jasmine just rolled her eyes before looking back at me.

"I'm coming with you," she said.

I blinked at her, surprised by her decision. Then I shook my head. "No way. I won't put anyone else in danger," I said.

"You're not going to be able to rescue anyone if you're dead," Jasmine said bluntly. "You may be an überwitch and all, but even you can't take all of them on if they catch you alone. And if they take you out, then the rest of us are toast. Face it. You need us just as much as we need you."

I began to argue with her, but then Sascha took a step toward me and put her hands on her hips. "I'm in too."

Then it was Jinx's turn to stand up. "We'll be your backup."

Before Emory could chime in too, I cut her off. "Someone has to stay here to watch the others and continue the training if something goes wrong." Emory was a little younger than the rest of us, so it made sense to me that she would stay behind. Besides, if she did have to give the others bad news, I could trust her to be able to handle it.

The others looked resigned in their decisions to come, and although I hated to admit it, my going alone might not have been the best thing for Fallon. Someone would need to get him out of whatever mess he had gotten himself into while I tried to hold off our enemies.

"All right. You can come, but everyone else stays put," I said. "And you three do *whatever* I say. No buts. We've seen what the Parrishables are capable of."

"What if they find us here while you're gone?" Emory asked.

"That won't happen," I said, turning to look at her. I hadn't told them why the cabin was our best bet for safe hiding. Mostly because I hadn't felt it was important to bring up until now. "This place is sort of enchanted."

"What are you talking about?"

No point in keeping it a secret anymore. "My mom told me a long time ago that this cabin was bewitched to be invisible to the outside world."

"Invisible? Like no one can see us?" Sascha asked, her eyes growing big.

"More like, whenever anyone comes looking for us, they'll get redirected so they won't end up here. Not exactly invisible, but they won't be able to see us if they can't find the place," I explained.

"Did they do that because of the Parrishables?"

"Not sure. Don't even know who cast the original spell," I said, shrugging. "So I don't think we have to worry about any crazy mountain men anytime soon."

"How does it work?" Jasmine asked. "I mean, we found it, so it can't be impossible."

"I think it has something to do with knowing that the cabin itself exists and your intentions or something. I've been coming here since I was a kid, so I knew where to go. And I brought you all with me. Now that I've brought you here, you'll always be able to find it again," I said. I was reminded of my mom again, and this time I smiled. "My mom used to love the fact that it was impossible for Dad's work to contact him while he was here on vacation. The phone calls just never went through."

"Weird," Jinx said. "But it makes me feel a lot safer being here now that I know."

The others nodded.

"Hate to break this up, but time's a-wasting," Jasmine said, pointing at the watch that was still suspended in the air. "And the longer we leave Fallon out there, the farther we'll have to go to find him."

I nodded in agreement and then stood up. "I'm ready if you are."

"Are you sure?" Jasmine asked, surveying my getup from head to toe. Looking down at my dark couture outfit topped off with a pair of black studded pumps, I wondered what she was talking about.

"What? You can't fight in heels?" I asked finally.

Jasmine shook her head at me and started to walk out the door. "Just don't come crying to me when you wipe out."

"They can double as weapons you know," I joked, before snatching the watch out of the air and clutching it tightly.

Chapter Fourteen

Jasmine sat shotgun and held on to the timepiece, guiding me on where to go. We'd been driving about a half hour when we were instructed to turn off the highway and pull into a town that looked familiar to me. Yet it wasn't until I saw the buildings looming ahead that I knew why.

"Fallon ran away to . . . the mall?" I asked incredulously.

"You've got to be freaking kidding me," Jasmine said before reluctantly directing me to enter the giant parking lot.

I pulled up to a spot about thirty feet away from the entrance to the Orange Hill Mall and let the engine die before stepping outside. Taking a deep breath, I closed my eyes and allowed myself to enjoy the quality of air down here in the valley.

God, I love the smell of retail in the afternoon.

"I can't believe I'm saying this—because, hello? We're at a mall—but what was Fallon thinking?" I said.

Jasmine led the way since she still had the watch, and I began to strut toward the big revolving doors. I was vaguely aware of people around me; my eyes focused on the most heavenly place I'd ever known. It was like seeing a mirage in the desert. I just couldn't keep away, even though I knew it wasn't as innocent as it looked.

"I'm not sure Fallon *was* thinking," Sascha cut in. Since we'd left the car, her eyes had grown big as she took in all the stores in front of us.

"In a way, it was actually quite smart," Jinx said thoughtfully.

"How do you figure?" I asked, not sure where she was going with the comment.

"Well, it's less likely that anyone's going to attack us here, in front of all these people," she said, pointing to the hundreds of shoppers we'd already passed on our way in. "I mean, they wouldn't be that stupid, would they?"

"We're talking about mass murderers with magical powers here," I answered. "I doubt they're worried about being seen."

As we walked across the threshold, we passed a group of guys who looked like they were around our age. The four of them surveyed the four of us in a not-so-subtle way and then gave nods of approval. Sascha let out a girlie giggle, at which Jasmine promptly groaned. Thankfully, our admirers headed into the nearest store and left us to do what we came here to do. Sascha looked after them longingly before speeding to catch up with us.

We weaved in and out of people as we tried to stay on course with where the watch was guiding us. Finally it brought us to the entrance of one of the busiest stores in the mall, the minute and hour hands both pointing us inside. As we walked in, we avoided the gaggles of girls all desperate to find something to make them look either skinnier or curvier in specific areas.

"Whoa, guys," Jasmine said, stopping short just inside the doors. I glanced at the watch, and saw that the metal hands were now spinning around the clock frantically.

I looked around. "He's gotta be here," I said. "Let's split up and try to find him as quickly as possible."

I followed a group of girls onto an escalator to my right and watched the others take off in opposite directions as I headed to the second floor. At the top, I sped off to cover as much ground as I could. The floor wasn't huge by any standards, but going through the whole store would take time we didn't have. I started to rush through the maze of jeans and hoodies, looking for the one person I didn't want to see and yet had to find.

I took a corner too quickly and immediately ran into something. I staggered backward and nearly fell, but before I did, a hand reached out, catching me underneath the arms and depositing me back onto my feet.

"Whoa," a guy's voice said. "You okay?"

I adjusted my jumper and then looked up at the person who'd saved me the embarrassment of having to admit to Jasmine that she might have been right about the heels. And then I saw him.

To put it bluntly: he was beautiful.

And not just in an easy-on-the-eyes sort of way. But in an international-male-model kind of way. His hair was so black it was almost blue, and it spiked up in the middle with just a hint of bad boy to its tips. As my gaze shifted to his eyes, I nearly gasped.

Because I knew those eyes.

I'd seen them as I jogged down my block and then again in the rearview mirror as we left town. Up close, I could see that they were a stormy gray color, rimmed with thick lashes. The level of his hotness was unreal.

"I'm fine," I said, once I'd found my voice again. Then I smiled and pushed my purse, which had slipped during the collision, back onto my shoulder. "Nice catch," I added.

"Thanks," he said, smiling back at me. The dimples that erupted on both cheeks nearly disarmed me completely. Then he looked at me closely before his eyes widened and he seemed to step back surprised. "Wait, don't I know you . . ."

"Sort of," I said, cutting him off. "I think we live on the same block, but we haven't actually met yet."

"Well, we should probably rectify that, shouldn't we?" he asked, holding out his hand. "I'm Asher."

I put my hand in his and my heart began hammering in my chest. I couldn't believe the reaction I was having to just touching him. Guys hit on me all the time, but I'd never been affected in this way. Yet here I was, acting like it was my first time talking to a boy.

"Hadley," I said.

"I know," he answered matter-of-factly.

This threw me off and I felt my blood turn to ice. Suddenly he didn't look quite so innocent.

"How do you know my name?" I asked, the sweetness leaving my voice.

My eyes darted around the store, searching for either Fallon or the other twitches—anyone who could help out if I needed it. I mean, it couldn't just be fate that I was running into this beautiful stranger here, could it?

Asher chuckled and ran a hand through his hair. "My aunt told me about you."

I looked at him suspiciously and then began to walk away in order to search for the others and get as far away from this Asher as I could. True, I didn't yet know if he was dangerous, but getting involved with anyone right now would be a bad idea in general.

Especially if he's disarmingly cute.

"Hey! Where are you going?" he asked as he caught up with me.

"Away." *From you.*

"Well, that's not very neighborly of you," Asher said, sounding let down. "And here, I thought you were like, Miss Social Butterfly. I was told there'd be a welcome wagon?"

"Looks like you should fire your informant," I said, wondering why he'd been asking about me in the first place. I still hadn't found Fallon, and this guy was managing to distract me. I stepped into the dressing room and called out Fallon's name. There was no response.

"You looking for your boyfriend?" Asher asked as I spun around, heading back toward the middle of the store.

"I don't have a boyfriend," I said without thinking. Out of the corner of my eye, I saw him smile, and then cursed myself for giving him any personal information.

"That's good to know," he said, still following me.

Despite my horror, I felt myself start to blush. I made a beeline for the escalator so he wouldn't see my reaction to his flirting.

"So who are you looking for?" he continued as he stepped onto the moving steps behind me.

"Why are you following me?" I answered, evading his question.

"I wouldn't exactly call it following you. You ran into me, remember?" he said, chuckling and running his hand through his hair.

"And yet, you're still here," I said, trying my best to sound annoyed.

"Look, my aunt offered to take me shopping and I needed a few things, so I came along. It's just a coincidence that we ran into each other," he said easily.

"You just happened to be at the same outlet mall as me, when there are at least three others that are closer to home?" I asked. I began to walk around the bottom floor where I'd left the others, hoping I'd run into them and that Fallon would be in tow. We needed to get out of here. Quick.

"What can I say? My aunt loves her Chico's and this is the only one in the area. What about you?" he said smugly. "What are you doing all the way out here? Maybe it's you who's stalking me."

My jaw dropped. "You wish."

"Oh, do I?"

"Seems like it."

"You think pretty highly of yourself, don't you?" he asked. I blinked. The question surprised me, because the answer was of course, yes, I did. But that was mostly because I had high self-esteem. I never understood those girls who complained about how fat they were or how bad their hair looked. Even if it was true, what was the point in pointing it out? The rest of the world was going to be tough enough on you, why join in on the negativity?

But what rendered me almost speechless was the fact that faux-hawk here was more brazen than any guy I'd ever met. No one had ever challenged me like this, and I couldn't decide if I hated him or admired him for it.

"Well, you would know, apparently," I said, bringing back up the fact that he knew more about me than I did about him. "What about you? You must think you're pretty important, crashing my afternoon and all," I said, narrowing my eyes at him. "FYI, I'm here with my friends."

As I said this, I did a final sweep of the lower floor and frowned when I realized Sascha, Jinx, and Jasmine weren't there. Jasmine still had the watch, so it was likely that the tracker had moved and the others had gone to follow it. They probably thought it would take too much time to go looking for me.

I turned on my heel and began to stalk over to the exit.

"Do you want me to leave?" he asked from behind me. He was being coy now, testing me. I could tell him to go, put a little magical persuasion into my words and watch him as he walked away.

But I was torn.

On the one hand, he wasn't completely horrible to talk to and he was definitely the first guy my own age who had ever piqued my interest for longer than, like, a second. On the other, he'd practically told me he was stalking me and not in a sexy kind of way.

"You never *did* tell me why you're on me like a shadow. How about we start with that and see where it goes?" I said, not telling him to leave, but not letting down my guard either.

He smiled, showing off his dimples again, and for a moment I got lost in the totally cute cheek craters. I started to smile back flirtily and then stopped myself.

Oh my God, did I want to be flirty? Was I really flirting with this stranger who appeared to be following me and, not only that, didn't seem to fawn over me like everyone else usually did? What was I thinking?

His hotness was no doubt addling my brain.

"Well, the truth is—"

His sentence was cut off by a loud explosion. The sound startled us both so much that we stopped in our tracks. Looking in the direction of the noise, I could see smoke rising above the outlet buildings a few hundred feet in the distance. Screams were mixed in with shouts.

"What the hell was that?" he asked, looking over at me.

"I don't know, but it can't be good," I said. "I'm going to find out."

"Seriously?"

"Of course," I answered without thinking. "Someone could be hurt and need my help."

"What, do you know CPR or something?" he asked me, giving me another one of his lopsided grins. It was then that I realized how closely we were standing. If I were to just get up on my tippy-toes, our lips would be perfectly level . . . not that I was thinking about kissing him or anything. It was just an observation.

Another scream pulled me out of my daydream and I began to walk backward, putting some distance between us as I did.

"I've gotta go," I said, and turned to run.

I'd barely gotten a few steps before I felt him come up beside me. I looked over at him, startled. "I'm going too," he said.

"Fine," I said as I somehow managed to jog in my heels. I didn't have time to argue with him. "But I'm going to need you to stay out of my way if anything happens."

"What, like you're Wonder Woman or something?" he responded sarcastically.

I gave him a look that told him I was being totally serious about this and waited for him to agree. "Fine. I'll let *you* be the hero today."

I was about to respond with something equally snarky, but as we rounded the last corner, I took in the scene in front of me and nearly froze with fear.

But I couldn't. Members of my coven were in trouble and there was no way I was ditching them now.

With a force I didn't know I had, I propelled myself into the bedlam before I could talk myself out of it.

Chapter Fifteen

By the time I reached the center of the fight, I'd already lost track of Asher, and to be honest, I was too distracted by everything that was going on to worry about him. I had more important things to be concerned about.

Like the fact that at the moment Jasmine was being cornered by two people. The woman to her left appeared to be in her twenties, had wild red hair, and wore loose-fitting black harem pants and a dusty white V-neck tee. She squinted at Jasmine like she was concentrating, but there was a huge grin on her face.

The man creeping up on Jasmine's other side was older—at least forty—with a salt-and-pepper mustache and hair to match. He wore a long cape-like jacket that fluttered behind him as he moved.

I was still at least twenty feet away when they attacked. Only, instead of touching her, they seemed to be hurling insults at her. No, not insults.

Magic.

Light burst through the air as spells were sent Jasmine's way and she tried her best to avoid letting them hit her. But she couldn't dodge it all, and I watched in horror as she was thrown backward with such force that when she hit the wall behind her, it knocked her out. She landed in a heap on the ground, not even flinching as she slammed into the hard surface.

"Jasmine!" I screamed, even though I knew she couldn't hear me. The other strangers gathered in the area heard me cry out, and began to cast in my direction as well. Magic was being sent every which way around the dead end and things were already on fire from where certain spells had landed. Although most shoppers had fled the scene once the fight had broken out, I could still see a few left in stores, checking out the action from the windows.

After a brief glance around, I could see that there were about three attackers for each one of us and we were already losing. Everyone was under fire.

Including me now. I felt an invisible force zip past me, narrowly missing my head, and without thinking about the consequences, I began to run.

I had no idea whether or not Jasmine was still alive, but I headed straight for her. The man and woman were still standing over her, casting spells while she was down. No way was I letting them continue to hurt her. My eyes darted around until they landed on a few mannequins that were on display outside a nearby store. With a flick of my hand, I pointed at the plastic bodies and then over at our enemies.

"Shifagin momentus!" I yelled with as much force as I could muster. The life-size dolls flew from their spots and crossed the space, hitting Jazzy's assailants and knocking them back onto the ground. When they didn't get up, I thanked the universe for helping me hit my targets and rushed over to Jasmine.

Crouching down, I touched my fingers to her neck, trying desperately to find a pulse. I didn't really know what I was doing, but I'd always seen people do it on television, so I figured there had to be *something* there. Finally I found the point I was looking for and let out a breath when I felt her pulse beating strongly.

"Help, Hadley!"

My head jerked in the direction of the scream and what I saw made my stomach drop. Jinx and Sascha were standing back-to-back, fighting off their own group of attackers. They'd been backed into a corner, and now it looked like their assailants were about to take them down too. The girls held their arms outstretched as if they were trying to fend off the others' next moves. Dark, burned spots decorated their clothes where spells had hit them. I was surprised the two were still standing, although by the looks of Sascha, it was just barely.

I didn't want to leave Jasmine on the ground by herself, but I knew that if I didn't get over to Sascha and Jinx, they'd be in just as bad shape. Or worse.

In a split-second decision, I cast a spell that overturned a nearby bench and sent it to the spot right in front of where Jasmine lay, so it acted as a sort of barricade.

It was the best I could do with the situation at hand.

Then I headed for the others.

As sparks flew from all directions, I sprinted toward the girls, hitting several scary-looking men with stunning spells along the way. They fell around me like flies, but I didn't have a chance to enjoy the victories. I leaped toward the guy closest to Sascha. Putting all my weight into it, I kicked my right foot up into a roundhouse kick and felt the familiar thud as it landed on the side of the guy's face. He made a sound like "oof" and then staggered backward. Not allowing him a chance to recover, I followed it up with a stunning spell.

The guy's body began to seize as if I'd jolted him with a Taser, and he hit the ground, rolling around in agony. I was tempted to keep the spell going, but every second I spent punishing him took me away from confronting the rest of them. So I moved on to the next guy, who'd lunged at Sascha and started to hit her. I grabbed ahold of the back of his shirt and simultaneously kicked the backs of his knees before dropping my weight to the ground and taking him down with me. Using the momentum of his fall to my advantage, I rolled onto my back and then placed my feet against his lower back. Grunting with exertion, I launched the man ten feet into the air, and he landed with a crack behind us.

Thank you, cheer muscles.

I rocked backward and then popped up onto my feet to see if Sascha was okay. She was trying desperately to fend off one last girl and was barely able to get a round of spells in before she was hit again. Overwhelmed by the sheer amount of spells being cast, Sascha backed up until her feet hit a garbage can behind her. A look over at Jinx showed that she wasn't much better off. I could see at least one person lying a few feet away, unmoving, but at least four others had replaced him. And Jinx appeared to be having trouble breathing while bruises began to form across her face.

I couldn't help but feel guilty over the fact that I hadn't been there to prevent all this from happening. If I had come alone, like I'd originally planned, I would've been the only one getting hurt.

Sure, I would've lost, but at least everyone else would be safe.

And I'd had no idea so many would be after us. Since there hadn't been any reported sightings of the Parrishables in hundreds of years, we'd been clueless as to how many members they actually had. It was clear that we'd highly underestimated them in more ways than one.

One look around the courtyard made it clear that years of witch classes and a day of round-the-clock training had in no way prepared us for the battle with a centuries-old evil coven.

I started to dive back into the fray when I was hit hard from behind. Falling to my knees, I struggled to pull in air, the wind having been knocked out of me. I looked up at Sascha and Jinx, who were now being overtaken from all sides, and tried frantically to get back up onto my feet. But a swift kick to my side landed me on my back and face-to-face with my enemy.

"You must be Hadley," the man sneered through snaggle-teeth. He straddled me, placing his knees on my chest, making it even more difficult to breathe. His cartoonishly large muscles flexed under his tight T-shirt as he reached for my neck. "The reverend is *really* interested in you."

A squeak escaped my throat as I attempted to cast a spell, but that was all that came out. His hands were so big that they reached completely around my neck. As a last-ditch effort, I flailed my legs, hoping I could at least distract him long enough to get away. Even with my years of combat lessons, the position I was currently in left me with few opportunities for escape.

Spots began to swim in front of my eyes and I realized I was on my way to passing out. But just as the lights were dimming, I caught a sudden flash of something as it rushed toward us.

There was a loud thud as something collided with the body above me and I gasped for air as I finally broke free. My body was exhausted and I wanted to give myself time to recover, but there was none. I had to help whoever had helped me.

That's when I remembered that Asher had been in the area. I'd lost track of him once I'd arrived and hadn't seen him since. I prayed that he'd honored his word and hadn't gotten involved.

At the same time, I was happy that Asher couldn't have been my enemy. Otherwise he would have disarmed me back in the store. He'd definitely had the opportunity.

But by the time my eyes fixed on the bodies that were now facing each other several feet away from me, I had no idea what I was going to find.

"Fallon?"

Where the hell did he come from?

"You okay?" he asked, his gaze never leaving the enormous man he'd pushed off me.

I wiped a trickle of blood from my mouth. "Yeah. I think so."

There was another loud explosion from the direction of Sascha and Jinx. Without looking over to survey the damage, I nodded toward Fallon.

"Go help the others," I said, narrowing my eyes menacingly at the bouncer-looking guy. "Leave him to me."

Fallon didn't stop to ask me if I was sure, he just took off running and joined the brawl, tossing people aside as he ran through the crowd like a battering ram. It was an amazing feat, considering how small and skinny he was; you'd never consider Fallon to be intimidating, unless maybe he was armed with a computer. He certainly wasn't the superhero type.

Then again, none of us really were.

I took a second to watch as he landed by the girls' side in the middle of the circle that had formed around them. Jinx was now lying unconscious behind Sascha. I wondered if that had been the loud noise that I'd heard. As I squinted, I saw blood pooling quickly around her. With Fallon now in the mix,

Sascha was finally able to crouch down to try to help her fallen friend. Fallon never slowed, even though spells were flying all around him. He just planted his feet and began shouting out every spell he'd ever been taught.

Angry that I'd been incapacitated while Jinx had been hurt, I turned my full attention back to the other guy.

"Earlier you said someone was looking for me. Who is it?" I asked him as we began to circle each other like animals stalking their prey. I sent a stunning spell his way, hoping to stop him from moving long enough to get what I needed out of him. But he sidestepped it easily and then laughed.

"You mean the good reverend? Oh, yes, he's got a *special* interest in you all right," he answered and then lunged forward as he sent his own spell zipping my way. I darted to the left just in time.

He said it was a reverend who was leading their group, but it couldn't possibly be *the* reverend. Not Samuel Parris. He would've died hundreds of years before. So there had to be a new reverend in town. One who had taken up his predecessor's evil ways.

"Why is he interested in us? We've never done anything to him," I answered, my teeth clenched angrily. "The Cleri always kept to themselves. You had no reason to hurt any of them!" I wasn't just talking about Jasmine and Jinx. I was talking about our parents. And by the smile on his face, I could tell he knew it.

Annoyed by his smugness, I shouted another spell at him and this time he barely escaped the blast. He reached up and touched his singed hair.

"You may be right, girlie," he said, nodding in agreement. "But *they* would've made it much more difficult for him to get what he *really* wanted."

This time I was expecting the magic that came my way and danced around it gracefully.

"Oh yeah? And what's that?" I asked, expecting him to refuse to tell me any more. I raised my arms in preparation to hit him with the stunning spell but paused for his answer.

He stopped walking and cocked his head to the side, looking at me curiously. "You don't know, do you?" he asked, sounding surprised. "Girlie, all of this is about *you*!"

Then he pointed both his arms my way and said a few words that sent me flying backward and onto the concrete, hard. The shock of the pain that suddenly flew up my tailbone was nothing compared to what I was feeling about what he'd just said. Having trouble standing now, I counterattacked from where I lay on the ground.

My eyes had started to water, but I could still see him as he advanced on me. "For the life of me, I can't understand why, though. You cast like a *girl*." He said it like it was a bad word.

That's it.

Before he had a chance to say anything else, I put everything I had behind my spell, feeling my body buzz with a power I wasn't used to. When it left my fingertips, it crossed the space and hit him square in the chest. His body went stiff and he fell forward onto the ground.

I walked over to him, the sound of my heels drowned out by the noise around me. Standing above him, I tapped him lightly on his behind with the toe of my studded pump. "I *am* a girl, you idiot. Now how does it feel to have your butt kicked by one?"

Then I spun around and rushed back toward the rest of my coven members.

Fallon was still holding his own and his bravery was impressive, but I could tell from the way the others were advancing on him that it wouldn't be enough. And I couldn't stomach anyone else getting hurt. Even someone who was partly responsible for everything that was happening.

We had to get out of there, and quickly.

Instead of joining them, I stopped running and closed my eyes tightly. With a deep breath, I tried to focus all my energy on what I was about to do. I'd managed to do the spell only a few times, and even then it had lasted only a few seconds and had been directed at just one person. Since holding a spell required major concentration and enormous power, it would take a particularly strong witch to be able to pull off what I wanted to do. And I wasn't sure I had what it took.

Hell, my parents might not have been able to do this spell.

But I had to at least try. We needed a distraction and the others were too busy or hurt to help out.

Recalling everything Jackson had taught us about tapping in to our powers, I visualized the energy coming up from my toes, coursing through my body, and bursting out my hands and head.

"Immobius totarium!"

I felt the force leave my body but had no idea whether it had worked. I was too afraid to open my eyes and risk seeing that I'd failed. I could still hear scuffling and shouts around me, which wasn't a good sign, but I was almost sure *something* had happened.

I just didn't know if it was going to be enough to save us from our impending doom.

Knowing that every minute I kept my eyes closed was putting me and the rest of the Cleri in danger, I finally forced myself to open them. And smiled.

Briefly.

The rest of the members of Team Bad Guys had frozen in

their tracks, some midstep, others as they were casting spells. I was tempted to unfreeze one of them and force him to tell me who the traitor was, but I wasn't sure I'd be able to control the spell enough to cut him loose without letting go of the others, too. And given the state of my coven, that was a risk I wasn't willing to take.

I closed the distance between me and the rest of the Cleri and motioned toward the parking lot. "We've got to go!"

Fallon still hadn't let his arms drop to his sides, clearly not trusting the frozen figures around him. I had to respect his skepticism, but I needed his help if we were going to get out of there in one piece. Sascha looked a little shell-shocked and hadn't even noticed that the chaos around her had come to a stop.

"Fallon! Sascha! We have to get to the car!" I shouted, attempting to snap them out of it.

Jasmine emerged from where she'd been lying behind the bench and groaned, clutching her head. Sirens began to sound in the distance and I rushed over to where Jinx was sprawled and crouched down to pick her up.

"Sascha, go help Jasmine. Fallon, grab Jinx's other side," I commanded. When we lifted her limp body, I noticed with terror that she felt cold and her clothes were completely soaked in blood.

There was so much blood for such a small girl.

I started to feel sick as it dawned on me that Jinx hadn't even cried out when she'd been wounded. The quiet girl had remained that way through the whole thing.

Shuffling as fast as we could through the parking lot and to the car, we scrambled to get inside. Fallon, Sascha, and a dazed Jasmine pulled Jinx across their laps as I climbed into the driver's seat.

I wasn't sure how long I was going to be able to hold back

the attackers; for all I knew, the spell had already worn off and they were about to burst into the parking lot behind us. But I had to at least try to keep it going until we were out of town. So I attempted to split my focus between holding back the Parrishables and starting the engine and pulling out of the lot. The others were crying and shouting from the backseat, but I tuned them out as we entered the flow of traffic on the highway. Once I felt that we had enough of a head start, I finally turned around to assess the damage.

A wave of fear and nausea swept over me. Within a matter of minutes, Sascha's bruises had grown into full-blown welts and she was looking more like she'd been hit by a truck than beaten up in a fight. Jasmine was fading in and out of consciousness and I worried she was suffering from injuries that I couldn't see.

But it was Jinx who had me truly worried. The blood had soaked through her entire shirt and had even seeped onto Sascha's and Fallon's clothes. There was so much of it, though, I could hardly believe it was all hers. I grabbed my jacket from the passenger seat and passed it to Fallon in the back.

"Where is it all coming from?" I asked, watching him in the rearview mirror as he tried to find the source. Finally he pulled up Jinx's shirt to reveal a blackened hole in her side. It looked like she'd been hit by lightning. The skin was charred as if she'd been burned, but blood was flowing out of the gash like lava out of a volcano. I was mesmerized by it for a few seconds and nearly veered into the median. Swerving back into my own lane, I placed both hands on the wheel so that I didn't hurt anyone else before we could get Jinx to the hospital.

"Fallon, you have to stop the bleeding," I instructed with a voice that was much calmer than I felt. "Take my jacket and press your hand firmly over the wound."

He looked in my direction, horrified by what I was asking him to do. "I'm going to hurt her if I do that," he stammered. It was the first time I'd seen signs of his age since he'd shown up at the fight, and for a moment I felt bad that he had to be here instead of off doing normal kid things. But life wasn't fair.

We all knew that now.

"She's going to die if you don't," I responded gently.

He looked back down at Jinx's face and then whispered, "I'm sorry," and did as I said. Sascha began to sob again and Jasmine's head was lolling back and forth like her neck was made of rubber.

I knew it was risky to stop before getting to the cabin, but I was afraid of what would happen if I didn't get the others help. So I pressed my foot on the gas and crossed four lanes of traffic to follow the first sign I saw for a hospital.

I just hoped it wasn't too late.

Chapter Sixteen

"Where were you guys?" a voice rang out across the room as we trudged inside. It was hours after darkness had fallen, and I had no idea who was talking. In fact, I couldn't have been sure at that moment that I hadn't imagined it. The events of the day had been so surreal that I wasn't processing reality very well anymore.

I didn't bother to answer and instead walked straight past the others who'd been at home the whole time and entered the kitchen. I needed to be alone to think. There'd been too much going on at the hospital for me to even begin to sort out what had happened at the mall—who had been hurt and what I'd learned about the Parrishables.

How could they expect me to just talk to them like everything was okay? We'd been attacked and I was pretty sure that our enemies wouldn't have stopped until we were . . . could they have actually killed us? I mean, taking out a bunch of adults was bad enough, but would they really have been able to kill a bunch of *kids*? It had sure looked like things were headed that way before I froze everyone and got us out of there.

I hated to think about what might've happened if the spell hadn't worked.

I went to the fridge and retrieved a bottle of sparkling water before collapsing at the kitchen table. I took a big swig and stared blankly out the window.

"They're asking questions out there," Fallon said, traipsing in a few seconds later. "What are you going to tell them?"

"Nothing yet," I said.

I didn't even glance up as Sascha joined us at the table. She still had on the same blood-stained clothes from earlier and I couldn't stand to look at the reminder of what had happened to my friends because I couldn't protect them.

"Are you kidding?" Fallon asked. "We were gone the entire day and now we just showed up in the middle of the night looking like extras from a *Texas Chainsaw Massacre* movie. Jasmine and Jinx are in the hospital and you expect the others *not* to wonder what's going on? You can't just ignore this and expect it to go away."

The combination of stress, fear, and exhaustion was finally catching up with me and I could feel myself begin to lose it. I was like a rubber band that was being pulled all the way back—I knew I was about to snap.

"What am I supposed to say, Fallon? That our worst nightmares came true today? That the Parrishables really *are* after us and they're not going to lay off just because we're kids? They'd have filleted us alive if they'd had the chance. Or maybe you want me to let everyone in on the fact that we're down two people, one of whom is currently fighting for her life! We got away today because we were *lucky*. And chances are, we're not going to be that lucky again. Is *that* the kind of honesty you want me to dish out?"

"Yes!" Fallon yelled back. "This is exactly why I took off earlier. You keep treating us like dumb kids, when we're in this thing too. You're not the only one who can handle bad news, Hadley. We *all* lost our parents back home. We're *all* being chased by these guys. We *all* deserve to know the truth!"

"You want to be treated like an adult, Fallon? How about *not* running off, so we don't have to chase after you and endanger our lives to save yours," I said.

It wasn't what I'd intended to say, but I was emotionally bankrupt and physically drained and once again Fallon had pushed me to the brink.

"I may have left, but you know as well as I do that *this* was not my fault," he said nastily. "I heard what that guy said to you back there."

My heart began to race double time and I suddenly felt faint as I realized what this could mean. Was it possible that Fallon had heard what the muscle-head and I had talked about at the mall? The noise levels had been so loud and we were all so focused on *not dying* that I'd figured our convo had been lost to everyone else.

But apparently it hadn't.

"Admit it! *You're* the reason the Parrishables are after us," he accused, confirming all my fears. "Everything *always* has to be about you. And that's what's getting people killed. I just don't get why everyone thinks you're so special!"

"Enough!" Sascha screamed.

Fallon and I both jumped at the sound and pivoted to see her standing now. We'd been so entrenched in our argument that we hadn't even heard her get up from her chair. Sascha had been silent the entire ride home, so her outburst was enough to render us quiet for the time being.

"Hadley, don't you *dare* make him feel like this is all his fault.

We're *family* now and we will *always* help one of our own," Sascha said, giving me a look. Then she turned to Fallon. "As misguided and careless as they may be."

This was both of our faults. I looked down at the floor and thought carefully about what to say next. When I finally spoke, it was directed toward Fallon. "You think I'm *happy* that some crazy reverend guy is obsessed with me?" I asked.

Then, before I even knew it was coming, I began to laugh.

I'm not sure if it was because I was tired or maybe I'd finally lost it, but suddenly what he was saying seemed like the funniest thing in the world. Fallon's face morphed into astonishment as I leaned back in hysterics. And then the reality of what he'd said hit me and I laughed so hard I began to cry.

I cried because he was right.

I still had no idea why, but the reverend's henchman had made it clear that I was the reason all of this was happening. Which meant I was responsible for the deaths of our parents. And the fact that Jasmine and Jinx were both injured, so swollen and bruised that they needed round-the-clock medical care, was because of me too.

Dammit, I'd been trying everything in my power not to go there. The last thing I wanted to do was relive the experience of being in the hospital where we'd just left the others. It had been hard enough being there the first time. But I couldn't stop my brain from recalling what had happened, like it was a movie on repeat.

By the time we'd gotten to the hospital, the two girls were in pretty bad shape. Smelling salts had done the trick to wake Jasmine, although the doctor said she'd hit her head so hard that she had a concussion. Even though she was awake now and talking, she needed to be monitored closely for the next forty-eight hours to make sure there wasn't more serious damage.

They checked out Sascha too, but besides the fact that the poor girl looked like a human punching bag, she wasn't too worse for the wear.

Jinx, on the other hand, had been rushed into emergency surgery because her injuries were so severe. When the doctor assigned to Jinx's case questioned us about what had happened, I'd told her that we'd been jumped by some gang members at the mall and I wasn't sure what they'd hit Jinx with. This was technically true since I hadn't seen the spells they'd used on her. And what else was I supposed to say? My friend was hit by a spell? Yeah, right.

The reality was that whatever they'd used to attack her, they'd gotten her good. The hole burned into her side was over an inch in length and the bad guys had somehow managed to knick her liver and cause internal bleeding. I knew things were bad on account of all the blood, but apparently ripping open your internal organs is even worse. As they wheeled Jinx off to the restricted area where they'd attempt to put her back together, the nurses promised me she'd be in good hands and ordered us all to go home, since visiting hours were over and we wouldn't be able to help her from the waiting room anyway.

And now I was realizing that it was all my fault.

When I'd cried all I could, I wiped my eyes clumsily with the backs of my hands and turned to face them both.

"Look, Fallon, I didn't ask for any of this. I was happy just being a cheerleader at my high school. Leading the student council and going to homecoming. I was *fine* with leaving the big-time magic to the professionals—like Ellen DeGeneres or Christopher Walken—and just doing my own thing at home," I said quietly. There was no fight left in me. "But you're right. I don't know why they're after me, but they are. People are hurt because of me."

"You're not the only one they're waging war on, Had,"

Sascha said, finally having calmed down. "Like I said, we're in this together."

What she said set something off in my head and suddenly everything seemed clear. I knew what I had to do to make everything right.

"Maybe we shouldn't be," I said, reaching over and grabbing my purse off the back of the chair.

"What are you talking about?" Fallon asked.

"The Parrishables are after *me*. Not you guys, just me," I said, pointing to myself unceremoniously. "You're safer here without me."

I began to walk out of the kitchen and toward the front door.

"Hadley!" Sascha pleaded. "You can't go."

I stopped halfway down the hall but didn't turn around.

"I have to," I said, tearing up again. "Keep training. Take care of each other."

Remembering what Emory had shared with me, I wrestled with whether or not to warn them. I was still no closer to knowing who the traitor was and wasn't sure I should say anything to them either. In the end, I decided to give them something in the middle.

"Be careful."

Then, without another word, I walked out the door.

It took me an hour of driving to stop shaking. And even when I did, I couldn't seem to shut off my mind. It just kept whirring as I obsessed over what I was doing. I'd left my coven, the only people in the world who knew about the battle that was growing in the magical world. I'd left the remaining Cleri members to fend for themselves, in a cabin they barely knew, with no adults to take care of them.

But I had no choice.

The Parrishables had gone after our parents so that they couldn't defend me. They'd hurt Jinx and Jasmine because they were at the mall with me. Anyone who was close to me was in danger of being hurt—maybe worse. No, too many people had already died because of me and I wouldn't let anyone else join them. Even if it meant facing my enemies alone.

I knew that going home was dangerous. I wasn't stupid. Even with my advanced powers, it was going to be a long shot that I'd be able to defeat them if they all came at me at once. But at least I could draw them away from the rest of the Cleri and give them a chance to make it out of this alive.

It also meant I wouldn't be distracted worrying about them.

I could give 100 percent of my attention to destroying the Parrishables. I could train twenty-four hours a day if I wanted to. I'd up my combat training until I was the ultimate fighter and come up with a plan to go after them. With the element of surprise and my magical abilities, I might be able to overtake them. After all, hadn't they already admitted that I was a force to be reckoned with? Even if I didn't know why, it had to mean I had a chance of winning.

And right now, that was enough for me.

So I headed home, because I figured it was the last place anyone would think I'd go. I mean, who would be crazy enough to head back to the scene of the crime? Besides me, of course.

As I pulled up to the place I used to call home, I partly expected the lights to be on inside and my parents to be anxiously waiting for me to get home safely before they could go to bed. But instead, the whole place was dark. Though barely any time had passed since I'd left, the lawn somehow looked a little straggly to me and the whole place gave off an abandoned feel.

So as not to send the message to my enemies that I was

back home and open for an attack, I drove right past my house and parked a few streets away. After exiting the car, I rushed through yards, hoping that I could make it to the house undetected. The sooner I got inside, the better I'd feel. I let myself in the front door, locking it behind me, and then stood there listening for any noises that might mean I wasn't alone in the house. When my paranoia was met with silence, I relaxed and found my way through the darkness to the stairs, knowing exactly where to step after years of sneaking up and down for midnight snacks.

Once I'd reached my bedroom, I went inside and closed the door behind me. I performed a spell that I'd nicknamed "What happens in this room, stays in this room" because it allowed me to move around unseen and unheard. After I was done casting this spell, I would be able to do anything I wanted, and to anyone outside, the room would appear empty and dark.

Only when I was finished casting did I turn on the light. I took a deep breath and ran over to my bed, throwing myself onto the mattress and taking in my familiar bedroom smell. Flipping over onto my back, I looked around the room, analyzing everything.

It was exactly the same, so either no one had bothered to break in after I'd left or they'd been so good at snooping that they'd managed to make it look like they were never here. The thought of someone else being in our house while I was gone filled me with anxiety. As I felt it creeping up my chest, I forced myself to get up and focus on something else before the unease took over my brain.

Heading back downstairs, I began to cast the same spell as the one I'd performed on my room in each of the other rooms of the house, so that no matter what I did inside, people outside would still assume nobody was home. And because it took more than one person to cast a protection spell around a whole house, I settled for setting noisy alarms instead. That way if someone *did* break in, at least I'd know about it and have a chance to get away. But before I booby-trapped the back door, I walked outside to check on the note I'd left my dad. If he'd gotten my message, he would've written back. He still hadn't called me, which made me think they'd found him, just like they'd found Mom and the others. But if by some miracle he had managed to get away, I liked to think he'd try to get to me somehow.

I retrieved the magic rock and looked inside, seeing with dismay that my original note was still there and appeared untouched. The air I'd been holding in escaped my lips and, sadly, I replaced the rock before going back inside and setting the final alarm.

Climbing the stairs seemed nearly impossible, but I forced my legs to move and finally made it back up to my room. I sealed the door behind me and climbed into bed. I didn't even have a chance to give any thought to what I was going to do next before my body gave in to sleep.

Chapter Seventeen

When I woke up the next morning and reached over to my cell phone to see what time it was, I nearly fell out of bed in shock. I'd slept for about fifteen hours but hadn't dreamed, and I didn't remember falling asleep. My initial plans to begin training today appeared to be out of the question now that the day was practically over.

I got up and stretched, feeling every single muscle as it screamed in pain. As athletic as I was, cheerleading had in no way prepared me for the damage of magical warfare. My tailbone throbbed with every step. I went over to the mirror that was hanging on the back of my door and surveyed the damage. I might as well have been rolling around in the dirt, because that's how torn up I looked.

Somebody was badly in need of a shower.

Making it my first order of business, I headed over to my closet and swung the doors open to survey my choices.

Hello, clothes! Oh, how I've missed you!

I ran my hand across the rainbow of materials, feeling the familiar twinge I got over fabulous fashion. Given all that had happened in the last week, this particular passion had taken a major backseat to everything else. But it wasn't until I stood there in front of designs by Carolina Herrera and Vivienne Westwood (both fellow witches, I might add) that I realized just how much I'd been ignoring that part of me.

That wasn't the only thing I'd suppressed, though. As I touched the stretchy polyester fabric of my cheerleading uniform, I felt the pang of sadness grow even heavier. And then my heart sank into my stomach as I had a horrific thought.

If the Parrishables were going after everyone I was close to, then could that include my best friends? Sofia, Trish, and Bethany weren't witches, but that didn't necessarily mean they were free from danger. In fact, it was possible that if the Parrishables couldn't get at me while I was with the rest of the Cleri, they might go after my friends to lure me out. I'd learned from the mall incident that they weren't worried about the nonmagical world knowing they existed. The Parrishables could attack at any time, knowing that I would come running to save my friends. And I would, because although they were able to flip their way across a field, my cheer-mates didn't stand a chance against the Parrishables.

I had to make sure they were okay.

Looking back at my uniform, I realized that my teammates would be lining up to cheer on our football team in less than half an hour. If I rushed to get ready, I could probably make it to the game before halftime.

Ahhh, halftime.

If I was being honest with myself, checking on the others wasn't the only reason I wanted to go to the game. The truth was, I missed cheer, desperately. It had been the biggest part of my life for such a long time that not having it now felt like going through another loss. It was the one thing that always made me feel like myself again.

And if there was a possibility that I wasn't going to win this fight with the Parrishables, then this would be my last chance to be a regular sixteen-year-old doing what she loved. Even if I wouldn't be able to cheer along with the squad, I'd still be able to cheer them on, to feel the excitement of the crowd and dance to the music. I'd have to stay out of sight, but it would be like my final performance before retiring my pom-pons.

I hadn't realized I'd needed this, but I did. And I deserved it.

As soon as I'd made the decision to go, I got moving. I looked at myself in the mirror again and made a face at what I saw. It was not pretty. Even though I had no intention of being seen, I couldn't take the risk of going out looking the way I did. Just like celebrities when they go out of their house without makeup on and then are bombarded by the paparazzi, you never know when you might need to impress.

The problem was that I didn't have enough time to take a shower or primp. But I *did* have time for a spell.

"Renewbus freshimo perfecto," I said, waving my hand in front of my face. The dirt began to fall off me like my skin was repellent. I gave my body a little shake to get rid of the last remnants of my awful day. Next, color began to appear on my face like it was being applied by an invisible makeup artist. A subtle green shade swept across my eyelids followed by a thick black liner around the rims. My eyelashes thickened and grew darker, curling up slightly at the ends. I began to flush pink and my lips grew glossy, the light in my room catching their perfectly reflective surface.

My hair went from messy to loose curls within minutes, and once the ends had stopped winding this way and that, I gathered the shiny locks up into a high ponytail and secured them with a rubber band. Then I put on a pair of jeans and a black hoodie, so I wouldn't draw any attention to myself while at the game. Satisfied with my overall look, I snuck out the back door and across two blocks to where I'd parked my car the night before. Getting inside, I took a second to look up and down the block in case anyone had followed me. When it appeared I was in the clear, I turned on the engine and began to drive.

I could hear the buzz of the crowd before I even pulled up to the stadium. That and the fact that I was stuck in game traffic for about a mile before I was even able to park my car made me feel like I was back in my element. My body was humming and I couldn't have wiped the smile off my face if I'd tried. Not that I'd want to—a smile was a cheerleader's best accessory.

The row of parking spaces usually reserved for student athletes—which allowed for the cheerleaders to leave as soon as the game was over—had already been taken by the rest of the squad, since they'd gotten to the field about two hours prior to kickoff. So I had to settle for parking with the fans, which meant I was much farther away from the entrance. This was actually okay, since I wouldn't be going in the front entrance with everyone else. I needed to go in the back way if I was going to avoid being seen.

Locking up my car, I then headed in the opposite direction from the crowd, weaving in and out of cars until I reached the fence that closed in the stadium. Taking a hard left, I moved around the perimeter until I approached the area directly behind the bleachers. People weren't supposed to hang out back there, so I figured it would be the safest place for me to be. Looking around to be sure that no one could see me, I did a quick spell to separate the chains in the fence long enough for me to slip through and out of sight.

I snuck forward until one of the spaces between the bleachers was eye level. The roar of the fans was muffled from my current position, but I had a perfect view of the field. And best of all, the cheerleaders.

They were finishing up a chant and I watched with admiration as they held their final poses: three Scorpions in the back. Sofia had finally become flexible enough to pull her leg up behind her until her shoe was hovering in the air right above her head. She'd been trying to pull off a Scorp all year, but hadn't really mastered it until now. The fact that she'd managed to do it while I was gone was just a dip in the moment.

I began to clap for her accomplishment before realizing that no one could hear me, and let my hands fall back to my sides.

You're not here to cheer, Hadley. You're here to check on your friends. And say good-bye.

A quick sweep of the girls on the sidelines showed me they were all there. Bethany and Sofia were now splitting middle in the front row and Trish called the cheers from the far right back. My usual spot. It was hard not to feel jealous that Trish was currently living the life I wished I could get back. In fact, now that I saw they were all safe, the reality of what I was missing truly hit me.

My life would never be the same again.

I would never just be a cheerleader with normal teenage problems. A girl who spent her nights at games and her days running her school. My parents were most likely both dead, so they wouldn't be around to see me graduate from high school and help me with my college applications or give me advice on what career I should have. If I wasn't able to beat the Parrishables, I could forget about ever having a boyfriend or getting married one day. My life as I once knew it was over.

"Sixty seconds!" Coach yelled out over the noise of the crowd.

I watched as the others lined up for the beginning of the second quarter, chatting to each other excitedly and waving to their friends in the crowd. When the players took their places on the field, Trish called out a touchdown chant and the others got ready to perform.

Just one last time.

I took a step back and got into position right along with my teammates. Then, from under the bleachers, I clapped my hands together and cheered my heart out. I matched every motion, dance, and jump they did and jumped up and down when the team made a touchdown. Focusing on the task right in front of me allowed me to leave my worries and stress behind. It was the first time in forever that I really felt like myself.

And I wished it didn't have to end.

But it did. And I decided I'd rather leave on a good note and not press my luck by hanging around. So I began to back up, silently saying my good-byes to my old life as I went. Except, all of a sudden, I saw a set of familiar eyes looking in my direction through the slats in the bleachers. No, not in my direction, directly at me.

Asher.

I quickly crouched low to the ground, terrified that he'd actually seen me. Was it even possible? Asher would've had to look through a space the size of a bread box into a section of the stadium that no one should've been in and that was hidden under darkness. Maybe he hadn't spotted me at all and it was like those portraits where the eyes followed you no matter where you went in the room.

It was just an illusion.

I slowly stood back up, expecting to see his eyes still on me, but when I took a peek, the only people I saw were fans and students walking by as they chatted excitedly. There wasn't a dark-haired faux-hawk in sight.

Asher was gone.

Or maybe he'd never been there in the first place.

Either way, I was surprised by the sadness I felt when I discovered that he wasn't there. Logically I knew we were both better off. I'd come back home because I thought that the people I cared about would be safer without me around. I wasn't sure how I felt about Asher yet—we'd only ever talked once—but I certainly didn't want to get him killed.

Still, it would've been nice to have the chance to see what was there.

With a sigh, I turned around and walked away from the noise of the fans. Climbing through the magical hole I'd made to get in, I sealed it up behind me and then headed for the car. Trudging back like I was doing the walk of shame, I pulled my hoodie up over my long, dark hair and tried to shield my face from anyone who might recognize me.

At least I knew that my friends were okay. Maybe the Parrishables wouldn't go after them, like I'd thought. There was even the slightest possibility that I could convince the Parrishables to give up this witch hunt and I could go back to being me.

With a final look at the game going on behind me, I began to drive away.

A girl can dream, can't she?

It was harder coming home this time. There were no expectations of anyone being there to greet me. And instead of feeling better after seeing Bethany, Trish, and Sofia, I just felt worse. I couldn't explain it. Maybe I was having an identity crisis, because I no longer fit into a world I used to *own*. And I resented it.

I tossed my keys onto the kitchen counter and said the spell that would set the alarm behind me. The silence in the house was deafening and I looked for something to fill the void. Turning on the television in the living room, I sat down to think about what I was going to do next.

It felt like I'd slowly been losing myself since the fire in the warehouse and that it was time to get back to the heart of Hadley. Something had to bring her back to life or at least give her something to live for again.

And then there was a knock at the door.

I shot to the ground, even though I knew the spell was still on the house that made it impossible for outsiders to see or hear what was going on inside. The rapping came again, this time a little louder, and I carefully picked myself up and crept over to the locked front door. A peek through the hole revealed there was no one there.

The third knock had me clutching the wood while straining to see outside. I was cautiously curious, but there was no way I was going to yell through the door and let the faceless person—or people—on the other side know I was home.

"Hadley!" a guy's voice called, just loudly enough for me to hear in my entryway.

"Asher?" I asked, finally feeling safe enough to talk.

"Can I come in?" he asked.

I briefly wondered if it was wise to do what he asked. Then he'd be able to come back anytime he wanted.

Or was that just vampires?

I shook my head as I struggled to make a decision.

"I need to talk to you about yesterday," he said when I didn't comply right away. Then he paused. "Are you all right?"

"I'm fine," I answered through the door. Closing my eyes, I forced myself to say what I knew I had to. "You should go home, Asher."

Please stay.

He didn't even consider my request. "That's not going to happen," he said firmly. "If you don't let me in, I'm just going to stand out here until you do. I need to see for myself that you're okay."

I was annoyed by how stubborn he was being, but also touched by how sweet the gesture was. But he was creating a problem for me now. Either I could let him in and put him or myself at risk or I could let him stay outside and possibly draw even more attention to the house. At least inside with me, he'd be a little safer than he would be alone.

And he might just be the thing I needed to jump-start the new phase in my life.

I disarmed the alarm spell and unlocked the door before letting him inside.

"You have *got* to stop stalking me," I said, ushering him in, and locked the door up tight behind us.

He chuckled. "There you go again, assuming everything's about you."

It was almost exactly what Fallon had accused me of back at the cabin, but when Asher said it, it sounded sweet. So I went with it.

"Well, isn't it?" I asked coyly.

"I guess that's the question of the day," he answered, glancing around our living room. It looked like it always did. Mom had kept our house beyond clean and everything was meticulously organized. "I've always wondered what the inside of this house looked like."

"Well, mystery solved, I guess," I said, walking around the couch and sitting down. He did the same. "Is it everything you expected?"

He flashed me a smile that showed off his adorable dimples. There was a sparkle in his eyes. "Nothing about you is what I expected."

A wave of dizziness swept over me as I realized that I actually wanted him there. With me. Alone. And that's when it hit me: I liked him. This had never happened before, at least not to me.

Oh, for witch's sake.

He leaned forward and looked into my eyes like he was trying to guess what I was thinking. "What? No comeback?"

The TV provided us with noise to fill the silence. As I tried to think of something cool to say, I discreetly wiped my hands on the seat cushions next to my legs. They were so sweaty all of a sudden. But I wasn't the only one who seemed nervous. A glance down at Asher's leg showed that it was bouncing about a mile a minute, which actually made me feel calmer about the whole situation. It was so bizarre, but when other people got stressed out, that always seemed to be when I became most focused. Maybe it was because someone had to take charge and I always felt better when that someone was me. It made me feel more in control.

So I did the only thing I could think of that would help me regain control over this situation.

I was honest with Asher.

"You're not what I expected either," I said.

And then I leaned over and kissed him.

Chapter Eighteen

His lips felt good on mine and we kissed feverishly at first, quickly melting into each other. I didn't even stop to think if it was a good idea; I just did it. Our lips parted as we got more comfortable with each other; he tasted faintly of black licorice, a candy I'd never really liked until now. I toyed with the idea of leading him upstairs to my room, but then thought better of it. First off, I wasn't sure I wanted to be alone with him in a room with a bed on account of the fact that we barely knew each other. For all I knew, he could be a normal high school student by day and a psycho serial killer at night. A cute serial killer of course, but still.

Besides, there was no reason to head upstairs, anyway—we didn't exactly need more privacy in a house that was already empty. I *was* its only occupant, and it wasn't like anyone was going to come home and catch me making out with a boy I hardly knew.

Other kids my age would die for the opportunity to have

their house to themselves so they could be alone with a cute guy, and here I was wishing my parents were around to catch me. Life could be really messed up sometimes.

I couldn't keep my mind on what Asher and I were doing while I was thinking about my parents and what had most likely happened to them. Talk about a mood killer. So with the hand that had just been running up Asher's chest I gently pushed him away until we were on opposite sides of the couch, staring at each other.

"What's wrong? Are we going too fast?" he asked, out of breath. I seemed to be having the same problem.

"No. No, that's not it," I said, shaking my head.

"What is it, then?"

I couldn't exactly say that I'd suddenly lost my appetite for him because he made me think of my dead parents. Not only would that make him as depressed as I was now, but if he asked what happened to them, I'd either have to lie and make something up, or tell him the truth and then attempt to explain what had been going on in my life lately. Neither of these options seemed viable to me. Not if I wanted to try to get back on track with Asher.

"I've sort of got a headache and I'm not sure when my parents are getting home," I said finally. Technically this wasn't a lie; I *wasn't* sure when my parents would be home—if my dad was coming home at all. I knew I wasn't telling him the entire truth, and I didn't want to start a potential relationship based on lies. Technicalities . . . now, those were a different thing entirely.

"Do you want me to go?" he asked. I could tell by the sound of his voice that he didn't want to. I smiled. He'd asked me this question once before and I didn't have an answer for him then. Now I did. It might not have been smart, but . . .

"Not at all," I said reassuringly. Then I stood to leave. I needed to take a minute to collect myself and try to put aside the thoughts of my parents, which had blocked me in the first place. "Hang out. Get comfortable. I'm just going to get some Tylenol and I'll be back. Can I get you something to drink?"

Asher looked happy to hear that he wasn't being kicked out of the house just yet and did as I suggested, snuggling back into the middle of the soft cushions. "Sure. I'll take whatever you're having."

"Okay. The remote's there if you want to look for something else."

I gave him a smile I hoped would make up for the fact that I'd put us on ice for the time being and then retreated into the kitchen. The Tylenol was up in the corner cabinet and after shaking two out into my palm, I tossed them into my mouth and chased them with a swig of root beer. Truth be told, my head *was* throbbing—well, my whole body hurt, really. After everything that had happened yesterday, I knew that what the doctor ordered was probably just a good night's sleep. But with any luck, I wouldn't be going to bed anytime soon, thus the need for Tylenol. Snagging another can of soda from the fridge, I went to leave when something outside the window stopped me in my tracks.

But upon closer inspection, nothing was there. Nothing I could see, anyway.

The nights were so much brighter here than they were in the darkness of the woods. The weird thing was that I'd felt safer back in the isolation of the woods than I did in our suburban neighborhood. I'm sure it had something to do with the fact that I was constantly surrounded by a dozen other kids back at the cabin, and here it was just me and Asher. Not that I was complaining. It was just that I'd grown comfortable with having lots of people around me.

Strength in numbers and all that.

I looked around the backyard. Things were already starting to look bad now that no one was tending to it. The grass was an inch too long and a brownish color I'd never seen before. There was a pile of decomposing blackberries on the ground near the fence from where the neighbor's bush had grown over the side. I turned to get a better view of the rest of the yard and as I did so, there was another flash of movement out of the corner of my eye. I leaned toward the window until my forehead hit the glass, and struggled to identify what it could have been.

When I still didn't see anything, I chalked it up to an overactive imagination and exhaustion. What I'd seen was probably a squirrel or bird, or maybe even a leaf being blown across the yard. In other words, nothing I needed to worry about.

"You get lost in there or something?" Asher called from the living room.

Taking one last look at my yard, I backed away from the window and turned to where my guest was waiting. My very cute guest, who seemed to like me. Well, enough to make out with me, at least.

When I got to the room, I tried to hide my smile as I saw Asher cuddled up under my mom's fuzzy red blanket. He'd wrapped it around his body and up and over his head like Little Red Riding Hood. Between his innocent expression and the fuzzy material framing his face, he looked absolutely ridiculous.

And I *so* wanted to kiss him again.

"You are such a geek," I said as I walked over to him and placed our drinks on the coffee table. Plopping down on the couch next to him, I pulled my legs up to my chest and cocked my head to the side. "Are you cold or do you just like the look?"

"Well, I definitely think I can pull this off," he answered

coyly. He moved slightly closer to me. "But I might be a little cold."

"Oh, yeah? Well we can't have that, can we?" I leaned toward him and began rubbing his arms through the blanket to try to warm him up.

"I'm still cold," he said slowly. "Hey, I've got another idea of how you can warm me up."

"Oh, right. Subtle, Asher. You may be a good kisser, but you'll have to take me out on a date before I do whatever *you're* thinking," I said, feeling myself start to blush. Because the truth was, I was thinking it too. Maybe not tonight, but possibly (hopefully) sometime in the future.

"I was talking about kissing!" he exclaimed, feigning shock. "Why don't you get your mind out of the gutter."

I snorted and crossed my arms over my chest.

"Okay, well then there *is* something else you can do for me," he continued.

"I'm not doing that, either."

"You can tell me exactly what happened back at the mall yesterday," he said, suddenly serious.

My smile faded and my mouth went dry. He had brought up the one subject I didn't want to talk about. I knew it was naive to think that maybe he'd forgotten all about it, but after spending this whole time without mentioning the fight, I thought we were going to just pretend it never happened. But now he was bringing it up and I had no idea what I was going to say.

So I said the first thing that came to my mind.

"Okay, we can kiss," I said quickly, and moved toward him.

Asher leaned away from me and placed his hand in between us. "No way—you're not getting out of this one," he said. "Now what was with you going all G.I. Jane and running headfirst into that fight? It looked like—"

"It was a gang fight," I said quickly, blurting out the lie before I had a chance to think about it.

Asher blinked at me. "How could you tell they were a gang? They didn't look like gang members. Some of the people were *old*. Like thirty or something. And things were sparking," he said. Then he lowered his voice like he was sharing a secret with me. "I think some weird stuff was going on. I don't exactly know how to explain it—"

"They were a gang of magicians," I said. Even as I said it, I wanted to kick myself. What an incredibly stupid answer. Where the hell was I going with this? It's not like he'd believe magic was real, and that people were casting spells on each other, in public no less. "I mean, I read in the paper a few weeks ago that there are gangs out there who use the kinds of tricks that magicians use to distract their enemies. That's probably what you saw."

No way was he going to fall for this. No way.

"Do they have gangs for everything now?" he asked incredulously. It seemed like he was actually pondering the idea.

No. Way.

"I guess so," I mumbled.

"But that still doesn't answer why you ran in there," Asher said, turning the spotlight back on me. To my dismay. "You could've been hurt or something. They could've sawed you in half. It's not like you're some kind of secret superhero or something . . ."

"Um, I don't know why I did it," I said, starting to chew on my bottom lip, but then stopping when I realized I was taking off my lip gloss. "It was just my first instinct, I guess. I thought maybe someone could use my help."

"Well, did they?"

177

I looked down at the ground guiltily. "Yeah, they did." I immediately made a mental note to call the hospital and check in on Jasmine and Jinx once Asher was gone.

"Well, I'm glad you're okay, Hadley."

"You too," I answered.

At least there was that. Somehow Asher had managed to disappear during the fight and avoid the kind of damage that was inflicted on the rest of my coven. Come to think of it, I couldn't remember seeing Asher at *all* during the fight. Which was weird because he was right behind me when I first got to the courtyard; I had no idea what had happened to him after that.

"Where *did* you go during the fight, anyway? I was kind of worried you'd gotten hurt when I couldn't find you," I said, lowering my voice.

"You thought the evil magicians had kidnapped me?" Asher asked with a chuckle.

"Go ahead and laugh, but that fight was intense. A lot of people got hurt, you know," I said sincerely. "I'm glad you left before they got to you, too." I wasn't accusing him of bailing. In fact, being that he wasn't magically inclined like me, it was much better that he'd taken off. He would've been *so* out of his league if he'd jumped in.

"Well, it looked like you had everything under control," he said.

He obviously hadn't stuck around long enough to see much, because I'd never had anything under control. That's what I'd wanted everyone to believe, but I'd just been trying my best to get everyone out of there alive—myself included. For someone who was used to excelling at pretty much everything, the fact that I'd failed at keeping everyone safe was incredibly frustrating.

Before I could dip back into another funk—one that I

couldn't pull myself out of—I tried to change the subject. Attempting to put as much magical persuasion into my words as possible, I silently willed Asher to forget about earlier and focus on right now.

"Let's talk about something a little more . . . sexy," I said, giving him a suggestive smile.

He smiled back. "Like?"

"Like how hot you look in that furry red blanket," I said, giggling.

Asher rolled his eyes and pulled the blanket tighter around his face. "Wait, *this* is what does it for you? Are you sure you're not just trying to hide something from me?"

I leaned toward him boldly, until my lips were once again touching his. The butterflies in my stomach began to flutter and my head started to swim with feelings I'd never experienced. As our kiss deepened, Asher pulled me closer until I was lying flat against his chest on the couch. My brain started to question my heart over what was right and what was safe. What was I doing here, in my empty house, with a mere high school boy, when so much was already going on? Logically I knew that starting to date a relative stranger was potentially dangerous, but maybe that was part of what attracted me to him. The fact that it was the opposite of what I should've been doing might be the very reason I was doing it.

After all, I had an ancient evil coven out to get everyone I was close to. If I really cared about Asher, I wouldn't be pulling him into my web of violence and death, right? I'd encourage him to go home and stay far, far away from me instead.

But I didn't *want* him to go. I wanted to be there, pressed up against his chest, becoming familiar with the way he kissed. So I kept kissing him.

Almost as soon as I'd resolved to keep going, a scratching

sound pulled me out of my make-out sesh. I tried to figure out what it was while continuing to kiss Asher. I ran my fingers through his spiky hair and grabbed a hunk of it, pulling his face tighter to mine.

There it was again. A scratching sound barely loud enough to discern, but now I knew I hadn't imagined it. This time I stopped what I was doing and strained to hear where it was coming from.

"What? Was that wrong?" Asher asked, looking concerned.

"No. Shhh," I said, touching my fingers to his lips to keep him quiet.

We sat there like that in silence. The house creaked like older structures sometimes do, but that wasn't anything unusual. I could hear water dripping from the sink in the kitchen and it was making me need to pee. But besides that, the house was still.

There was nothing out of the ordinary, from what I could tell.

"Guess it was nothing," I said, taking my fingers back from their place on Asher's lips. I shrugged and leaned back in to kiss him again.

"I think you're amazing," he murmured between kisses. I started to smile as he said it, because I'd been thinking the same thing about him. I couldn't believe that I was actually considering dating a high school guy. I'd be breaking my own rules if I kept in the direction I was going with Asher. Then again, would anyone really care except for me?

I was still considering this when suddenly my world exploded in light and pain.

Next thing I knew, I was on the floor in front of the couch, my head pounding. I felt something wet trickle down my forehead and drip into my eye. Wondering why I was sweating,

I reached up and wiped at my brow. When I pulled my arm back, blood covered my hand.

What the . . .

Looking to my left, I could see that Asher was on the ground as well, only he seemed to be asleep. But he didn't look peaceful. People who fell asleep usually looked peaceful and that's not what this was.

He looked . . . dead.

Still confused and now worried about Asher, my eyes darted around the room for some sort of explanation for what had just happened.

And that's when I saw them.

Several figures stood in the doorway, looking ready for a fight. As I watched, more appeared from the kitchen area, surveying the scene. Before I had a chance to yell out, they were already rushing toward me, spells flying.

Chapter Nineteen

I rolled out of the way right as an older man with messy long hair and a goatee shot a spell my way. The carpet singed less than a foot from my face and my eyes widened as I imagined what would've happened if it had hit me and not the floor. I tried to put the thought out of my mind. Scars *so* weren't a good look for me.

I took cover under our glass coffee table just as one of the guys ran across the room and leaped into the air. I was terrified that he would hit his mark, but I stayed still for just a few seconds longer. My heart was racing and everything in me screamed to move, but I forced myself to stay put.

Finally, just before my attacker's heavy black boots went crashing through the glass above me, I shot out of the way, missing the fatal blow by milliseconds. Shards of glass sprinkled down like crystal rain, but I didn't stop to shield myself. Instead, I thrust my leg up and kicked the guy as hard as I could in the side of the head as he leaned down to take a second try at me.

With nowhere to go since he was stuck in the frame of the coffee table, the guy fell over the side and landed with a thud. When he didn't get back up, I assumed the layer of glass on the floor had slowed him down.

With one guy down and two closing in, I turned back to Asher, who was lying facedown a few feet away. "Asher! Wake up!" I yelled at him. I didn't know what I would do if he didn't answer. I needed him to get up. Even if it was just so he could get out of there intact.

But he wasn't moving. I was about to screech at him again when I felt a shot of magic hit my lower back and make its way up my spine, exploding in mind-crushing pain seconds later. Without thinking, I spun around to look my attacker in the eyes. When another girl around my age looked back at me, I blinked with surprise.

"I heard you think you're something special," she sneered. Her hair was as blond as mine was black, but darkness clouded her features. She was pretty, though. If she'd gone to my school, she probably would've been competition.

"Funny, I haven't heard *anything* about you," I said, placing my perfectly manicured hands on my hips and popping my hip out like I was posing for a picture.

This seemed to piss her off and she started to advance on me slowly. I knew I should put my hands up to protect my face in case she lashed out, but I wasn't going to give her the satisfaction of thinking she had me worried. I'd sparred enough with my dad to know that I was ready for whatever she threw my way.

I waited to see whether she was going to come at me with a spell or with her fists, bending my legs slightly so I was ready for either. When she was within striking distance, she raised her fist and I knew we were settling this civilian-style.

No magic it is.

Her knuckles made contact with my hands as I blocked each hit she threw my way. The girl was putting so much energy into each blow, I knew it wouldn't be long before she tired herself out. So I stayed on the defensive and allowed her to go crazy. As soon as I saw her chest heaving, I waged my own attack.

I struck fast and hard, but the difference was, I knew where to hit her so she'd end up on the ground. Three strikes and she was out, lying on the floor next to her partner in crime, unconscious but not dead.

"Guess I *am* that good," I said, looking down at her.

Two more roundhouse kicks and I'd taken out a few more guys as they came into the room to join their fallen friends. One managed to get a blow or two in himself, but my adrenaline was running so high I didn't even feel it. They came at me one after another through the kitchen door and I alternated between hand-to-hand combat and spells, doing whatever I could to keep up with them. Just as I threw a woman back over the couch with a tossing spell, I looked over my right shoulder and saw that still more were appearing.

"Oh, come on!" I screamed. "How many of you *are* there? You know one against a thousand isn't exactly fair."

"What the hell's happening?"

I looked back to see that Asher was awake now and thoroughly confused by what he was seeing in the living room. And why wouldn't he be? He'd been knocked unconscious and woken up to people shooting sparks from their fingers and tearing up my formerly quiet house. There were nearly a dozen bodies on the floor around him and though there seemed to be a lull in the rush of bad guys, I knew it wasn't over.

Asher's eyes grew wide and he tried to get up but couldn't

seem to make it. Apparently the hit he'd taken was still affecting his lower extremities.

"What's going on, Hadley?" he asked, looking straight at me now.

What was I supposed to say that wouldn't have him running for the door or get us both killed? I could hear more footsteps hitting the floor of the kitchen and there was no way to explain what was going on while defending us both. I had to think fast to come up with an excuse that wouldn't leave Asher asking too many questions.

"Angry magicians," I said, before turning around just in time to dodge a punch from a young guy who was screaming something indiscernible at me, and then threw one of my own. He stopped talking as his nose exploded in blood, and I screamed out in pain. Hitting him felt a lot like punching a brick wall.

"What can I do?" Asher asked, trying again to stand up. This time he succeeded.

"Nothing," I said, magically sending a pair of chairs and the nearly destroyed coffee table flying at the open kitchen doorway to try to block anyone else from coming in. I held my focus on the spell and watched as people began to pile up against the barrier.

"This is insane. Are you . . . Hadley, are you in a gang?" There was hesitation and the slightest sound of fear in his voice. Oh, great. The guy I liked, or thought I liked, was scared of me. Guys didn't want to date girls they were scared of. Unless that was their thing, I guess, but as far as I knew, Asher wasn't *that* guy. As all of this ran through my head, I watched Asher look from me to the door and back again, like he was just now realizing that the furniture couldn't be holding up itself.

I had to get him out of here before he started asking more questions and got himself killed in the process.

"I am definitely *not* in a gang," I said, trying to split my concentration between the spell and Asher. The spell was getting weaker and so was I. We'd been fighting for close to ten minutes already and I was beginning to run low on energy. Whoever was on the other side of my barricade was throwing their own magic at the problem and so it was becoming a major struggle of wits and spells. I had a feeling I was stronger than them, but I wasn't sure how much longer I'd be able to keep it up. "Asher, get out of here. Go get help."

He didn't respond and I began to think—well, really, hope—that he was already gone. But then I felt him come up behind me and touch me softly on the shoulder. "I'm not going to leave you here alone."

He still liked me! I just about melted hearing him say that, but knew that I couldn't let my guard down—otherwise we were both going to be in a lot of trouble. No, he *had* to leave so I could take care of this myself. No one else I cared about was going to end up in the hospital again. And as gallant as he was, Asher couldn't help me.

"Do you trust me?" I asked him.

He paused. "I do."

That was all I needed to hear. Facing him, I fell into his arms and kissed him long and hard. There was a fever to our connection, the kind of heat that's ignited when you think it might be your last kiss. Something weird happened when we kissed this time, though. I began to feel the magic I was still directing toward the barricade at the door grow stronger, and it became less difficult to hold in place. In fact, it almost felt easy. Like I'd just gotten a power boost.

Whoa, talk about creating sparks.

I reluctantly pulled myself away but noticed that I was still all tingly from our kiss. I'd never felt this alive before. And if I was going to get us out, it was going to have to be while I was still feeling strong.

To do that, I really needed Asher to leave.

I looked at Asher and put as much conviction into my words as I could. "Go. Get. Help," I pleaded. I felt a little bad about using my powers on the guy I liked, but this wasn't the time to be worrying about ethics. It was time to stay alive. "Now!"

He opened his mouth to argue, but nothing came out. Instead, he just nodded and began to step away. But something in his eyes told me he was trying to fight it. In the end, my powers won out and I watched him grip the doorknob tightly before walking out the door.

As soon as he was gone, my abilities took a nosedive and my body began to shake with exertion. It was like the natural boost I'd gotten from our kiss had left with Asher and I suddenly didn't have the same will to fight that I'd had before. The feeling of his lips on mine started to fade and instead, all I felt was fatigue.

This was bad. I'd never felt so depleted of my powers in my whole life. The Parrishables seemed to be growing stronger now and the force of their magic was pushing me backward. My feet slid across the floor until I hit the couch and fell back over the arm and onto the cushions.

And then they were making their way through the door, coming at me faster than I could've thought possible, only now I couldn't seem to move. I'd run out of juice, and holding them back while Asher escaped would be the last thing I did.

At least I hadn't let *everyone* down.

Just then, there was a huge crash, but with all the noise going on around me, I couldn't tell which direction it came from. And being that I still felt paralyzed, I couldn't move my head to see what was going on.

Please don't be back, Asher.

"Leave her alone, you crazy magicians!" Asher yelled out. He sounded far away and my heart leapt when I realized he was shouting from his place just outside my front door. My persuasion had succeeded in making him leave, but I hadn't been clear enough apparently. If I could just make him go farther away, I could finally let go. I was so tired.

"Asher, go home!" I tried to say it out loud, but I could no longer speak. I couldn't cry, either, although I wanted to. Without me to defend him, Asher wouldn't stand a chance.

"What the hell is he talking about?" I could hear someone else talking now—and they were much closer to where I was lying. They were in the same room as me, for sure.

"No clue. Magicians? Is that the new slang term for witches? Are we magicians now?" another person asked.

"Guys, cut the chitchat and help Hadley!" This voice I recognized. But it was still highly possible that I was hallucinating, so I tried not to get my hopes up. Instead, I focused on the noises around me. It was clear the fight was not over, but for some reason, none of the flying spells were hitting me.

Time ticked by excruciatingly slowly until suddenly Sascha was at my side, leaning over me and hurling spells at people as they advanced on us. I tried to smile at her to show her how happy I was to see her, but I'm not sure my mouth moved. I wanted to tell her how much I'd missed her.

All of them.

As my eyes adjusted to focus on the beautiful face of my friend and savior, she was suddenly yanked away from me. As she struggled in and out of my sight line, I was able to make out a guy standing behind her holding her in a headlock. She scratched at his wrists and forearms and strangled sounds escaped her lips. Then, just as quickly as he'd come up behind her, he disappeared and Sascha was gasping for air.

"Is she okay?"

Emory.

When I knew it was her, a wave of calm washed over me. There was something about knowing she was there that made me feel closer to my mom. And right now, I was scared about what was going to happen next. It was times like these when I just really needed my mom. And now that she was gone, Emory was the closest thing I had to that comfort.

"I'm not sure. She looks fine, but something's going on with her," Sascha said, leaning back over me as something exploded overhead and debris rained down around us.

"Leave her alone!" Asher was still yelling at everyone. He had no idea that those who'd just come in were members of my coven.

"We're not trying to hurt her," another person said. "We're here to *help* her."

Sascha started moving in and out of my line of vision and I could hear her throwing spells in the direction of our enemies. The explosions drowned out most of my thoughts except for one. I didn't want them thinking that Asher was one of them and hurt him by mistake.

I opened my mouth to tell them as much, but nothing came out. Another wave of exhaustion washed over me and my eyelids started to flutter closed. After that, I had to rely on my hearing to find out what was going on around me.

Was this it? Was this what dying felt like? If it was, I didn't get what everyone was so scared of. I mostly felt like I was about to drift off to sleep. And I was so tired, I almost welcomed it. Not that I wanted to die or anything, but I wouldn't have minded the chance to rest. The shouting was still going on around me. Things were breaking and I felt something wet hit my cheek.

As I began to float away, someone took my hand. And then the oddest thing happened. My hand began to grow warm, like I was holding a heating blanket. After a few seconds, the warmth became a tingling that spread from my hand up my arm and to my neck. By the time I felt it on my face and around my head, I realized what was happening.

Someone was giving me a jump start.

My energy started to come back little by little. The power I was feeling traveled down my body and into my legs, my muscles twitching with—I wasn't exactly sure what. Excitement? Energy? Whatever it was, I wasn't sleepy anymore. In fact, I was feeling totally rejuvenated.

My eyes sprang open and I sat straight up on the couch, scaring Emory and making her jump about three feet away. I was still holding Sascha's hand and looked down at our entwined fingers and then up at her.

I had no idea what she'd done, but I was incredibly grateful. As I tried to tell her this, her hand slid from mine and she hunched over, placing her hand up to her forehead. I took a moment to study her face and saw that she was pale and looked a little sick. At first I worried that she'd been hit by a stray spell, but I quickly realized it was something else.

"What just happened?" I asked. "Are you okay, Sascha?"

"Yeah. I'm just . . . light-headed. It happens sometimes when I do this," she answered quietly, still staring at the ground.

"What *did* you do?" I asked.

A body sailed over our heads and crashed into the entertainment center in the corner of the room. Sparks flew and shorted out a nearby lamp. Still, given the magic that was being cast around the place, there was plenty of light.

"Let's talk about this later," she said quietly. I was just now noticing how loud and chaotic it was in the house and tried to shield her from things that were flying around us. "You need to help the others."

She was right. I didn't want to leave her there, especially when she was looking so frail, but the others seemed to need my help. There might have been more of us at the moment, but the Parrishables had more experience with fighting dirty. And they were pulling out all the stops.

"Hadley! You're okay!"

Oh, God. Asher.

I swung around to see him inside the house again, being held back by Fallon, Peter, and a girl named June. My persuasion must have faded when I'd almost passed out before, allowing Asher the free will to do what he wanted. Now he was trying to escape, but they had a tight grip on all his limbs. If he hadn't looked so worried, I would have commended them on a job well done.

"Let him go, guys. It's cool," I shouted, putting as much influence into it as I could. "He's on our side."

Those seemed to be the magic words, because as soon as I spoke, they let go and Asher stumbled forward. He was by my side within seconds and right there, with everyone watching, he pulled me into a hug. I clung to him, just happy to be back in his arms.

Over Asher's shoulder, I could see Emory rush toward the door where more of the Parrishables were coming in. With a cry befitting a battle, she disappeared into the kitchen. I moved to go after her, afraid of her being back there alone, but Asher held me tighter.

"I know you're strong and fully capable of kicking anyone's ass and I totally believe that you can take care of yourself. I even respect you for taking charge in messed-up situations," he said, a little bit breathless from the struggle. "But don't you *ever* tell me to leave you behind again. You know I'll say yes to just about anything you ask, because, well, I like you, but when I thought you might be hurt back there . . . So from here on out, we're in this together. You're stuck with me, so you better get used to it. And don't even try to talk me out of it, because I'm the one making this decision."

I fought the smile that was threatening to break out. He'd just admitted he liked me. Sure, it was under the guise of telling me what to do, but in this case, I thought it was kind of sweet. Because, did I mention that he liked me?

I moved in to kiss him again, but something flew through the door and landed on an armchair in the corner with a thud. It was Emory, back from the kitchen, hurt but still alive. Thank God. She began to yell something at me, but before she could, a pillow raised up from its place on the floor and pressed itself up against the redhead's face. Emory began to struggle against the invisible force, but it was too much for her. After a few moments, she went still.

"No!" I shouted and started off in her direction.

But before I could make it even a few steps, I was being pulled backward like a rubber band snapping into place and was thrown against the ceiling like a fly caught on sticky paper. I fought to move my head, my arms, even my fingers, but something held me there. As I stared down at the battle that was going on beneath me, I could see that there were about a dozen people packed into our tiny living room going head to head, fighting for their lives.

And then I caught sight of my adversary, the reason I was currently pinned to the ceiling.

He was dressed in black pants, a matching shirt, and a floor-length, worn-looking brown leather jacket. It was old, but not in the distressed kind of way that you'd find in a trendy store. It looked more like it had been lived in.

Moving up to his face, I wasn't surprised to see the blackness of his eyes. We'd learned early on in magic class that when witches practiced dark spells, the caster's soul turned dark as well. And since the eyes were the window to the soul . . . well, you get the idea. Only the darkest witches' eyes ever turned black, and now that they were staring back at me, the effect was chilling.

A shiver ran down my body. Still frozen in place, I could do nothing to stop it. I was powerless.

He gave me a crooked smile as if he were reading my mind. But he couldn't . . . could he? I knew it was something my mother could do, but I'd always thought it was because the gift ran in families. The thought that a stranger—someone who wanted me dead no less—could know what I was thinking was beyond upsetting. I felt violated. But as soon as I realized what he was doing, I built up the wall in my mind to at least try to block him out. Given the fact that I couldn't move my body, it was all I could seem to do to fight against him.

In response, the man chuckled and winked at me.

"Well, you're certainly not a disappointment, are you?" he said. And then with a flick of his wrist, he lifted his spell and left me to drop to the floor below.

Chapter Twenty

I watched as I got closer and closer to the ground in what seemed like slow motion and wondered what would happen when I hit. Would my bones crack instantly? I'd never broken anything before, although I'd always wondered how I'd managed to escape that rite of passage.

But if I was seriously hurt in this fall I might not be able to get myself—let alone everyone else—out of there alive. Maybe I'd be able to convince enough of the others to get out, so it wouldn't turn into a total slaughter. This thought nearly made me sick to my stomach. Or maybe it was the fact that I was falling so quickly now that my insides felt like I was on a roller coaster. Either way, I wasn't feeling too hot.

I was seconds away from going splat all over my living room floor when I clenched my eyes shut. Right as I was expecting to feel the floor come up to bite me in the ass, the strangest thing happened.

My body began to slow down, resisting gravity as if I were

attached to an invisible bungee cord. And then I was being pulled sideways, arms and legs flailing as I tried to somehow navigate the flight. I had to open my eyes because I had no idea what had just happened. And what I saw didn't make any sense.

The guy in the trench coat was still there, only now his eyes were following me as I flew across the room. He seemed oblivious to everything that was going on around us. Peter and June were taking turns shielding each other and knocking bad guys down, and Asher was in the middle of pounding on another guy near the front door. Sascha was still recovering from reviving me earlier, but Fallon had moved to her side, deflecting spells as they were thrown his way. The Cleri were too busy fighting others to go after the guy who currently had his black eyes trained on me. So he just stood there, smiling that eerie grin of his like he was actually having *fun*.

"Shifagin momentus!" someone yelled out, barely audible over the noise in the room. A few moments later, my body hit the soft cushions of the couch with an "oomph." The landing may have been better than hitting the floor, but I still ended up having the wind knocked out of me and had to take a moment to get air back into my lungs. When I could breathe again, I jumped up from the couch and stood in a defensive stance. I knew I had someone to thank for making the couch move four feet backward to soften my fall, but there was no time. Trench-coat guy was steadily walking toward me, still smiling, which made me totally uneasy.

Just as he was raising his hand to cast yet another spell, I muttered the words to a bubble spell that trapped its caster in the safety of an impenetrable, circular force field. I felt the strength of the guy's spell hit my bubble, but—thank God—it held.

This time, trench-coat guy's mouth twitched even though the smile was still plastered across his face.

"I knew you'd be a worthy adversary," he said, as if we were the only two there.

I watched with horror as Fallon knocked out a man who'd jumped over the couch to get to him and Sascha. Then he ran straight toward trench-coat guy. Just as Fallon was opening his mouth to let out a spell, Trench Coat flicked his wrist, tossing Fallon into the air like he was a rag doll. I screamed his name, but that was all I could do. Luckily, Asher turned around just in time to see Fallon coming toward him and reached out to help cushion his fall. The bad guy was still talking, as if he'd just swatted at an annoying fly.

"I've been waiting a long time to meet you," he said with an almost animalistic snarl. "Everyone else was just too easy to defeat. Or too damaged. Or too . . . *predictable*. I needed a challenge. And that's where you come in."

"Like *you're* the first person to tell me that I'm challenging," I said, sounding a lot more like myself than I had in days. The only problem was that it was taking all my concentration just to keep the bubble around me intact, and I needed to try and pull the others into it with me.

"Pretty *and* funny. That's a powerful combination," he said with an evil chuckle that would've sounded totally normal in a horror film. "I don't think we've been formally introduced. I'm Samuel, leader of this coven. And you're Hadley."

I was so surprised to hear him say my name that I nearly dropped the spell. "How do you know who I am?" I asked before I could stop myself. I immediately wished I could take it back. The last thing I wanted was for him to know he'd rattled me.

"Oh, dear girl, I make it my business to know who's out there in our world. I've been watching you for quite some time now. You see, every magically inclined person lets off a sort of footprint—an enchanted calling card, if you will," Samuel said, gesturing around the room. "Your kind of power screams across state lines. I've been following your work for years."

"Some people would call that stalking," I answered.

The fight was still going on around us, but we continued to focus only on each other. This wasn't easy considering that I could see the others struggling to stay standing. And here I was, with my protective bubble keeping me safe. I began to step back so I could bring the others into it. By this time, Emory had woken up and was fighting her way over to Sascha.

"There's that wit again," old black eyes said. "You know, I could use someone with similar talents in my group. Join my team and we could be unstoppable."

"I'm a cheerleader. I'm already a part of a team, thank you very much. And to be honest, you're not exactly my type. You know, being evil and all."

He narrowed his eyes at me and took a few steps in my direction. I involuntarily took a few steps backward, feeling the desperate need to get as far away from him as possible. When Samuel saw me move, he stopped in his tracks. He reached up to rub his jaw as he thought about his next move.

"I have a feeling you'll change your mind," he said, his eyes growing even darker than they'd been a minute earlier. The blackness in his irises swirled like a storm growing deep within him. "Bridget did. In the end, anyway. You will too."

It hit me with the force of a slap even though I was still under my spell's protection. Samuel? Bridget? Could it possibly be true? Was this sadistic witch really Samuel Parris? But that was impossible because that would make him over . . . *three hundred years old*. No way was this guy over the age of forty. Either that or he'd aged *really* well. And if that was the case, I was going to make it my mission to figure out how to bottle the secret and become rich and famous after creating my own skin care line.

But right now I had more important things to worry about. I needed to get all my friends out of the house without taking another trip to the hospital. A look around showed that they were still on their feet—even Fallon after Asher's great catch—but people were starting to slow down. Emory had finally reached Sascha and was helping her up, while Peter and June had joined Asher and Fallon in fighting off the rest of the baddies left in the room. We needed to leave before everyone got so tired that they started making mistakes. Because mistakes led to injuries.

I had to stop this bizarro one-on-one convo with this possibly undead witch ASAP so we could get the heck out of here.

"Funny, I heard she wanted nothing to do with you in the end." I didn't divulge how I knew this, but stated it as fact. "Speaking of traitors, how did it feel to betray your own coven? I mean, I'd be afraid that any coven I built after that would either never fully trust me or would eventually do the same thing to me. Glad I don't have to worry about that."

He was silent for a moment, seemingly mulling over what I'd said. Was he holding himself back from going off on me? I was taking a huge risk by talking to him this way; I had no idea whether he was who he said he was, but either way, he had his own army, and it didn't seem like they were going to stop until they'd gotten rid of us all.

Another reason we had to get out of there right away.

Samuel had a whole gang of people standing between the two of us now, but maybe I could use his numbers against him. Making a split-second decision without even knowing if it would work, I said a few words under my breath and thrust my now solidified ball of a force field toward the closest of Samuel's group. Just as I'd hoped, the gelatin-like ball picked up speed and sucked the first guy in and continued to pick others up as it turned into a huge orb of bad guys hurtling straight for the leader of the pack.

Samuel was able to dodge the human bowling ball at the last minute by diving behind an overturned recliner, but it didn't matter. The distraction had still managed to give us plenty of time to slip away and out the front door without any more damage being done or anyone else getting hurt.

I was the last one out, and as I went I tossed a sludge spell behind me, the sidewalk turning into a sort of sticky tar mess so that anyone who followed us would stick to the ground. Eventually they'd get out of it—either the goo would break down when the spell wore off or if the guy was smart enough, he'd take off his shoes and go barefoot—but by then we'd be long gone.

"Get in your car!" I yelled, surveying the group to make sure we had everyone. Emory and Fallon carried Sascha, since she was still looking a little out of it from earlier. Peter and June followed quickly behind them. For now, the whole group appeared to be intact.

"Asher, over here!" I motioned for him to follow me the few blocks over to where I had parked and had the car unlocked before he'd even reached the passenger side. Jumping inside and hot-wiring the car with a few choice words (I'd left my keys somewhere in the house during all the drama), I then slammed my foot down on the gas and the car lurched forward, peeling out as we made our exit. I met up with the other car a few blocks away, before we all got back onto the highway to head to the cabin. Every few seconds I'd glance back to make sure they were keeping up.

Once we'd been driving for at least twenty minutes, I finally allowed myself to let up on the gas and trust that, for the time being, we weren't being followed.

For now.

"What the *hell* was that?" Asher asked once I'd stopped driving like I was in the Indy 500. The sound of his voice breaking our silence startled me as I'd been pondering what our next move should be. I started to answer, but he cut me off. "And don't give me that crap about magician gangs. Magicians or not, that was *magic* back there. You guys were doing actual *spells*. But not fun ones like making cake appear out of thin air or guessing cards. That was a battle. The kind you don't walk away from."

My mind raced to come up with an explanation that would be less crazy than the truth, but in the end nothing I could make up would sound any saner. And I was sick of lying to Asher. It somehow felt wrong. Like, if I was trying to start a relationship with someone, I didn't want to base it on a plethora of lies. After everything he'd just seen, I doubted he'd believe me anyway. Better to come clean and deal with the consequences later. Even if it turned out that Asher wanted nothing to do with me or my crazy life.

I hoped all this didn't scare him off for good.

My stomach twisted into knots as I prepared to do what I knew I had to. "Asher, I'm a witch," I said, saying each word carefully like it might help the meaning sink in. "I come from a long line of witches. My mom could do magic. My grandmother, too. As far as I know everyone in my family tree has had some ability to cast."

I left out the fact that my super-great-grandmother was the first witch to be executed at the Salem witch trials and was quite possibly the most powerful witch of all time. And that it looked like the apple didn't fall far from the tree in my case. It didn't seem important to the story, and I was nervous about overloading him with too much heavy information all at once. That discussion was more of a fifth-date kind of topic.

"You were right that it was a battle, Asher. And those guys back there? They're the bad guys. *Really* bad guys. They've been hunting down other covens for centuries, wiping out anyone who could threaten their rise to power. And now they've found us. The people who helped us out at the house tonight are members of my coven, the Cleri. Just over a week ago the Parrishables—those are the bad guys—they attacked our parents at a coven meeting and burned the place to the ground, with everyone still in it."

I chanced a look over at Asher but he wasn't saying anything.

"After that, those of us who were left went on the run, escaping to the only place I knew would be safe. And then we started to train. We hid and we trained, trying to perfect all the spells that we'd been taught by our magic teacher. But it wasn't enough. Because when they found us at the mall, they ended up putting two of my friends in the hospital. One even had to have emergency surgery."

Now I was unloading everything on him. All the stress and upset I'd been letting build up inside me in order to shield it from the others came spilling out. It was hard not to choke on my words when I thought about Jinx and her injuries, but I kept going. I had to.

"Then I found out from one of Samuel Parris's goons that it's really me that they're after, and if the Cleri hadn't been with me that day, they never would've gotten hurt. So I left. Figured they were better off without me. But it was all a *bad* idea—well, good because I ran into you, but bad because of that total slasher scene back at my house.

"Now it looks like we'll have to go back to the cabin where the rest of the Cleri are staying, because so far it's the only place that the Parrishables haven't been able to find us. And on top of that, I've pulled you into my witch fit and put your life in danger too! Asher, you're the last person I'd ever want to get hurt and I'm not sure if you should even be around me anymore, but I also don't know if it's safe for you to be out there by yourself now. I don't know what to do."

I looked over at him again, scared that he'd call me a psycho and jump out of the moving vehicle just to get away from me. But his butt stayed glued to the seat and his face remained neutral, both reactions I hadn't been expecting. I waited patiently for him to say something. Finally, he cleared his throat and broke the uncomfortable silence.

"So, you're a witch," he said in a way that was like, "So, you're seventeen" or "So, you're a redhead." It brought a feeling to my heart that was indescribable. He didn't care that I was a witch. Or that I did magic. Or that I was *different*.

I'd told him my big secret and he hadn't gone running for the hills. My mind boggled at the fact that he seemed to be taking it all pretty well. I never would've expected it.

"So, what next?" he asked, settling back into his seat, more at ease than I would've expected of someone who'd just found out that witches existed.

"That's it? You're okay knowing that they're after us and all?" I asked, surprised but happy. "I mean, I'm kind of a liability right now. Trouble seems to follow me around these days."

"Oh, you're trouble all right," he said with a smile. "But like you said, they've already seen me, and it won't be any better out there fending for myself than here with you. Besides, I trust you to keep me safe; I'm sort of not ready to let you go just yet."

This made me blush and I was thankful that it was dark in the car. Taking my hand off the wheel, I placed it on his and linked our fingers.

"So don't," I said.

Chapter Twenty - One

The whole gang of us trudged into the cabin in silence. It wasn't necessarily that we were trying to be quiet; it was that nobody had much to say. I'd been wondering during the trip home—when I wasn't busy beaming over how understanding Asher had been about everything—whether it would be weird now that I was coming back. I mean, the last time I was there, I'd pretty much ditched them. Of course, in my mind I'd had reason: I was just trying to keep them safe. Still, I could see how they might've interpreted my exit as abandonment.

On the other hand, they *had* come looking for me in the end and that had to mean something. Since we'd all been in separate cars, I hadn't had the chance to talk to any of them and gauge how they were feeling.

All I really knew was that it felt oddly good to be home— odd because the cabin had begun to feel more like home than anywhere else.

It was about 11 p.m. as we walked in the front door of the

cabin, and I was expecting the house to be quiet with all its inhabitants asleep. But as I walked into the living room, I saw that almost everyone was still up. It was possible they'd been waiting in the same spots since the others had left to find me; people were leafing through magazines or had books open, and a few were just sitting there staring off into space. But when we shuffled in, all heads and eyes turned to us.

Here we go.

I was trying to figure out what to say—whether I should apologize for leaving or thank them for coming to my rescue—but it turned out I didn't need to say anything. Almost immediately, I was tackled from the side in a hug. I looked down at my attacker and saw Penelope, a thirteen-year-old who I'd come to associate with horses, because she always wore the same pony necklace every day. We'd barely said more than hi to each other; she sort of stayed in the background of our coven and was rarely seen or heard. And now Penelope had attached herself to my lower half, hooking her arms around my waist with a surprisingly strong grip for someone her size.

"Please don't leave us again," she whispered. Her voice was inaudible to anyone but me. There was so much emotion behind her words that it nearly broke my heart.

I looked up at the rest of my coven. Judging by their faces, I thought they were happy that I was back too. They weren't annoyed or looking to fight with me. Their smiles ranged from relief to joy to excitement and that's when I knew.

The cold war was over.

There would be no hard feelings, between them or me, and we *would* move past this. Hell, we were already past it in a way. They were glad for my return and so was I.

"I promise I won't take off again," I said, glancing down at

Penelope, who was full-on crying now. "You guys are stuck with me whether you like it or not."

I felt a tap on my shoulder and spun around to see someone else I hadn't expected.

"Jazzy!" I screeched, reaching out to grab her. But she was too quick for me, throwing her hands up to ward me off before I could get to her. I'd forgotten she wasn't the mushy-gushy type, so I settled for giving her a grin instead. She smiled back and I knew she was just as happy to see me.

"What are you doing here? When did they let you out?" I asked after taking a moment to pull myself together.

Jasmine waved off my question. "I'm fine. You really thought a little rumble like that was going to keep me down? Nah, I'm tough. Have you seen these muscles?" She pulled up one of her sleeves, showing off her scrawny arms.

I couldn't help but laugh. "Very impressive," I said. "But really, are you sure you're okay?"

"Thanks, *Mom*, but I think I'll be fine," she said semi-sarcastically. "I just couldn't take lying there like that any longer. It was like prison, only cleaner. The doc said I just had to take it easy the next couple of days and sent me home with some of these." Jasmine shook a bottle of what I assumed were painkillers. She talked a good game, but I could tell her head was still hurting, as she winced at the quick motion.

"And Jinx?" It hurt me to ask, but the question was on my mind, since Jasmine had made it home.

"She's still at the hospital. They were able to stop the bleeding and she even woke up for a little while. But they've got her all hooked up to these monitors and they're giving her meds that have her sleeping round the clock. They said there was no use in sticking around since she won't be conscious most of the time anyway. So I came by myself."

"Is she going to be okay?" I asked hopefully.

"That's the rumor," Jasmine said, shrugging. She was playing it cool, but I knew that Jinx's condition was hitting her pretty hard.

Hearing that Jinx had made it through her surgery and that the docs were feeling hopeful about her recovery made me feel like I could finally breathe again. Of course, I'd always hoped she'd be okay, but a part of me was constantly waiting for the bad news. Now that the more pressing crisis appeared to be over, another question popped into my head.

"Wait, how did the others find me, anyway?"

"That was all Fallon," Peter said, walking in the front door with Sascha, Emory, and June in tow. Fallon, however, was nowhere to be seen. When Peter saw the look on my face, he chuckled. "We were surprised when he suggested it too. But he insisted that you'd be at your house. Said it would be the last place we'd check and the first place you'd go."

"Good guess," I said, surprised by how right he'd been. I looked around for him, but saw that he still hadn't come inside.

Pete shrugged. "He saw how close you were to your parents when we were all there after the fire and figured you'd go there before disappearing for good."

"So he came after me, even after I told him not to?" I asked.

It was hard to believe that what Peter was saying was true. Since when did Fallon do anything out of the kindness of his heart? Or at least without some sort of evil motivation behind it. Did he finally realize that my powers were in a whole different league than his and decide it would be better to have me around? Or were his motives more sinister than that? I couldn't ignore the fact that each time the Parrishables had attacked, Fallon had mysteriously shown up to save the day.

The others nodded. "He started coming up with the plan about an hour after you left."

"Well, that was nice of him, I guess," I said, still bewildered.

None of this derailed me from the fact that I was back with my coven (well, most of them, anyway) and had a whole new perspective on this war with the Parrishables. None of us could do this on our own. Yes, it might be safer if the others had never met me, but as of right now, there was no spell to turn back time. So it looked like they were stuck with me. And I with them.

Thank God, because I'd learned—almost at the expense of my life—that as powerful as I was, I wasn't strong enough to bring down an entire coven on my own.

"Who's he?" Peter asked, a bit of a growl creeping into his voice. He was just being protective of his family, so I ignored the fact that he was acting rude toward our guest.

"Yeah, who's the honey?" Jasmine asked, nodding to the space over my right shoulder. Turning to follow her gaze, I saw that Asher was standing a few feet behind me, trying not to get in the way, so that I could have some time to reconnect with my friends. It was sweet of him to give me some space, but I also noticed that he hadn't retreated far enough away that he couldn't be at my side within seconds. It looked like he was keeping his promise to not let me out of his sight anytime soon.

I walked over to Asher and placed my hand on his arm protectively. The gesture was not lost on the others. I may as well have flashed a neon sign that said, "He's okay and he's mine," because everyone seemed to relax a little.

"Everyone, this is Asher. Asher, this is the Cleri."

People gave him variations of hello and a few showed off shy smiles. The guys mostly grunted and walked away, probably to complain about another man invading their territory. Especially one as good-looking as Asher. I wasn't worried, though. They'd all get over it when they realized he wasn't a threat—he was here only because of me, not to take his place as the alpha male.

"Hadley, we never wanted you to leave before," Sascha said. "I know you think we'll be safer without you, but we won't. We can't afford to lose you now."

I crossed the room and knelt down next to her, noticing how weak her voice still was. She was at least sitting up now, but her face was pale and she looked drained. All because she'd worked her magic on me back in my living room. Without her, I would have been done for. As far as I was concerned, she and the others were the reason I was still alive.

"Then you won't lose me, Sascha," I said, laying my hand on hers just like she'd done to me back at my house. "Because I think you're right. We need each other."

I looked up at everyone in the room. During the drive home, I'd managed to find time to do some thinking about our next steps. Now that I had everyone's attention, I knew it was the best time to let them in on what I'd decided. I only hoped they'd see things the way I did.

"So, I have good news and bad news," I said, standing up and making my way to the middle of the room so I could see everyone better. "The bad news is that our fears have come true. The Parrishables are back and they're out for blood. In fact, I don't know how it's possible, but I think I was attacked by Samuel Parris himself tonight."

Gasps escaped from a few mouths and whispers erupted around me.

"Creepy old guys aside, they're strong. *Really* strong. And they're a lot more experienced in fighting battles," I said. "They know how to find us and that we're running scared. And if we keep letting them ambush us, they *will* take each and every one of us out."

I'd been pacing the floor as I talked, but now I turned around and looked into the eyes of my fellow Cleri as I continued on.

"But we're strong too," I said, emphasizing each syllable. "I realized something tonight, guys. They want our *power*. I mean, think about it. They wouldn't be coming after us otherwise. It may not seem like it, because we haven't had much experience using our magic in a fight, but it's true. Like Sascha said, Samuel basically confirmed it tonight. He wants us gone because *we're a threat*."

"Yeah, but the Parrishables sort of handed our asses to us at the mall," Jasmine said. Realizing she'd just said this out loud, she stood up a bit straighter. "I mean, you know I'm always looking for a fight, but I'm not sure everyone *else* is ready."

Emory stepped up. "What I think Jasmine's trying to say is, how can we possibly go up against the Parrishables? We need to train, but there's no time. We're willing to do whatever you want us to, Hadley, I think you know that. But we need to do something more. Otherwise, how will it be enough?" Emory said.

The others were staring at me now, waiting for me to say something. They were nervous, and honestly, so was I. What I was about to ask them to do was not only dangerous but scary. I needed them to put all their faith in me and what I was about to say without any proof that it would end in anything other than bloodshed. But I could feel it in my bones. Together we would be enough.

"You're right. In order to beat the Parrishables, we have to *be* more," I said.

I watched as everyone began to look around at each other, wondering what I was getting at.

"And even if we up our game, we *will* be risking our lives. I wish it wasn't true, but it is. It's not fair that this random group of people wants us dead, even though we've never done anything to them," I said. I hated that other kids our age were worrying about who was going to ask them to the winter semiformal and we were stuck here stressing over whether or not we'd still be alive long enough to even go. "Plain and simple—this sucks."

"Uh, Hadley? Is this supposed to be a pep talk or a pity party?" Jasmine asked, a hint of sarcasm in her voice. I resisted the urge to roll my eyes and continued.

"This sucks—but it's not over," I finished. "You guys did some amazing stuff while going up against the Parrishables tonight. It made me think that we may be selling ourselves short about our ability to fight back."

"Maybe you should've gotten checked out at the hospital when the others were too," Peter said. "Sounds like you may have amnesia or something."

"No, really. Just hear me out," I said. I was happy that Peter was joking around, because it meant he was starting to feel better. Turning my attention over to Sascha, I went on. "I know you did something earlier tonight. Something I've never seen before."

Sascha looked at me wide-eyed, like she'd just been caught with her hand in the cookie jar.

"Now, either I was out the day Jackson taught us how to do that or you learned it somewhere else."

"Um, it sort of just came to me," she said helplessly. "Look, Hadley, I'm sorry, I know we're not supposed to—"

"Why are you apologizing?" I asked, cutting her off. "If you hadn't followed your instincts and done that voodoo that you do, I don't think I would've survived that fight back there. I owe you my life. Don't you *ever* apologize for using the power you've been given. Any of you."

Even though Sascha looked embarrassed by the sudden attention, I knew that she was feeling honored by the compliment. The color had even begun to return to her cheeks and she was starting to look alive again.

"And I think most of you know by now that Emory has some unique gifts of her own." I turned to look at my new friend. "I've never met anyone who has abilities like you. Communicating with those who've passed . . . do you have any idea how *special* that is? How special you *all* are?"

I surveyed the room and realized I was growing to care about everyone in it—even Fallon, who'd finally appeared in the doorway behind me. They were my friends, my soul mates, my family. But I couldn't forget that one of them was a traitor, either. One of our own was planning to sell us out. I just hoped he or she wasn't more powerful than the rest of us together. Once I knew what special abilities each of us had, I'd also know what the potential traitor was capable of. And traitor or not, the coven was tighter than ever.

"You're all probably wondering why we were hit so hard at the mall and earlier tonight. How we can possibly win a fight against the Parrishables? What's so different about us now that will lead us to a victory? Well, the answer is you—you and your individual gifts are what's gonna keep us all alive. That's what will make us stronger than them. The natural gifts that run through our veins—passed down through our ancestors— that's something the Parrishables don't have. Our individual powers. And that's how we're going to get rid of them once and for all.

"Starting now we're going to teach each other everything we know. Every spell you've ever created, whether you think it's relevant or not, can help us win the fight against our enemies. And for those of you whose powers can't be taught, we're counting on you to hone those skills and use them when the timing's right. Of course, all of this means more training, but not just in our magic. We need to become proficient in hand-to-hand combat, because we've learned the hard way that they're not limiting the battle to spells." I looked over at Sascha, who still had yellowing circles of bruises decorating her jaw and cheek.

"We have to truly learn how to fight, and I'm not going to lie: it's going to be hard, really hard, and you're probably going to hate me before this is over. But I don't care, because this is what's going to keep us from ending up like our parents. And if you have to yell at me and talk about me behind my back to do it, so be it. I'm not letting you all down again. We *will* win this thing."

They were hanging on my every word, and even without asking, I could feel it in my heart . . . they were ready to do what had to be done.

"I'm not sure whether we're being watched or followed, but I think we need to assume that the Parrishables *will* come looking for us," I said. "And I don't know about you, but I'm tired of waiting around for them to find us. They were looking for a war and now they've found one."

Chapter Twenty-Two

Apparently, all you need to do in order to light a fire under someone's butt is land your friends in the hospital. Because once the violence gets real, people tend to come around to doing whatever it takes to survive.

The next day when everyone had woken up by 8 a.m., gotten fed and dressed, and assembled in the living room all ready to go, I knew that what I'd said the night before had really sunk in. It was also proof that all had been forgiven, which made me happier than I could describe.

But when I strutted into the living room, pulling on the jacket of my magical designer knockoff track suit (bright red, of course), I saw that everyone was already there, waiting for me. Considering how late we'd all been up the night before, I figured I'd be dealing with a bunch of cranky kids, all more interested in going back to sleep than doing work.

That wasn't the case, though. I think this was partly because after my big speech the night before, we'd spent another hour ironing out the details of how to prepare for our inevitable battle with the Parrishables. This included a serious powwow about each of our biggest secrets.

We went around the room as people recalled everything that could possibly give us an advantage over the Parrishables. Besides Emory's ability to talk to the dead and Sascha's talent for transferring her power to others in order to help them heal, we were all a little surprised to find out that still more had their own gifts to contribute. For instance, Jasmine was like a human mood ring and could see others' auras, which would be helpful in foretelling people's intentions. Fallon was somehow able to pick things up really quickly. Like someone who had a photographic memory, he could try a spell once and would never forget it. Like magic memory or something. Of course, just because he knew how to *do* the magic didn't mean he could always execute it correctly. That was all dependent on the strength of the caster and the time they put into working on the spells.

After going through all this, we began to work out how we could use these things to our advantage. Those who didn't have special powers contributed in other ways, like by sharing their favorite family spells. It turned out that even the most tight-knit coven kept some things from each other.

"Whoa, Hadley, cute outfit!" Sascha said as I walked into the room. "You always have such cute clothes! I'm totally jealous."

I looked at her choice of sweatpants and a tank top. She saw me taking in her outfit and then made a face. "I didn't know we'd be training when we went shopping before," she said, sounding slightly ashamed.

I looked around the room and saw that she wasn't alone. No one was quite as fashionable as I was, but then again, that was usually the case no matter the situation. And of course, I'd had a little help.

I thought it was time for me to give them a little help too.

"Actually, if you like it so much . . . you can have it," I said, deciding that I knew which spell I was going to teach the group first.

For a minute, she looked like she didn't know whether or not I was kidding. Once she realized I was being serious, her eyes grew wide and she shook her head. "No, I couldn't take your outfit, Hadley. It looks crazy expensive, and besides, I'm pretty sure we're not the same size."

I gave her a sly smile. This was going to be fun. "I didn't mean you should actually take *mine*," I said, turning to look at everyone else around the room. "Listen up, guys, I've got your first lesson of the day right here."

I proceeded to teach everyone my glamour spell. I had no idea how this was going to help us win the war against the Parrishables, but who was to say we wouldn't need it for something? At the very least, we'd all look good in the heat of battle. After all, outfits really did make a difference. Why do you think sports teams wear uniforms? Fashion is something that unifies people.

Plus there's just no excuse for a bad outfit. If I was going out, I was doing it in style.

"That is the coolest spell *ever!*" Sascha exclaimed when she finally managed to replicate the dress that Taylor Swift had worn to her last awards show.

"Not bad, Had. I just figured you stole all your clothes," Jasmine said. She may have been playing it cool, but I'd already seen her switch from one black getup to another, trying hard not to smile the whole time.

"Okay, who's next? I know you've all got something up

your sleeves that you didn't show us last night, so step up and share it now," I said. "Even if you think it's insignificant or that we can't possibly use it against the Parrishables, we want to hear it. Because the truth is, you never know what will come in handy, and the more prepared we are the better."

A few seconds passed before anyone said anything. Finally, Jasmine rolled her eyes and joined me at the front of the room.

"Fine. I guess there's *one* spell I can teach you all. It's not a big deal or anything, just something I've done on occasion. You know, when I'm hanging out by myself and I'm bored," Jasmine said. She walked over to the couch and picked up a cushion. Then she threw it straight at Peter. He caught it just before it hit him in the face. "Do me a favor, kid, and hold the pillow."

"Why, what are you going to—"

He hadn't even finished his sentence before Jasmine yelled, "Exbiliby totalitum!" and pointed in Peter's direction. There was a loud pop and then it was as if it were snowing indoors. I reached out my hand to try to catch some of the white stuff. It was soft and cushy. Then I noticed the gaping hole that was now in the pillow Peter was holding in his trembling hands.

"Seriously?" I asked incredulously.

"Oh. Sorry about your pillow," she answered nonchalantly as a big puff of stuffing landed on her shoulder.

"Forget the pillow—how could you think that wasn't a big deal?"

She made a face. "I don't know. I did it a few times as a kid and then my parents forbade me to do it anymore. So after that I could only do it when I was sure they wouldn't find out about it. Besides, when is blowing stuff up ever considered a *good* thing? I mean, that's why kids go to juvie."

Jasmine showed us how to do her spell and we spent an

hour or so practicing it. Not on any more of my mom's pillows, mind you. I felt it was important to have some fun with our training this time, so we took a stash of balloons that I found in an old dresser drawer of mine and filled them up with water. Placing them on various spots around the property, we made a game out of watching them explode into showers of glistening droplets. A few of us got so good at it that we even took turns holding the targets in the air and being soaked while standing beneath them. It was like our own version of a dunking booth.

After that we made it a point to turn every lesson into a game of some sort. And as the days went on, the others became more vocal about the spells they'd discovered on their own. It had been naive of me to think I was the only one who'd expanded upon our mandatory lessons with Jackson.

And the creativity in our group! June showed us how she'd discovered the right words to extend her time in the air when she jumped; it wasn't quite flying, but she *did* defy gravity a bit. A guy named Brick, one of Fallon's buddies, taught us how to conjure up a hologram. Of course, he'd only ever used it to scare his younger female neighbors, but I could see how this particular spell could come in handy. We learned how to write words in the sky (Peter), how to make it snow in small amounts—like a personal snowstorm—(Josephine), make a person literally tongue-tied (Emory), and give someone a nose-bleed that wouldn't stop (Fallon).

By the end of each day, we were all exhausted but happy with our accomplishments. We never would've had the chance to do spells this potentially dangerous had it been up to Jackson and the other adults. They would've argued that we were too young to take on that kind of responsibility. Well, seeing as we didn't exactly have a choice about it now, I figured the more we knew, the better.

"Great job today, everyone. Really good!" I said.

The sun was going down in the distance and the sky was giving way to brighter shades of blue, pink, and orange. Temperatures were higher than usual and I'd been forced to shed my jacket early on. I think I'd even managed to get a tan while we were outside. But now with the sun dissolving and the breeze kicking up, my bare arms began to grow chilly. I snatched my jacket from its spot on the porch and tugged it over my body, covering the rising goose bumps.

I was about to head inside to get something to eat when I heard someone clear her throat behind me.

"Um, Hadley?"

I turned around to see Emory standing with her arms behind her back, looking a bit flushed. She'd been with the rest of us for the beginning of the day, learning all the same spells we had, but then those with special skills were given some time to work on their own. While this was going on, I sent the others to start working on the physical side of combat. This was one of the only things Asher could get involved in, since it didn't require magic. Just stamina and strength.

Because of the way we were breaking up our training format, I hadn't seen Emory in a few hours by this point and was interested in hearing how things had gone.

"Hey, Emory. What's up?" I asked, walking back over to her. "How was your private session?"

"It was good. Really good, actually. At first I was kind of nervous about giving all the spirits access to me, but after I started to let go, things became clearer, if that makes any sense," she said. Emory began to play with the bracelet around her wrist. This one was a chain of real violets. "Hadley, when I was channeling, your mom came through again. There was some stuff she wanted me to tell you."

I raised an eyebrow, my heartbeat quickening at the thought of communicating with my mom again. But I wasn't sure how I was supposed to react to the news that she was trying to reach me from beyond the grave. As amazing as it was to talk to her, it was also a reminder of what had happened. That I couldn't see her or talk to her anytime I wanted. In that respect, it was almost more difficult than not having her around at all.

"My mom never was one to hold back from telling me what to do," I said, laughing nervously. "What did she have to say?"

Emory looked around as the rest of the coven made their way either inside or to relax in the setting sun. She lowered her voice. "She's actually here right now. Is there somewhere we can go that's a little more . . . private?"

"Sure," I said, butterflies fluttering around my stomach. I had no idea what to expect, but I motioned for Emory to follow me anyway. "Let's go for a walk."

We turned away from the house, heading toward the woods and the growing darkness. The farther we walked the quieter it got; pretty soon all I could hear was the sound of our feet walking over leaves and sticks. Whenever a branch would crackle, I worried that it was coming from behind us or off to the side. Logically I knew I was the one making the noise, but knowing what our enemies were capable of, I couldn't help but be on edge. If I wasn't so worried about the others hearing what she was about to say, I wouldn't have been venturing from the safety of the house at all. But I reminded myself that the invisibility spells that covered the house also extended to the land around it.

When I was sure we were far enough away from the others to talk openly, I slowed my pace and turned to face Emory. "She's here?" I asked. The longing came through in my voice even as I tried not to let it. I reminded myself that this was

Emory I was talking to and didn't have to be worried about losing control in front of her. Sure, I was the leader of our group now and it was important for me to stay strong, but Emory wouldn't judge me. She wasn't like that.

"Yes. She's been here the whole time, actually. Sometimes she just comes through louder than others. Today she was particularly vocal."

"That's my mom," I said jokingly.

"She says she understands why you went off on your own," Emory said. She paused then, and looked down at the ground nervously.

Why was she nervous? I was the one getting the lecture.

"She says it's not going to be enough. If you try to defeat the Parrishables you *will* lose. *We* will lose."

"Thanks for the vote of confidence," I muttered, my heart sinking over what my mom was telling me. The last thing I wanted to do was disappoint her. Especially after all that had happened. And my biggest fear was that I would lead the others to their deaths. Hearing that it might actually happen deflated all the confidence I'd had before.

Emory took a step toward me and lightly placed her hand on my arm. "She says that a great leader knows when to admit defeat. She feels really strongly that you need to put the lives of the coven ahead of your own."

I nodded, because at this point there wasn't much else for me to say. She was right and deep down I'd known it. Nearly losing the fights at the mall and my house had proven that much. I just hadn't been strong enough to do what needed to be done. I'd been too weak to truly offer myself up in place of the others.

"There's something else. She says you know who the traitor is among you."

I blinked. "I do?" I asked, still distracted by my thoughts.

Since my mom had first told me that I couldn't trust someone in the coven, I hadn't gotten any closer to figuring out who it was. But if I was truly being honest with myself, I'd always had my suspicions about one specific member. Had I been right the whole time?

Emory paused and looked at the space over my right shoulder. She squinted and after a few seconds, turned her attention back to me. "Yes. She says you know who it is and you must send them away. Now."

"I don't have any proof, though," I said. Thinking someone was bad at his core was one thing, but actually banishing him from our coven . . . that would be much more difficult. At least if I had evidence, I wouldn't feel bad about it. Still, this was coming from my mom and she'd never steered me wrong before.

Emory shook her head. "She says you don't need it. She's insisting that you're right. She says you need to do it now, before it's too late. This person's intention is to turn you over to the Parrishables."

My head started to spin. Could he really help the Parrishables destroy us? The truth was, I just wasn't sure. I tried to push the thought way down and bring my focus back to what Emory was saying.

"And that's it?" I asked, hoping she might have better news for me. So far, it had all been a bust.

"Sorry, Hadley. That's all she's telling me," she said.

I sighed. It was *so* like my mom to be totally cryptic about something this important. "It's all right, I'm used to it by now," I said.

So once again, I'm doing everything wrong. Fantastic. At least I'm consistent.

"Maybe she's wrong, Had," Emory said supportively. "Or confused."

"You didn't know my mom," I said, like this explained everything. I began to walk back to the house and Emory fell into step beside me.

She was quiet for a few moments as we both tried to take in what had just happened. I could feel the redhead's eyes fixed on me, although I wouldn't return her look. Finally she spoke up. "So what are you going to do next?"

That was the million-dollar question, wasn't it? Everything was always so complicated. I couldn't help but long for the days when I just had to worry about homework and disagreements with my mom.

"What I have to do."

Chapter Twenty-Three

I spent the rest of the evening agonizing over what my mom had told me through Emory. Could I really leave everyone again? It had been difficult enough the first time; I wasn't sure I had it in me to do it a second. And the idea of just giving up made me want to throw up. It went against everything I'd ever stood for.

It was also particularly confusing, given that my mom had always been the one to encourage me to fight. All those lectures about preparing for a possible battle . . . why would she have pushed so hard for that if she was just going to tell me to wave the white flag in the end? Unless she knew that things would be much worse if we didn't.

Frustrated and more confused than ever, I chose to sleep on it. The decisions I had to make were too big to reach in one night. I knew time was of the essence, but I really felt like I needed a little time to digest it all. So I put on my cute pajamas of capris and a cami with little seagulls all over them and slipped under the covers. Magic took a lot out of you, and we'd been going strong for most of the day. My whole body was sore from tensing up during the spells, and I could feel small bruises forming in spots where the others had hit me with both their fists and spells. It was a good hurt though, the kind that came with knowing that you worked a hard day.

Even so, I was looking forward to getting a good night's sleep. That's why, when I heard a light knock on my door just as I was drifting off, I wished I could ignore it. But when it happened again less than a minute later, I threw the covers off and padded reluctantly to the door. Ever since getting back, I'd been trying my hardest to show the others that I wanted to be there and that we were a team, not just a coven of individuals. Which meant that I couldn't just do whatever I wanted to with no regard for anyone else. Even if I was currently debating whether to stay or go.

Besides, if there was anything I *did* understand from what my mom had been trying to tell me, it was that I needed to stop thinking only of myself. She'd seemed pretty clear on that. So I plastered a smile on my face before unlocking my door and opening it.

"Hey. You weren't already asleep, were you?" Asher asked quietly. He was leaning up against the door frame and looked unbearably adorable. It was like something out of a movie. In fact, maybe I'd already fallen asleep and this was a dream.

Then I grew sad. How was I supposed to leave Asher, too? Especially since I'd been the one to get him into this mess.

"Uh, no," I said, looking back at the bed that I'd obviously just been lying in a few seconds before. With a quick glance down at my pj's, I crossed my arms over my chest and tried my best to appear awake. "Not yet, anyway. What's up?"

"Oh, nothing. I just didn't get to see you much today.

Thought maybe we could hang out or something." He looked at my outfit and then smiled. "Unless you want to go to bed."

"Nice try, Asher," I said sarcastically, hearing the flirtatiousness in his voice.

"There you go with your mind in the gutter again," he said, wagging his finger at me.

"Please, like you weren't trying to get into bed with me."

"Well, if you insist!" He breezed past me and jumped halfway across the room, landing with a thud on my mattress. I watched with amusement as he lay back, crossed his legs at the ankles, and folded his arms behind his head. "You coming?"

I paused for a second, trying to decide what to do. Then with an exaggerated eye roll, I closed the door and locked it behind me. If there was a possibility that this would be my last night with Asher, I was willing to take the chance of being alone with him. I highly doubted that anything serious was going to happen with a house full of kids.

At least *I* wasn't going to let anything happen with everyone else downstairs.

"Fine, you can stay. But this is strictly a PG sleepover, got it?"

"So that means freezing each other's underwear and having pillow fights?" When I gave him a look that said I wasn't amused, he added, "I'm a boy, remember? We never had sleepovers growing up. Now explain to me what goes on at these so-called slumber parties. And does kissing fall under the PG category?"

My face grew warm with embarrassment and my body tingled. As if I needed another reminder that I was really into this guy.

"Let's start with talking and see where it goes," I said, laughing at his bravado.

Once again I slid under the covers and noticed with relief

that Asher wasn't trying to follow me in. Instead, he stayed on top of the comforter and kept his hands to himself. It wasn't that I didn't like the idea of kissing him again, but I wasn't sure that now was the right time to be getting sexy. Not with imminent doom pressing down on us and all.

"So what do you want to talk about?" he asked when I'd settled back into my warm cocoon of a bed.

"Dunno," I said, thinking. "What's your full name?"

"Asher Aaron Astley the third," he answered.

I raised an eyebrow. "You're a third?"

"Yep. You know that the best things come in threes, right?" he asked.

"Oh, do they? Good to know."

"Now my turn. When did you know that you were a witch?"

"Wow, start off with something simple, why don't you," I said with a snort.

"Sorry," he said, and looked down at the puffy comforter between us. "We *could* just get straight to the making out. . . ."

"So, you want to know the *first* time I knew I was a witch, right?" I said quickly, ignoring his last comment. "Um, I think I was about three and there was this candy that I really wanted in a store, but my parents wouldn't buy it for me. I got really mad and started to throw a tantrum in the car and the next thing I knew, the candy was in my hands. I was already eating it by the time my parents noticed, and when they asked me about it, I told them it had just appeared. After that I think they realized they had to have *the talk* with me."

"The talk?"

"'Responsible magicking,'" I said, doing air quotes. "Letting me know that I wasn't like other kids, that my friends couldn't just conjure something up because they wanted it badly enough. That's how I found out I had certain . . . abilities."

"Didn't it freak you out?" Asher asked.

"Nah. It's all I've ever known. And I sort of already knew it before that day. My parents always thought they were being sneaky when they were casting, but the truth is, you can't hide anything from a kid. Especially one who's magically inclined," I said. "Okay, my turn. Where did you come from, Asher Aaron Astley the third? I mean, you just showed up one day and suddenly you're everywhere I turn. Why are you here?"

"Are you *sure* you don't want to just make out?" he asked with a laugh.

"Nuh-uh. I answered your question. You answer mine."

"Okay, okay. I guess that's fair," he said. He didn't speak again right away, but after a slightly awkward pause he continued. "I'm here because my parents passed away and I had to come live with my aunt."

Hello, mouth, meet my foot. I hope you feel comfortable in there.

I studied his face as I tried to figure out what to say in response. I decided that the truth was probably my best option. "I'm so sorry, Asher," I said, feeling horrible. Then a thought came to mind. "So you *do* understand what I'm going through."

"Yeah," he admitted, sadly.

I reached for his hand and slipped my fingers into his. Our skin made for a great contrast of colors; his was a dark caramel, mine was porcelain like a doll's. There was something oddly intimate about holding hands with someone. It was one of the few things you could do to show affection without it necessarily being sexual. I wanted to comfort him, to bring an emotional connection into physical territory. It'd been a long time since I'd found someone I wanted to be intimate with. And now that I'd found him, it would be even harder to let him go.

Asher looked up at me briefly and smiled in a way that

seemed forced. His face looked slightly pained, as if the memory physically hurt him. But then it was gone as quickly as it had appeared, and he was squeezing my hand back. He rolled over and stared up at the ceiling.

"Thanks. It's been a while now, so . . ." His words trailed off. "It gets easier." The pain in his voice told me otherwise, but I decided to believe him for the time being.

"How do you do it? Be normal after something like this, I mean." I was actually really curious to hear his answer.

"You think *I'm* normal?" he asked, chuckling and shaking his head. "I think you're the only one who'd describe me that way."

I rolled my eyes. "Okay, as normal as any of us are, anyway. You know what I mean."

"Yeah. Well, you start off waking up every morning thinking about them and being sad and angry that the universe has let such a horrible thing happen. Then you get up and go about your life," he said, absently tracing the design on the bedspread. "And then the next day you do the same thing. If you do it enough, eventually it starts to hurt less and you find that not every little thing reminds you of what you've lost. You never get over it completely, but over time, you create a new normal. And having a good distraction never hurts."

He made it sound so easy, even though I knew the journey he talked about had been anything but. Still, it gave me hope and also made me feel closer to him. I'd been feeling really alone in what I was going through since I couldn't bring up my grief to the other Cleri members. With them, I had to be the strong one. But with Asher, he not only understood, but he'd survived. Which also made him that much more attractive to me. Suddenly his offer to make out seemed more inviting.

"In that case, wanna be my distraction?" I wiggled my

eyebrows suggestively. The tension in his face relaxed into a sexy smile.

"Absolutely. Anything I can do to help. You know I'm here for you."

Leaning into him, I attempted to put the subject of our parents out of my mind.

I woke up with a start. A glance over at the empty bed space next to me told me that I was alone. When I'd fallen asleep, Asher had been in bed with me. We hadn't done much more than make out, but it had been enough to pull me even deeper into whatever was going on with us. This both scared and thrilled me at the same time. I hadn't felt this way about anyone before, so it was like entering into uncharted territory.

And now I was waking up after falling asleep alongside the guy that I was digging and he was nowhere to be found. I rubbed at my eyes to try to get rid of the sleepies and sat up to look around the room. Nope. Definitely not there. Maybe he'd just gone to the bathroom? Or to the kitchen to get a midnight snack? There had to be an explanation that didn't involve him ditching me in the middle of the night.

Right?

With only one way to find out, I got out of bed and tiptoed across the room. Slipping out the door, I made my way toward the room where Asher was *supposed* to be staying and pushed it far enough open to peek inside. I breathed a sigh of relief when I saw that the bed was still made and there was nobody sleeping in it. That meant he at least hadn't left me to go sleep alone.

Turning around and heading in the opposite direction, I made my way downstairs, being careful not to wake anyone up. People had been crashing all over the house since we'd gotten here, taking any spots that were available. It was sort of first come, first served around here, which meant that some unlucky individuals were always stuck with the floor in the living room or on a row of uncomfortable chairs lined up to make a sort of cot. Since it was crowded enough that everyone was practically on top of each other, I knew that even the slightest creak would wake the whole place.

As I crept past the living room, I glanced in to see who'd been stuck with the floor for the night, but to my surprise, the place was empty. There wasn't a single person lying on the couch, draped across a chair, or slumming it on the carpet. There wasn't anyone anywhere.

Now I was confused and getting a little worried. I continued on to the kitchen, hoping to see everyone sitting around, eating and gossiping. Even knowing they were holding a secret meeting without me would've been preferable to the alternative.

But there was no one there, either.

I was beginning to freak out when I heard the front door open and close, and footsteps coming down the front entryway. Hoping for some clue to where everyone had gone, I poked my head around the corner.

When my eyes adjusted enough to see who had just entered, I gasped in shock. I recognized the girl coming down the hallway, though I'd never met her before. She had dark hair that hung over one shoulder in a loose braid, wisps grazing her cheeks, which were wet with tears. As she came toward me, her floor-length skirt swished around her legs and then followed behind her with the force of her walk. Her eyes were intense as she turned at the stairs, and took them two at a time until she got to the second floor.

The girl was on a mission.

I quickly went after her, conscious of the fact that I was no longer being quiet. If my hunch was right though, that didn't matter. She was already gone by the time I made it upstairs, but I could hear her rummaging around and followed the sounds into my old room. I didn't have to open the door to see what was going on, since she'd left it open in her haste to find what she was looking for.

The girl had pushed the bedside table over to the wall, exposing a slightly dirty and dusty floor. Getting down on her hands and knees, she began to pull at the floorboards, until one of them gave way. I watched as she yanked another plank loose and threw it onto the bed behind her. Her hands disappeared into the hole she'd created and a few seconds later, they popped back out with an extra-large book and something shiny that reflected under the lights.

I took a step forward to try to see exactly what she was holding, no longer worried that she'd catch me. The girl turned away and sat with her back resting against the bed. She propped up the leather-bound book on her knees. I watched as she conjured a quill out of thin air, leafed through the pages until she came to the one she was looking for, and then began to write. The pen moved across the pages with an urgency I'd never seen before. It was as if she couldn't make her hand move fast enough, and after a few seconds she let go of the pen and allowed it to work its magic alone.

By the time the quill stopped moving, more than five pages had been written. The girl let her legs slowly extend until they were lying flat, like she was exhausted. Taking a deep breath, she reached to her side and grabbed the object that had been gleaming in the light. Inching closer to her, I could see that it was a ring.

As she slipped on the gold band, I was drawn even farther into the room, suddenly mesmerized by the jewel embedded in it. The size of the ruby took my breath away. It was bigger than anything I'd ever seen before, and for a second I wondered if it was fake.

The girl began to mumble words that I couldn't quite understand, either because they were in a different language or possibly just because she was speaking so fast I couldn't discern what they were. As I watched, the ruby began to glow bright red and the air around it started to radiate what I assumed was heat. And based on the fact that I saw beads of sweat starting to form on her forehead, I knew I was right. I halfway expected to feel the warmth myself.

Then the intensity went away and I watched as she put everything back in the floor and fit the boards back into place. Tugging at the table until it was once again covering the spot, the girl was careful to hide the treasures she'd taken so much care to keep secret.

"Do not worry, Mother, I will not forget you. The *world* will not forget you," she said to the empty room.

When I woke up back in my parents' room, tears were running down my cheeks. Without looking, I could feel Asher lying beside me and heard him lightly snoring into his pillow. Rolling over onto my side, I tried to process what I'd just been shown. Because I had no doubt the girl in my dreams wanted me to see what she'd done.

It was the first time I'd ever had a dream about Bridget's daughter, Christian.

And suddenly, there in the dark, with Christian's memories fresh in my mind, I knew that I'd been given a clue about what I was supposed to do next.

Chapter Twenty - Four

I lay in bed awake, waiting for the rest of the house to come back to life. It's a funny feeling, being the only one up while everyone else is asleep; everything's quieter. It's easier to hear yourself think. I'd always had the theory that you can't get bogged down with the stress of life when you're still in a horizontal position and those around you are snoring and dreaming. It had been a long time since the house had been quiet like this and I reveled in it.

I got to know the way Asher sounded when he slept. He breathed slowly and evenly, and he barely moved at all. I'd been told by friends who'd shared beds with me at slumber parties growing up that I was a thrasher, possibly due to my active dreams. At one point Trish refused to ever share a bed with me again.

But Asher was a calm sleeper. Not that I was watching him in a creepy kind of way. More like *observing* him as I waited for him to wake up. At one point, I could barely see him breathing, and I got so paranoid thinking that he might have died in the middle of the night that I pulled my compact off the bedside table to find out. Luckily, the mirror fogged up when I placed it near his mouth and I was able to relax, knowing I hadn't lost him, too.

As soon as I began to hear others move around the house, I decided it was probably an acceptable time to leave the comfort of my bed—and Asher. But I didn't want to ditch him. I knew from my dream what that could feel like.

There was work to be done before I could wake him, though. No way was I daring to breathe on him with my morning dragon breath. Nuh-uh. But getting up would mean moving around in bed, which could possibly wake Asher before I was ready, so I had to take a few shortcuts to achieve morning perfection.

Casting my freshening spell, I sucked in deeply, tasting the minty flavor as it played across my lips. With that out of the way, I turned to the next order of business: changing this mess into a success.

"Renewbus freshimo perfecto," I whispered.

I didn't need a mirror to know that my hair was transforming into waves that would glisten in the light. Various shades of concealer and makeup were appearing on my face, covering my flaws and highlighting my natural beauty. When I was sure I was boy worthy, I knew it was time to do what I had to do.

It was time for Asher to wake up.

"Quivable divanish."

I stayed as still as I could as the bed shook like a mini-earthquake. It felt a little like sitting in a vibrating chair—there was just enough movement to shake you out of whatever dream you were having. And that was exactly what it did to Asher.

"Whaa?" he asked as his hands flew to grip the comforter.

I, however, acted like it was Asher who'd woken *me* up.

"What's wrong?" I asked in my most sleepy, I-just-woke-up voice.

Asher was looking around the room now, his head flipping from side to side as if he could find the culprit that had suddenly awakened him. When he finally realized we were alone in the room and nothing was out of place, his eyes dropped and rested on me.

"Huh? Nothing. I must've been having a weird dream or something," he muttered.

"What about?" I asked.

"I have no idea," he said, shaking his head. His eyes roamed over my face as he noticed my morning glow. He smiled lazily. "Wow. You're really not a Hyde, are you?"

"A Hyde?" I asked, confused.

"You know, there're those girls who look great during the day, but when you see them first thing in the morning, you realize in reality they don't look anything like the person you fell asleep next to. You go to bed with Dr. Jekyll and wake up with Mr. Hyde."

"Girls don't like it when you compare them to psycho monsters, Asher." I said it like I was serious, but then let my mouth fade into a grin.

"I just mean that some girls wear so much makeup that you're surprised when you see what they *really* look like. And you're not like that. You really *are* gorgeous all the time," he said, turning over onto his side and propping himself up on his elbow. "Your girlfriends must hate you."

I burst out laughing. Not a great delivery, but I could tell he was trying to give me a compliment. "Only part of the time," I responded.

"Sounds about right," he said. Then, without hesitation, he

leaned forward and gave me a soft kiss. I happily kissed him back, grateful that I'd had the foresight to freshen up. But the sound of someone running down the hallway pulled me out of my fairy-tale make-out session.

I sucked on his lower lip lightly before falling back onto my pillow. "Everyone's getting up. We should probably do the same."

Asher reached over and wrapped his arms around my waist and rolled us until I was lying on top of him. "Let's just stay in bed for the rest of the day. The others can get along without you for a few hours."

I shook my finger at him, but didn't get up just yet. The offer was tempting—part of me wanted nothing other than to stay right there, enveloped in our little love cocoon—but I had work to do. Because the truth was, I wouldn't be around to enjoy these kinds of moments if the Parrishables wiped me out the next time we met. So right now, Asher had to come second.

"Have you *met* these kids? If I leave them alone too long, they'll burn the cabin down, leaving smoke signals for our enemies," I said. "So come on, get up!"

I threw the covers back and hopped out of bed.

"Ugh," Asher groaned, watching me cross to the bathroom. "You're really kicking me out?"

"Yep! Now go clean up and get dressed—because although *I'm* beautiful and smell like roses in the morning, you don't seem to have those powers," I said jokingly, and gave him a wink. "I'll meet you downstairs in fifteen and we'll eat breakfast together, okay? And if you're good, I may be up for another slumber party tonight."

"*Fine*," Asher said, sounding like it really wasn't. But he was smiling as he trudged over to the bedroom door.

When he finally disappeared, I threw on a classic look of

designer jeans and a black top that Kristen Bell had worn in an episode of *Veronica Mars*—one of my fave shows of all time—and turned the knob as quietly as possible. Poking my head out into the hallway, I was happy to see that everyone appeared to be downstairs already. When I was sure I wouldn't be caught, I tiptoed down the hall to my old room.

This was *really* why I'd been so eager to kick a cute boy out of my bed. Asher may not have remembered the dream he'd been having before he was shaken awake, but I could certainly remember mine. The dream about Bridget's daughter was as firmly planted in my mind as if it were my own memory.

And I was positive that if I pried up those floorboards, I was going to find all of Christian's secrets. This, I hoped, would help me finally decide whether I was going to stay or go. On the one hand, I wanted to do what my mom was asking me to do. She'd never steered me wrong before, and she had ventured beyond the grave to tell me to save the others by leaving for good. It didn't make sense to me, but it was coming from my mom and that was impossible to ignore.

That's what I was hoping my little scavenger hunt would help clear up. If there was something in that book of Christian's that could help us actually win the battle with Samuel, then I wouldn't have to leave after all. Maybe my mom hadn't had this info when she'd passed her message on to Emory to relay to me. So she wouldn't have been wrong, just uninformed.

I was happy to find my old room empty, and tiptoed inside. Closing the door quietly behind me, I turned the button in the knob until the lock fell into place. No good would come from someone catching me—with a traitor among us, I didn't want whatever I found to end up in the wrong hands. No, the fewer people who knew about what I was doing the better.

With the door secure, I put my hands on my hips and

surveyed the room. The furniture had changed from what I'd seen in my dream, so this wasn't going to be easy. Currently there was a twin bed directly over the spot where Christian had pulled up the boards, and beneath that, carpet. Thanks to me and my extreme dislike of hardwood floors at the age of six (they were cold when you woke up in the morning and weren't exactly comfortable to lie down on during slumber parties), my parents had installed wall-to-wall shag.

With a sigh, I began to push and pull the furniture until it was situated on the opposite side of the room. I'd already broken a sweat, and wished I could've let at least one other person know what I was doing just so I could have gotten a little help with the heavy lifting. But it was too late to do anything about that now.

Snatching a pair of scissors off the desk, I knelt down around where I'd seen Christian the night before and stabbed the blades into the crack near the wall. Jimmying around the edge of the carpet, I managed to get up under it after I pried my fingers in there too, and I started to pull it away from the floor. Using the wall as leverage, I planted my feet and pulled back with all my strength until I heard a ripping sound. One foot, two feet—when I'd loosened three feet of carpeting from the floor, I began to saw at the carpet, attempting to cut a hole big enough to get into the hiding space.

Five minutes later, I'd reached the wood underneath and was practically vibrating with excitement over what I was about to see. I tested out the wobbly boards, hoping they'd come up easily. I didn't really want to ruin my nail job and I'd done about as much manual labor as I could handle for the day. But all it took was a twist of my wrist, and I was moving the planks out of the way and tossing them on the carpet behind me.

When I looked into the hole, my heart sank.

It was empty.

The hiding place wasn't all that deep—less than six inches, I'd say—and after all that work I found myself sitting there staring at empty space. What had been the point of having the dream if I wasn't supposed to find anything? Just another stupid waste of time, dreaming about another crazy, long-lost relative.

I was about to put the floorboards back into place when I had a thought. Sure, it was a last-ditch effort, but it was hard to believe I could've done all this work for nothing. Crouching back over the hole, I carefully leaned down and reached my hand into the dark parts of the chasm.

Even though I was hoping to find something, another part of me was scared that my hand would touch something I didn't want it to—like something furry or slimy. As I thought about what might be hiding under the floorboards, my brain started to scream at me to retract my hand. But I forced myself to keep feeling around.

Finally, my fingers grazed something cold and hard. I pulled my arm back reflexively. As I willed my heartbeat to slow down and the pounding in my ears to go away, I realized that if there was any chance that Christian's stuff was hiding under this roof, I had to do whatever I could to find it. It would be worth touching something icky in the process.

Taking a deep breath, I reached back down and began to feel around again. It didn't take long—what I felt was small, hard, round, and cool to the touch. Based on my dream from the night before, I was pretty sure it was the ring that had glowed when Christian had put it on. Wrapping my hand around the jewelry, I pulled it out and looked at it triumphantly.

The ring itself was stunning. With a thin band of gold

encrusted with tiny diamonds, the ring glittered under the lights in the room. All these details led up to the traffic stopper: the enormous ruby sitting right in the middle. It was at least six carats, in the shape of a soft square with more diamonds surrounding it like a little army protecting its queen.

It was the kind of ring I'd dreamed of owning one day. Preferably given to me by my incredibly wealthy and attractive boyfriend, but hey, beggars can't be choosers. This was pretty cool too.

I wanted to sit and stare at the ring all day long, but I hadn't forgotten that in my dream, Christian had also been hiding a book. With the ring firmly in one hand, I reached back down into the darkness with the other.

My fingers searched the space, at first coming up with nothing. Finally, I touched something long, thin, and soft, like a string, and I had to force myself to grab hold of it, even though I was scared of what it might be. It was dragging something along behind it that made the tiniest scratching sound as I pulled it out.

Please don't be attached to a rat, please don't be attached to a rat, please . . .

But as my hand came back into view, I breathed a sigh of relief as I saw that what I was holding on to was a silk ribbon being used as a page marker for a book. The book that Christian had been writing in.

Crawling back across the floor, I sat down cross-legged against the bed, mimicking the position of Bridget's daughter. Slipping the ring onto my middle finger—no way was I wearing it on my ring finger, since it's totally bad luck—I waited for something spectacular to happen.

But nothing came. No heat. No tingling sensation. No magical surge of power. No glowing red light. Just a gorgeously expensive ring that would've been the envy of my friends. With a shrug, I turned my attention to the book.

The worn, leather-bound book was heavy in my hands. The pages weren't numbered, and there were too many to count. A quick flip through showed that not all of them were written on. Some were blank, but most were filled up with scribbles. At first glance, I thought maybe it was poetry because of the way the words were positioned on the page, all gathered in the middle with lots of white space on the sides. But a closer look proved it to be something much different.

What I was holding in my hands wasn't a diary or a compilation of poetry.

It was a spell book.

"Holy magic, Glinda," I mumbled.

There was page after page of spells. Each was labeled at the top; some pages held multiple incantations. We'd been taught only around fifty spells through magic school, but there were hundreds in here. More than we could ever learn in a lifetime, probably. And it appeared like more than one person had contributed to it. At first glance, I could see that some of the spells were seriously outdated, reflecting the time that Christian would have been growing up. Some, however, could span generations . . . and did.

Turning to a page that had been dog-eared, I read carefully through the words. As I began to understand what I had here, my adrenaline started pumping.

A Charm for Forgetfulness

When a cloudy mind is what you seek,
Just step inside and take a peek.
Create a storm to rain in the brain,

Make things muddy and then take claim.
As the mist takes hold and covers your secrets,
I'll make you forget just where you keep it.

Wicked. I'd never heard these spells before, and although they were a bit old and the wording was outdated, I was psyched to try them—I definitely didn't doubt their potency.

In other words, I couldn't wait to see how well they worked.

Bustling around to put everything back in its place, I was already working out what I was going to do with this new-found knowledge. Should I bring it to the entire group and try to have everyone learn as much as they could before the Parrishables found us? Or would I be better off keeping this news to myself, considering the traitor in the house?

Wait. Maybe there was something in the book that could help me with *that.*

I had my hunches of who was planning to betray us, but I still didn't feel comfortable shunning him without seeing the proof for myself. And though my mom hadn't been much help in telling me who the culprit was, it didn't mean that Bridget and Christian wouldn't be.

In fact, I was counting on it.

With a fire lit inside me, I opened the book back up to take a closer look and see if we couldn't find the stranger among us.

Chapter Twenty-Five

When I finally made it downstairs, about a half hour later, I found that everyone was awake and already practicing the spells in the backyard. My heart swelled with pride as I realized that I was no longer going to have to convince the other kids to train; they actually *wanted* to get better.

As I walked into the kitchen, my eyes drifted to Asher. He was sitting on the counter near the sink, sucking down a bowl of cereal. When he saw me, he shot me a grin, a line of milk dribbling down his chin. Heading straight to him, I leaned up against the counter, jutting out my hip as I looked up at him.

"I thought Trix were for kids," I said, nodding to the box of cereal on the counter next to him.

"That's just what they *want* you to believe. Trix are actually for *everyone.*"

"You're kind of tricky yourself, aren't you?" I asked, raising my eyebrow at him.

He paused briefly before shoveling more food into his

mouth. The break in eating was so imperceptible that I wouldn't have noticed it if I weren't looking for it.

"How so?" he asked, his mouth full again.

"Well, the plan you had to crash with me last night was pretty sneaky. You must've known that if you got into my room, I'd let you stay," I said.

He smiled. "I don't know what you're talking about," he said. "I was just coming to hang out. You're the one who invited me in."

"Liar!" I hissed, in mock shock. The truth was I'd have let him stay whether he'd asked or not.

"You can act like the jury's still out on me, but I know you think I'm awesome."

"A little overconfident, don't you think?" I asked.

"I like to think of it as realistic."

"Mmm," I murmured.

"Hadley? Are we learning new stuff today or going over what we learned yesterday?"

I turned to see that Asher and I were no longer the only ones in the kitchen. Emory and Peter stood by the back door, looking at me expectantly.

"We'll review a few things, but I thought we'd go over hand-to-hand combat today," I said, still staring at Asher.

"Cool," Peter said, cracking his knuckles. Then, looking over his shoulder nervously, he took another step toward me. "Hey, Had, you may want to take a look outside before we get started."

"Why? What's up?" I asked, not liking the way that sounded.

I walked quickly over to the back door, sweeping past them. Scanning the yard, I looked for anything out of place or potentially dangerous. My eyes landed on a crowd that had gathered off to the right of the yard.

In the middle of it was Fallon.

I immediately became suspicious as I watched him talk in hushed tones to the group. "What is he up to?" I wondered to myself.

Ever since we'd made it back from the run-in with Samuel and his crew at my house, Fallon had kept a pretty low profile. He was still showing up to all of our training sessions, but he'd barely been talking to anyone and there were whole chunks of time where I'd forget he was even around. I wasn't sure what had caused his sudden desire to fade into the background, but I was too busy to worry about it. Besides, a little time off from our constant bickering was kind of nice.

But now it seemed like he was back to his old self, which was not a good sign.

Crossing the yard, I thought about what I wanted to say. The group was in such a great place now—we were finally acting like a true coven and not just a bunch of latchkey kids— that I was hesitant to do anything that would take us two steps back. We needed to be fully unified if we were going to win this fight against the Parrishables. It would be bad if Fallon and I butted heads again now.

I couldn't let him know I suspected anything was off. That could derail my plan.

"Serenity now, serenity now . . . ," I repeated under my breath as I neared the edge of the group.

Plastering a smile on my face, I clasped my hands behind my back to avoid looking defensive and then pushed my way through the crowd to get to my frenemy.

"Let's talk about this later," Fallon said as soon as he saw me coming.

I resisted the urge to roll my eyes. "Fallon!" I exclaimed, trying to sound as genuine as I could muster under the circumstances. He would've known something was up if I hugged him, so I kept my distance but flashed him a welcoming grin. This apparently was enough to throw him off, because almost immediately he crossed his arms over his chest and narrowed his eyes at me.

"Hadley." He said my name slowly, deliberately. There was no kindness or friendliness in his tone. The way he was acting, you'd have thought he was angry at me. This didn't make any sense though, considering the last thing he'd done was attempt to save me from the Parrishables. Unless that's just what he wanted us to think and really . . .

Oh, man, I had to get to the bottom of this before I went crazy.

"You guys almost ready?" I asked, as if I didn't have a care in the world. A few nodded, while Fallon remained silent. "Okay, let's get started then!"

I left Fallon staring after me, slack-jawed, as I turned and walked away without challenging him about his sudden change in attitude.

If I wasn't already thinking about the next phase in my plan, then I might have taken a moment to laugh at the stupefied expression on his face. Instead, I took a mental picture and stored it away for the next time I was in need of a little cheering up.

"Let's start off with Jasmine's exploding spell," I shouted before walking over to the porch. I watched everyone break up into groups and begin to practice. Fallon circled up with a few of the guys and they each attempted Jasmine's spell. To my dismay, Fallon was the only one able to pull it off on the first try, shattering a potted plant on the railing of the porch.

Looks like somebody's been practicing.

My mind started to whir with possible theories. When

could he have managed to team up with our enemy without us knowing about it? Maybe I should have just confronted him when I'd first found out there was a traitor in the Cleri. But how was I supposed to know if he was telling me the truth when he denied having anything to do with the Parrishables? Which he would, of course. It wasn't likely that he'd stand up and say, "Oh, the Parrishables? Sure, I met them at the mall and handed over every secret we've ever had on a silver platter. Surprise! I'm a traitor!"

Yeah, right. Whoever was planning to turn against us wasn't going to admit it on their own—until our enemies were well on their way to destroying us, at least. Nope, I was going to have to get it out of them. And that's what had changed.

Thanks to the Bishop family spell book, I now knew just how to sniff out the double agent.

In the meantime, I joined Asher on the porch and began to wonder whether it was possible that the culprit could be anyone other than Fallon. Of course, once I looked at everyone as a potential suspect, it was easy to awaken my inner conspiracy theorist and realize that anyone was capable of turning on me. I wished it wasn't true, but I had to prepare myself for the possibility it was someone I'd come to care about.

Jasmine always *had* been a little hotheaded and quick to cast before she thought. Sure, she'd been knocked out at the mall, but the Parrishables could have done that to throw us off. With all that black in her wardrobe, she had darkness written all over her.

And Sascha definitely had it in her to be the mole. No one was *that* happy and friendly all the time. I'd never really thought of her as a threat before, but that would have made her the perfect enemy.

Then again, Peter's parents had been the first to disappear

and the only ones not caught in the fire. Could they have been a part of the Parrishables the whole time, and could their son be the one passing along information? He'd been one of the few who hadn't gotten hurt so far.

After enough thought, it became clear that any one of my coven members could have been the one to sell us out. But I hated feeling that way—like I couldn't trust anyone around me. So after a few hours of practice had gone by, I decided I'd had enough and it was time to unveil the culprit once and for all.

I knew exactly what words to say. Before I'd left my room, I'd committed the spell to memory.

"Hey, everyone! Can you all gather over here real quick? There's something I want to talk to you about." I looked around the yard to make sure everyone was still there. I hadn't sent any of the naturally gifted witches off to hone their crafts alone today and Asher was still hanging out beside me and watching the others train.

Once everyone was assembled on the grass in the yard, they stood there staring up at me as if awaiting instructions. I took a deep breath and smiled confidently at them. It was the moment of truth.

"Are we learning a new spell?" Peter asked hopefully. Over the past couple of weeks, he'd gotten increasingly good at mastering new spells. Maybe being around the other twitches had inspired him to finally live up to his full potential. Or maybe he'd tapped in to some evil magic mojo and was on a casting high from the power boost.

Guess we were about to find out which it was.

"Not exactly," I answered. "Actually, I wanted to talk to you guys about something. Ever since the Parrishables blew into town, they've had us running scared. And we've done a great job training for our day in battle. When we came here, I told you the cabin was a haven, a safe place to hide out in until we were ready. And although I thought it was true at the time, it's come to my attention that it's been infiltrated by the enemy."

Gasps broke out in the group and I tried to search their faces for one with guilt and shame written on it. But all I saw was genuine fear—kids were looking around as if the Parrishables were about to burst out at any second and attack.

Since no one had come forward, it looked like I was going to have to perform the spell after all. I thought maybe if I gave the person the chance to turn themselves in, they would take it. But no bother. Ever since I'd found the spell, I'd been looking forward to seeing how it worked, anyway.

"We have a traitor among us. Someone who plans on selling us out to the Parrishables. This person's been posing as a friend when they're really our enemy. And it's time to send them back to their true coven."

"Who is it?"

"Are you serious?"

"I'm going to kill whoever it is," Jasmine said with a growl that sounded completely genuine.

Clearing my throat, I concentrated on the lines I'd been waiting for hours to say:

> *You never can tell who is friend or foe.*
> *Ask them straightaway and they will not say so.*
> *Do not close your eyes to the truth in your heart,*
> *Or the knife might hit back before the curtains do part.*
> *Sun light the dark and let it be known,*
> *The traitor is caught and their lies are now shown.*

As soon as I began to say the words, I could tell they were working. It felt like there was an electrical current flowing through my veins. The energy surging through my body almost startled me out of continuing, but I kept going, reciting word after word until I finished the spell.

As I came to the last line, my hands began to shine brightly, light emanating from both palms. My arms began to shake with the magical power that was filling up inside my body, building and building until I felt like I might explode from the force. The spell wasn't particularly difficult—I'd performed harder ones on several occasions—but for some reason this one seemed to really affect me. Like it was coming from my very core. For a brief second, I worried that I had taken on something I couldn't handle.

Just when I wasn't sure I could take it anymore, the magic burst from my hands in two streams of light. I watched as the beams weaved around the group in front of me like slithering snakes, bending and curving as they looked for their targets. People were running around the yard now, scared they might be hurt by the streaks of light. I knew what they were really after, and that only one of them had to worry about what was going to happen when the light caught up to him.

My heart was racing from the intensity of the spell and anxiety over what we were about to find out. Then the heaviness in my stomach turned to nausea as I watched the first stream of magic hit Asher and the second hit Emory.

Chapter Twenty-Six

As soon as people realized they weren't actually the targets of my spell, and that Asher and Emory had been singled out instead, the reaction was immediate. People were confused, angry, frightened—all the emotions that came along with betrayal—and no one bothered to hide their feelings.

Except for me. Because this was the first time I'd ever been in this sort of situation. And I had no idea how to deal with it.

I'd always rolled my eyes when my friends said it, but at that moment I truly understood what they meant when they said they could feel their heart breaking. Because that's what it felt like to see the stream of light hit Asher straight in the chest. It was a deep ache, unlike anything I'd felt before. When I'd lost my mom, the pain was more like despair, like the feeling that nothing would ever be right again. But the betrayal of someone you cared about romantically? If I didn't know it was impossible for a heart to physically bust in half, I would have bet that's what was happening then.

I'd never felt so incredibly let down in my entire life, not by anyone. A dozen different thoughts started racing through my head, each one worse than the last. How was this possible? Had our whole flirtation been a part of the Parrishables' evil plans to overtake the Cleri? Would everyone hate me because *I'd* been the one to bring Asher into our coven? How had I been so stupid to fall for a stranger when I knew from the beginning that there was something sketchy about the way he kept turning up everywhere I went? And worst of all, what was I possibly going to do about the fact that the only boy I'd ever kind of loved was playing for Team Evil?

As much as I didn't want to admit it, that's what it had come to. I could no longer deny the fact that my feelings for this beautiful dark-haired boy, who had the most magnetic eyes I'd ever seen, had grown into something like love. Could I really turn my back on that? And if I *could* manage to ignore my feelings, how was I ever going to be able to trust another guy with my heart again?

Trust. It was such a small word that held so much power— and potential for pain. Asher had taken my trust and stomped all over it. So even if I *did* have certain feelings for him, he obviously didn't feel the same about me. Otherwise he wouldn't have conned me into thinking he cared about me when he'd just been planning to hand me over to the Parrishables.

That's when it dawned on me: someone like that didn't deserve my love *or* my forgiveness.

Asher was a traitor and there was no way of atoning for that. And I wasn't about to let my feelings put my coven in danger any longer. I narrowed my eyes at him as I came to my decision.

Asher looked down at where the light was illuminating his body and then back up at me. He ignored the madness that had erupted around us and kept his gaze steadily on my face. Despite the yelling and arguing that filled the air, Asher just stood there, mouth slightly open as if he was stunned into silence. And maybe he was. It was the first time I'd ever performed that spell, and for all I knew, it'd knocked the wind out of him on impact.

For the first time since we'd met, he *looked* guilty. Gone was the cocky confidence and sexy smirk I'd come to associate with him. Now he looked more like a deer caught in headlights. I was tempted to let him know there was nowhere he could run to escape my wrath, but it was too loud around us with everyone asking questions and threatening Emory and Asher for me to respond. And truthfully, I didn't trust my voice just yet.

Movement to my right diverted my attention just in time for me to see Jasmine and Peter grab hold of Emory. Right away she began to struggle, but they just held on tighter. I'd never seen Jasmine as angry as she looked now and I was thankful that I wasn't in Emory's position.

"Let me go!"

My head whipped around at the sound of Asher's outburst. Fallon had followed Jasmine and Peter's lead and he and a few of his buddies had surrounded Asher and were holding him in place. As I watched—drained by the spell and stunned by the results—they forced him off the porch and onto his knees. A fresh pang shot through my gut as I watched him struggle.

"Hadley! Hadley, look at me," Asher pleaded, his eyes sincere. "You *know* me. I never wanted to do any of this, you have to believe me."

"Actually, I don't, Asher," I said, the hurt coming out like hate. I turned to the rest of my coven members. The ones who hadn't betrayed me. "Don't let them go."

I walked down the porch steps to where Emory and Asher

were now kneeling side by side, both being held down tightly by the others. When I stopped in front of them, I refused to look at Asher. I was afraid that if I did, I wouldn't be able to handle the emotions that would flood my soul. So I kept my attention on Emory.

But the girl in front of me now wasn't the same person I'd come to feel close to over the past few weeks. Her calm, quiet, sensitive demeanor was gone. Sure, she was still dressed like she was on her way to church, but her face had transformed into something hard and ugly. Her lips had formed a perma-snarl and her eyes were so dark now that the whites were barely showing. I couldn't believe I hadn't seen the evil in her before.

"Why are you here and what do you want?" I asked her.

She gave me a smug smile but didn't respond.

"Okay, let's try this again," I said, my patience depleted. "What the *hell* are you doing here and what do you want?" This time I put all my powers of persuasion behind the questions, calling on all my will to force her to answer me. Apparently, my strong emotions helped to make the spell more powerful, because Emory's lips shook briefly as she fought against telling me what I wanted to know.

"What do you *think* I'm doing here?" she spat. "My leader sent me to gather information on the Cleri."

"Why did Samuel send you? And why does he even care about us? We're no threat to him!"

Emory snorted. "No threat? Are you kidding? Please tell me you're kidding," she said, shaking her head. "You want to know *why* Reverend Parris cares about you so much?"

"Yeah, I do," I said, placing my hands on my hips.

"Because you're the only one who *matters*."

We all looked at each other, confused, wondering whether that had been Emory's goal all along: to manipulate us into turning against each other so it would be easier to get to *me*. I still had no idea why *I* was so important to them, though. I was just a twitch, with really great hair and a natural talent for casting. Since when did that equal formidable foe? And if this was the case, then was I just putting everyone else back in danger by sticking around?

When I didn't say anything right away, Emory got bored and grunted before continuing. "How could you be so incredibly clueless? I swear, it's infuriating how talent is wasted on people like you," she began to rant. "If I had even an *ounce* of the power you have—"

"You can communicate with the *dead*! How much more power do you need?" Jasmine asked incredulously.

"I don't really see dead people, you daft twit," Emory bit back. "It's called lying. Look it up." Jasmine looked like she was about to pummel her, but I gestured for her to stop. She settled back into her spot next to Emory, still breathing heavily with anger. I couldn't have her knocking Emory out before I had a chance to find out what the Parrishables' plan was. Emory went on.

"I thought if you believed I could talk to your dead parents, I might be able to get you to do what I wanted. And by telling each of you that there was a traitor in the group, I figured you'd lose trust in each other and self-destruct. But, apparently, you guys will trust *anyone*." She glanced sideways at Asher, to which he began to shake his head emphatically. I ignored him.

"Why am I the only one who matters?" I asked.

I was still forcing Emory's will, and based on experience, I knew that she'd continue to tell me things even if she didn't necessarily want to. This particular power of mine was really coming in handy today, and I passed up a silent thank-you to my dad for having great witch genes. Emory might not spill *all* her secrets, but knowing even a little bit of the Parrishables' plan would put us in better shape than we were in now. And even better was that I hadn't divulged this part about myself yet. I'd been holding on to it like a secret weapon.

"Because you have *power*. Same reason we've hunted down your relatives. The magic that runs through your lineage rivals any other in the world. But you . . . you are the only one that Samuel has been able to find in all the world whose power rivals that of Bridget Bishop," she said. "So why do you matter? Because he wants you, Hadley. Either you can join him on our quest for magical dominance or you can die. We know which one Bridget chose. Personally, I'd love for you to join her."

"Why murder the others, then, if you only wanted me?" I asked, my voice a whisper. The last thing I wanted to do was cry in front of this hypocrite, but I could feel my emotions beginning to rage out of control.

"Samuel wanted them out of the way so it would be easier when we came for you," she said, shrugging. "If the elders had known you were our target, they would have rallied around you, making everything so much more complicated and annoying. So, we took the army out first to get to its queen." There was no remorse in her eyes. In fact, I'm sure she fully believed that the end justified the means. How could someone be so incredibly unfeeling? These were our *parents* they'd killed.

Our parents. Meaning, her parents should've been at the meeting in the warehouse too. How was she being so cavalier about this? "How could you do something like that to your own parents? Don't you care about anyone other than yourself?"

"Samuel turned my parents rogue a long time ago," she said, snickering. "They weren't in the warehouse that night.

They were standing with me, outside, watching it burn to the ground."

This time I started to lunge for her myself, but Fallon was behind me in a second, pulling me back so I couldn't scratch Emory's eyes out.

"Let me go, Fallon!" I yelled, reaching for her. But he wouldn't do it. He probably knew I could have killed her, which would definitely have started the war sooner than we intended. And deep down, we both knew I wasn't a killer. I drew a controlled breath and forced myself to relax slightly under Fallon's hands.

"Let. Me. Go," I instructed Fallon, without taking my eyes off Emory.

It wasn't my intention to use my powers of persuasion on him, but the words had barely come out of my mouth when Fallon loosened his grip. He stayed close, though, in case he needed to swoop back in. But by now I'd gotten my emotions under control. Not that I wasn't still mad, but I wasn't planning to strangle anyone to death anymore.

Taking a big step forward, I got so close to Emory that I could feel her breath on my face. Underneath the darkness of her eyes, I could see fear beginning to creep in. This would have made me smile if I hadn't already been so upset.

"Don't you *dare* talk about my family like that *ever* again. They were better witches than you'll ever be, and the Parrishables will burn for what they did to them. But right now, while you're still alive? You're about to know pain unlike anything before," I said deliberately. I moved another inch closer to Emory. Our noses were almost touching now, and I was officially invading her space. Oddly enough, I didn't care if she was uncomfortable, because I was about to make her wish she'd never infiltrated my coven.

"You were right about one thing, though," I said, this time my voice low and clear. I knew the others were straining to hear what I was saying, but this last bit was just for her. "I *am* more powerful than you could ever imagine, and you've gotten on my bad side. The Parrishables can come after me as often as they want. You may hurt me, you may slow me down, but you need to understand me when I say, *I will win.*"

I didn't wait for a response. Emory's pale face and dropped jaw were enough. I wasn't playing games anymore. It was time for the Parrishables to know what they were up against.

I began to walk away, hoping to collect my thoughts and maybe start strategizing on how to defeat the Parrishables. I'd gone only a few steps before Asher stopped me.

"Hadley, wait! I'm not *like* her. I had nothing to do with what happened to your parents. I didn't even want to do any of this. Hadley!" Asher tried to get to his feet, reaching out his hands like he might be able to keep me from leaving. The others pulled him back, refusing to let him get any nearer.

Emory took advantage of the scuffle to yank herself free of Peter's and Jasmine's grip, and she began to run toward the back fence and beyond it. To freedom.

"Grab her!" I screamed. A few of us shot spells her way, but we were still so shocked by the whole situation that none hit their mark. A few moments later, she was gone.

And part of me was happy about it.

"Hasta la pasta, biznatch," Jasmine said, looking in the direction of where Emory had disappeared.

With her went our best chance at learning more about what the Parrishables had planned. But all wasn't lost. We still had Asher. As hurt and angry as I was with him, I wasn't about to let him get away without giving us every bit of information we wanted.

"Tie him up in the shed at the side of the house," I told the guys who were once again holding Asher down. "Get him to tell us what the Parrishables have planned. And if he doesn't— kill him."

I didn't really mean what I said, and there was no way the others were about to off another kid their age unless it was in extreme self-defense, but Asher didn't have to know that. It would probably do the backstabber good to squirm a little anyway. Now he'd know what it felt like to be betrayed.

"What?" Asher asked, his eyes going wide. "Are you kidding me? Hadley, I'm not who you think I am. I'm—"

"Muflix sertikin," I said, directing the words of the mumming spell right at my ex.

I was through listening to his lies.

As soon as Asher was secured in the shed, I gathered everyone up and held a meeting. Now that we were rid of our infiltrators, we could get back to training—doubling our efforts this time. With a few of the older kids watching Asher and trying to get answers out of him, Sascha, Jasmine, Peter, Fallon, and I began to pore over my family's spell book. There was no way I was going to be able to learn the spells all on my own, and now that I knew who I could trust, I was ready to share the knowledge.

So, after teaching the rest of the group some basic hand-to-hand combat and defensive moves (blocking punches, kicks, and getting out of holds), I left them to practice, while the five of us read through and memorized as many of the spells as we could. If we were able to pull these spells off, it would give us the edge over the Parrishables, since these spells had been used by my family exclusively.

"Why are these spells so *long*?" Sascha whined.

We were all gathered up in my parents' room, since it was the biggest in the house, and I could still look out the window and check on what the others were doing. Everyone had taken up different spots around the room to practice the spells that had been assigned to them. Sascha was lying on a chair in the corner, her head dangling off the front and her back in the seat. She had her legs resting against the back of the chair even though she was wearing a skirt, which was creeping up her thighs. I wasn't the only one who noticed she was dangerously close to flashing everyone in the room. But if it was what helped her to retain the shielding spell she was currently learning, more power to her.

"I actually kind of like them," Jasmine admitted. She'd taken over the bed as soon as we'd entered, falling back against the enormous pillows and making herself comfortable. Peter had somehow managed to park his butt on the corner of the mattress, far enough away so as not to violate Jasmine's personal space. She didn't seem to mind him being there, though. Then again, who would ever be able to kick Pete off the bed? It would be like making a puppy sleep on the floor. "It's like we're taking it back to old-school magic. Way cooler."

"Your idea of cool is seriously messed up," Sascha answered sarcastically, and then stuck out her tongue. "I just wish they'd get to the point already."

"I actually think there's something to it." I was sitting on the window ledge, watching everyone below me practice, but turned back inside. "It's like, the more specific the spells are, the more potent they are. It's hard to describe, but when I did the spell earlier, I felt this surge of power unlike anything I'd ever felt before. It was like I was tapping in to something ancient."

"Well, these are definitely *old*," Fallon said with a snort as he flipped halfheartedly through the book. I flinched as he almost ripped one of its pages. I was still reeling from the fact that he wasn't the one who'd sold the Cleri out, and even though I logically *knew* he wasn't working for the Parrishables, I still didn't fully trust him. Unfortunately, I didn't really have a choice given the circumstances.

"I didn't mean ancient like outdated. I meant like . . . magic that's been built up over time. These spells are more intense than any we've ever been taught. If we're going to have any chance at beating the Parrishables, this is it."

"You. If *you're* going to have any chance of beating them," Fallon said quietly. "They've made it pretty clear that they're not worried about the rest of us. The only person they think is a threat is you. We're just casualties of their war."

I understood what Fallon was feeling and I was surprised that he was only bringing this fact up now. There was no malice or jealousy in his words. Just acceptance of his fate. Only, I didn't believe that what he said was completely true.

"I know it seems that way, Fallon, and if any of you want to get out before this thing gets really messy, I won't hold it against you. But they're wrong," I said, looking at him now with a new set of eyes. "They think I'm powerful, and yeah, maybe I am. But I can't do this on my own. I need you guys more than you know. It's because of the coven that we're all still alive."

Fallon began to shake his head like he didn't believe me, and the others looked a little doubtful themselves, so I pushed on.

"Why do you think Emory was trying so hard to split us apart? She knew that we're stronger as a group and that the only way they could destroy me was to destroy all of us," I said. "So maybe I am their target . . . but I have the ultimate weapons."

Everyone was silent as they let what I said sink in. I could see them start to perk up, and when they turned back to what they were working on, I knew it was with a renewed energy.

"Freaking Emory," Jasmine muttered. "I can't believe she duped us all."

"How could she sit in our witch lessons for years and then just decide to betray us one day?" Sascha asked. "It doesn't make sense."

"Sure it does," Fallon said.

We all looked over at him, surprised that he seemed to be defending her.

"How do you figure?" I asked.

"She's evil," he said, matter-of-fact. "You heard her. Emory and her family wanted power at any cost. The Parrishables offered her that and she took it. It's actually not all that complicated when you think about it."

"How can going against your own coven be uncomplicated?" Jasmine asked.

"Easy," I said, getting what Fallon was trying to say. "When you don't care about the people you're screwing over, you can do just about anything without remorse."

"Emory didn't care about anyone but herself and what she could get by joining the Parrishables," Fallon said. "We were just obstacles to be worked around."

"I could *kill* her," Jasmine said, her hands balling up into fists. "Speaking of, when are we planning to take these suckers out, anyway?"

That's what I'd been asking myself since Emory had run off. Because she knew exactly where we were hiding, it was no longer a good hiding place. Which meant we didn't have a lot of time before they came looking for us.

And I was through with being ambushed. The next time we

went up against the Parrishables, we were going to be ready and it would be on *our* terms.

"Tomorrow," I said. I was guesstimating how long it would take for Emory to make it back to Samuel and then for them to find the cabin. And though it was sooner than I'd have liked, we would be prepared. "The war starts tomorrow at dusk."

Chapter Twenty-Seven

Before I knew it, it was nightfall and the others started to filter in from outside, but the five of us remained in the room, memorizing spell after spell. There wasn't enough time to practice, and besides, most of the ones we'd deemed useful for our impending battle weren't exactly the kind of spells we wanted to try on each other. No one was volunteering themselves as guinea pigs, anyway. I'd have tested a few out on Asher, but I wasn't ready to see him yet—besides, I had much worse things in store for him.

At one point in the evening, one of the younger girls brought up some sandwiches for us to eat. We didn't bother stopping, just shoved the peanut-butter-and-banana sandwiches into our mouths as we worked. There was a sort of rhythm to our flow of learning. One of us took the book, read the spell, wrote it down, and then passed it on. Then we'd commit it to memory during the time that it took for the volume to make its way back around again, when we'd choose yet another spell to master.

By 3 a.m., every one of us was falling asleep sitting up and it was clear that anything we were trying to memorize wasn't going to stick. And if we were going to be fighting the Parrishables in the next twenty-four hours, we needed some rest. So we slept right there in our spots, giving way to all the wicked dreams our minds could come up with.

By now I knew mine weren't just products of my imagination. It was a fact I'd started getting used to of late. Tonight, I almost welcomed it, because I felt there was something I was still missing, some piece of information that Bridget or Christian could give me that would pull everything together. I couldn't imagine that the universe would bring me this far only to let us lose. No, there *had* to be something that I was missing.

So when my eyes itched with sleep and my lids grew heavy and threatened to drop, I lay down, snuggling into my covers next to Jazzy, and allowed my mind to be opened up to whatever wisdom the past had for me.

Before long, I was no longer in the cabin. I was standing on uneven ground and my feet were warm, as if they were wrapped in a heating blanket. The smell in the air was acrid, a mixture of smoke, ash, and the slightest bit of something foul. Like burning hair. Or flesh. The combination almost made me retch.

Fighting back the bile that threatened to come up, I realized exactly where I was. And then I saw it: I was standing on the site where the Parrishables had massacred the Cleri. My parents. My friends' parents. All cut down because of an immortal man who was insane with power. A man who saw us as a threat and would stop at nothing to ensure that he stayed in control of the magic world.

As I took a step across the rubble, and then another, ash

began to cling to my shoes and coat them like mud. But I couldn't worry about my clothes right now, because I was brought here for a reason—though I still had no idea what it was.

Why was I here? To pick something up, perhaps? To learn something? No answers came to me, so I continued to walk across the still-burning ground.

I was alone in the makeshift graveyard, with only my thoughts to keep me company. This was a dark place to be. Especially when all I had on my mind was revenge. I wanted the ones who were responsible for this destruction to suffer. Horribly.

"You realize this couldn't have been avoided."

The voice came from behind me, in a space that had been deserted only a few seconds ago. The sound both startled and comforted me. I realized quickly that I'd been expecting it all along. I whipped around to find myself staring at someone I knew well. However, up until then, I'd never actually had a conversation with her. I'd only ever been a witness to her life, never an active participant.

Right there in front of me, looking stunning in a bloodred frock, was my long-lost ancestor, the infamous Bridget Bishop. She looked nothing like the woman I'd seen in jail on the day of her death; here she was cleaned up, immaculate even. Her hair fell in gentle waves around her face and shone a vibrant midnight black color. A slight smile played on her lips, giving the impression that she was hiding a secret or had just told a dirty joke. And knowing what I did about her, this very well could've been true.

I'd seen her at her worst: dirty, helpless, proud, and fearful, but today she was prettier than I'd ever imagined. I could see now why women worried about their men when Bridget was around. Then I wondered if I had inherited that particular gift, too.

Before I could say anything, she continued. "It was a tragedy, yes, but there was nothing you could have done, my dear girl," she said, looking straight at me.

I didn't want to be impolite and keep staring at her without responding, so I cleared my throat and took a step closer. The air around us was hushed but for the crackling of fires that hadn't yet burned out. It almost seemed like there were little screams among the sounds, and I imagined everyone being caught in the flames.

"But I *could* have," I said, almost pleadingly. "If I'd just tried harder, followed my mom when she got that call. Maybe then I could've gotten everyone out in time."

She shook her head sadly. "The interesting thing about time is that it is fleeting. And it *was* their time to go. As it was mine long ago."

"That's not fair," I said. I knew I sounded like a little kid, but I felt like throwing a tantrum at the injustice of it all. I restrained myself from stomping my foot, but I didn't have as much control over my quivering lips and teary eyes. This poor woman, who'd suffered through more horror than most of us could imagine, didn't need to see me have an emotional breakdown. Not with how brave she'd been that day in 1692. I couldn't cry in front of her. It would be too embarrassing. So I changed the subject. "What about Samuel? He's like four hundred years old and he's still walking around like he owns the magic world. I think it's far past his bedtime, don't you?"

Bridget gave a chuckle. For a second I could imagine what things might've been like if I'd met her in her own day. Would I have liked her or would we have butted heads because we were so much alike? I wanted to believe that we would've been friends. We could've bonded over our mutual love of power and the color red.

"Samuel is a different matter entirely," she said gently.

"But why? What makes him so different?"

"Well, for one, he chose darkness over the light of the universe. His heart is black. So is his soul, and when it is time for him to meet his maker—which I anticipate will happen soon—he will be punished for all he has done. The otherworld does not take kindly to those who defy its laws. Which is why we are *always* to be careful of where our alliances lie."

Something Bridget had said stopped me. "Wait. So you think we actually have a chance of *winning* this thing? I mean, that's what I've been telling everyone, but to be honest, I haven't been so sure. . . ."

Standing among the ashes of my fallen coven members, I was finally able to admit it out loud: I thought there was a possibility we wouldn't make it out of this fight alive. But here was the first person slain in Reverend Parris's quest for total magic domination, and she was telling me there was a chance. We had a chance. Samuel's reign of terror might be coming to an end.

"As I said, we must be careful with whom we align ourselves. If you ask the right people for help, you will triumph. But this is a decision you must make for yourself."

"I thought we already had," I said, growing confused and then frustrated. "Why aren't you people ever clear about these things instead of talking in riddles? Just tell me what to do and I'll do it."

"The Bishop women are beautiful and passionate, but one thing we are not is indolent. I cannot give you the answers, but when you come up with the right questions I will be here. We are *all* here for you whenever you choose to call us."

"It doesn't feel like it," I mumbled, beginning to feel defeated. Between the vague advice and the fact that I was standing in the place where my mom had died, I was starting to think I'd rather be awake than dealing with all this.

"Look again," Bridget said, gesturing widely.

I turned slowly to find the previously empty space before me now packed with people. The first face I recognized was my mom's. She was standing at the front of the crowd, smiling at me. There were tears in her eyes, but I knew without asking that they were tears of joy, filled with pride. I resisted the urge to run to her and give her a big hug, because even though it was a dream, I knew that her presence wasn't tangible. There would be no hugs, no kisses, no comforting hands on my shoulders. So I stayed where I was and beamed back at her, hoping she understood how much it meant to see her.

Then I began to pick out other faces in the crowd. Peter's parents were there and so were Jasmine's. Fallon's hulk of a dad stood with his arm around his mom. Even my grandparents were there. But it was more than just my coven and immediate family. There had to have been hundreds of people standing in the crowd that was now stretching back as far as my eyes could see. Most of them I didn't even recognize, but I knew in my gut we were all connected.

And just when I began to understand what was going on, I started to shake violently, until everything around me evaporated and I found myself back in my room staring up at Fallon.

According to him, I'd been murmuring in my sleep. Given the dream I'd had, it made sense. But I couldn't worry about what he may have heard, because we were running out of time to do what we needed to do before the Parrishables showed up. There was no doubt in my mind that they were already on their way. Luckily, Bridget had given me the last piece in the puzzle of how to defeat them.

First, I let the others in on what I'd discovered through my dream. My theory, which I hoped would lead us to win, was a little far-fetched and I had expected some resistance— or worse, a flat-out refusal from Fallon—but everyone stayed silent as I explained what I believed Bridget was trying to tell me. By the time I was finished, the others in the room were on board.

Telling the rest of the Cleri had been easy, and afterward we went back to training in a last-ditch effort to prepare ourselves for what was about to happen. People were growing tired, and to be honest, we all could've used another month or so of intense practice, but by the time the afternoon started to give way to the night I knew we were as ready as we'd ever be.

I figured that the Parrishables wouldn't strike while the sun was still out. It wasn't that they couldn't; they'd done it before. It was a question of comfort. Darkness craved darkness. It was when they moved best and did the most damage. The night sky was like a security blanket for people like them. And with Emory free to tell the Parrishables everything we'd been doing and where we were staying, we were practically sitting ducks.

At least that's what they would think.

An hour before sunset, I gathered everyone together and went over one final time what we were going to do. I explained that just because the Parrishables had managed to get to us in the past, that didn't mean we weren't strong enough to stop them. This time for good. The exact words I used weren't important. It was the feeling that rippled through our coven that mattered. The over- whelming knowledge that we were going to win. And when I told every last one of them how we would do that, I could physi- cally see their spirits lifting up. They stood a little straighter and looks of fear were replaced with a determination and a confidence that hadn't been there before.

I knew that in order to maximize our chances, we had to wait for the exact right moment to take action and until then, there was nothing else to do but wait. So I told everyone to take the next hour for themselves and get in the best head space possible before the battle—watching the sunset, getting lost in a book, painting, gossiping with a friend—whatever it was that gave them some modicum of joy and comfort. They deserved that at least, because it was a real possibility that not everyone would have the chance again.

How would you spend your last hour alive if you knew it was your time to go? A teacher had asked us this question in a creative writing class and my answer had involved going to Paris (the carb capital of the world); making wild, passionate love to Zac Efron (I heard he was into magical chicks); and dyeing my hair blond (I wanted to see if they really *did* have more fun). But when it's actually a possibility, the reality is much different.

Now, instead of wanting to do things I'd never done before, I found myself wishing I could spend the time with my old faithfuls. I went upstairs and took a shower, taking special care to use all my favorite soaps and shampoos, getting lost in the scents that the different products created. When I got out, I carefully applied my makeup, opting out of using magic as a shortcut. Before life had gotten complicated, I used to love doing this. Taking the time to choose my colors, using opposing shades and blending them creatively across my eyes. Lining my lids with such intense precision that you'd have sworn I was born like that. Dusting the makeup brush lightly against my skin felt unbelievable. This was my quiet time. The time I let go of all the nonsense and stress that bogged me down.

I didn't realize how much I'd missed the ritual until I was faced with the possibility of never doing it again.

Getting dressed was more difficult. What does one wear to a war? How to be fashionable yet functional? I turned to TV shows and movies for inspiration on what the modern femme fatale was wearing these days and ended up in a skin-tight catsuit the color of a fire engine with hidden pockets to hold a few spells I'd written out, plus my lip gloss. Black boots extended up my calves, just skimming the bottoms of my thighs. The heels were short for me, only three inches, but still stiletto. Anything more than that and I might break an ankle or impale someone during a roundhouse kick. And the latter would mean destroying another pair of shoes, which I was so not into.

Just as I was putting the finishing touches on my hair (pulled back into a tight ponytail with a braid around the base), there was a knock on my door. One of Fallon's brood came in, wanting to update me on where they'd gotten with Asher.

Asher.

I'd somehow managed to forget about him a few times already that day, and for the last hour, I purposely hadn't let myself think of him at all. Now all the feelings came rushing back, undoing every last bit of Zen I'd achieved while getting ready.

I didn't want to think about him, but I needed to know what he knew.

"We've tried to get him to talk, but he says he'll only talk to you."

My stomach flipped. Talking to Asher was the last thing I should do. I didn't want to go into battle with my emotions all over the place, and that's exactly what would happen if I went to have a heart-to-heart with him now. But if I didn't, what would that mean for the Cleri and our chances in this fight? He might have knowledge that could be helpful to us. And I had to do what was best for the group right now, which meant talking to him when all I wanted to do was kill him. After all, so much of this was my fault in the first place.

"Fine. I'll be down there in a minute."

As soon as I was alone, I started to feel sick to my stomach over what I was about to do. But I commanded my legs to move and before I knew it, I was standing outside the shed that had become my ex's prison. Taking a deep breath to compose myself, I turned the handle and walked inside.

"Whoa. You look—" Asher managed to get out before I shot him a glare.

"Dangerous? Because that's what it would be to try and hit on me right now," I said, the threat hanging in the air between us. When he didn't respond, I continued. "So, what couldn't you tell the others that you can only tell me? And hurry up, I don't have a lot of time before your friends get here and try to *kill* us."

I avoided his eyes. Those dark, piercing eyes. The eyes that had made me swoon, that I longed to see myself in, that I wished were only for me. No reason to remind myself how I'd felt, considering we were about to fight, possibly to our deaths. Remembering my feelings for him would just make it harder for me to do what I had to do to survive.

"Had, you've got this all wrong," Asher said in a voice so sincere that my heart ached.

But I ignored it. "So you *weren't* sent here by Samuel and the other Parrishables to gather information on us?"

"Well, yeah, but—"

"And you *didn't* lie to me this whole time about who you were and why you were here?"

"Not exactly—"

"So your plan *didn't* involve getting close to me and making me care about you, just so you could turn me over to our enemies in the end?"

"Dammit, Hadley, it's more complicated than that!" Asher yelled in frustration. Hearing the shouts, one of the guards popped his head in to see if everything was under control and I waved him away while keeping my eyes on the cuffs that held my old flame in place. I'd taken a page right out of Samuel's book and charmed the locks to make it impossible for Asher to do magic. I wasn't sure if he'd tried to escape yet, but if he did, he was in for a rude awakening.

Once we were alone again, I crossed my arms and waited for him to speak. Sensing that my patience was dwindling, he sighed and softened his voice. "I'm sorry. I just need you to hear me out. . . ."

"Why should I?" I snarled back, the anger rising steadily in me like a flame.

"Because—I think I love you." The way he said it made him sound broken. His voice cracked and he couldn't continue.

I felt like I'd been socked in the stomach. Had he seriously just dropped the L-bomb on me after everything he'd done? He had to be kidding. Right? The thought was insane, yet something nagged at my chest, making me feel torn. Was it possible his words were more than just a plot to get free and finish what he'd started?

"Did you hear me?" he asked when I didn't say anything in response. "I—"

"I heard you," I said with less venom in my voice now. "I just don't believe you."

His face fell. "Look, did Samuel make me come here and befriend you? Yes, but it's not because I'm one of *them*. You know how I told you my parents died a little while back? Well, Parris did it. My parents had a feeling that he was back and they were going to take us away, get us somewhere safe. But he hunted us down...."

Horror flooded me as I imagined what he must have been playing back in his head right now. If what he was saying was true, he'd been through the same harrowing experience as me. But that didn't justify him switching teams, and I told him as much.

"After he"—his voice caught on the words—"killed my parents, he took my sister and told me that if I didn't do what he said, he'd kill her, too. So you see? I didn't have a choice! She's my sister, Hadley. What was I supposed to do?"

My anger began to fade as I realized I believed him. I tried to put myself in his shoes and knew that I would've done the same thing. Well, not *exactly* the same thing.

"Why would they come after your family, Asher? You're not a part of the Cleri," I said, not yet seeing the connection.

"Yours wasn't the only coven in the Salem area that posed a threat to Parris and his plans back during the trials," he said. "If you weren't with him, you were against him. He must have been searching for us ever since our family fled from Massachusetts. Guess we didn't run far enough."

I let what he said sink in as my conflicted feelings battled it out in my head.

"You could have been *honest* with me, Asher," I said finally, lowering my voice. I took a few steps farther into the room, still not daring to get close enough for him to touch me.

"Really? How was I supposed to do that? You know, you're not the easiest person to get to know. And then once I *did* get to know you, I knew I couldn't come out and tell you who I really was because I figured you'd react like *this*." He motioned to the handcuffs with his head.

"Can you blame me?" I asked.

He paused and seemed to think about it. "I guess not," he said, sounding defeated. "But you have to believe that once I realized I had feelings for you, all I could think about was how I could fix all of this and *still* save my sister. Because . . . because I can't live without either of you."

He was telling the truth. I knew it. And not in that naive he-wants-to-make-out-with-me-so-he-must-love-me kind of way. I knew it because I'd never been so sure of anything in my life. Closing the distance between us, I knelt down in front of him and took his hands in mine. The spark of electricity that had always been there between us felt like fireworks now. I could no longer deny it: we were meant to be together. But I still didn't fully trust him, and for that reason, when I leaned forward to kiss him, I left his cuffs in place.

Our lips had just touched when a loud boom sounded to my right and I watched with horror as the side wall exploded into pieces around us.

Chapter Twenty - Eight

Before I had a chance to recover from the shock that half the wall was gone, a pair of boots appeared through the debris. I'd been tossed to the ground when the explosion rocked the shed, and there wasn't really anywhere for me to go, since one of the remaining walls was right behind me. And I couldn't exactly leave Asher behind, helpless with his arms bound. If what he'd said was true, Samuel was his enemy too.

I lay there, too stunned at first to move. Eventually the dust cleared and gave way to the outline of an enormous man. He was raggedy-looking and had two girls with him; they all looked rather pissed and were coming straight for me.

"Hadley, let me out," Asher hissed at me. "I can't help you with these things on my wrists."

I didn't even have a chance to decide to let him go or not before the first girl lunged at me. Rolling a few feet away, I pushed myself up onto my feet and took a defensive stance.

"I was thinking about remodeling, but this wasn't exactly what

I had in mind," I said, looking at the structure they'd destroyed.

The girl gave me an annoyed look. Guess Sammy's pack weren't the joking types. No matter. I could be serious, too.

"What are you waiting for? Come and get me," I said, beckoning her forward with my finger.

That was all the encouragement she needed. Without waiting for another invite, she ran at me, raising her leg to strike me in the side. I might've been more worried if she hadn't been wearing metallic stretch pants and out-of-date orange tennis shoes. An outfit that tacky didn't give me much confidence in her abilities. If your look has expired, chances are, so have your fighting skills.

Just like I'd thought, she was totally predictable, and I reached for her leg and used her own momentum to toss her right past me and into the far wall. She landed with a thud and then remained on the ground.

Satisfied that she was down for the moment, I turned back to the other two. Neither of them had bothered to move from their spots. The girl looked a little less sure of herself now that I'd done away with her friend. She shifted her weight from one foot to the other as if she was trying to decide whether she should stay or run. Finally, she looked over to the guy for direction.

Her buddy wasn't as hesitant and gave me a nasty smile. His leer made me uncomfortable, though I didn't want to show it.

"Who's next?" I asked, already knowing the answer but hoping to move things along, and away from Asher, who was still cuffed behind me.

The brute in front of me only grunted in response and then lifted up his arms to prepare for a spell.

"Tiamus perplexigun!" he shouted, pointing in my direction.

I attempted to get out of the way in time, but I felt the buzz of the charm hit me on the back of the leg as I sprinted to the right. It felt like the electric shock from one of those joke hand buzzers—only this one moved through my body, up my legs, past my stomach, and then down my arms toward my fingertips. I figured it would just pass through my hands and out the other side like a lightning bolt. In fact, I was starting to wonder why he'd bothered to send such a weak spell my way when my hands connected tightly at the wrists and stuck that way.

Looking down at them, I was horrified to see they were bound together. Not with handcuffs like I'd placed on Asher but instead with what seemed to be an invisible force. It felt like little magnets had been implanted into my wrists. I tried to pull them apart, but they wouldn't budge.

The skeezy guy laughed. He was enjoying seeing me struggle. It was all I could do to force myself to stop and think, racking my brain for any spell I'd ever been taught that could get me out of his hold. But then I was being pulled across the floor, as if led by a rope attached to the ties that bound me. Fighting against it the whole way, I dug my heels into the floor and listened to them scrape across the surface as he willed me closer and closer to him. I didn't want to know what he planned to do once he got his hands on me.

Finally, something Jackson had said in one of our classes popped into my mind. I stopped fighting and moved forward willingly. A smile broke out on my adversary's face. He thought I'd given up.

Just as I was nearly close enough for him to reach out and touch me, I pulled on the magic rope and flung myself at him as hard as I could. This was the last thing he'd expected me to do, so when I hit him, he lost his balance and fell backward, landing hard on the ground.

As soon as he was down, my wrists sprang free, exactly as

I'd suspected they might. Many years before, we'd been taught that a spell like this is useful only as long as the caster is concentrating on his powers. Oftentimes if you're able to distract the spell caster enough, their mind will wander, letting go of the spell and allowing you time to get away.

Stunned at what had just happened, the hulk of a man looked up at me. I waved and threw him my own devilish smile. Then, before he could recover, I sent a piece of the roof falling down on top of him, ensuring that it would take the Parrishable quite a while to climb his way out from beneath the rubble.

"Hadley!"

"I'm kind of busy right now, Asher," I warned, my gaze now fixed on the only other girl left standing in the room.

The girl looked over at her friend, who was lying on the ground, and then over at the unconscious guy just a few feet away. It was as if I could see her thought process: "Do I run and risk the wrath of my coven leader or stay and most likely get my ass kicked by this girl?"

Apparently, it wasn't a very difficult decision. A few seconds later the girl took off, running back through the hole that used to be the door to the shed.

"Good choice," I said, watching her disappear. I started to follow but heard some shuffling and then a throat clearing behind me.

"Had! Let me out of these so I can *help* you," Asher said, lifting his arms to show the cuffs that were still locked in place around his wrists.

I paused and considered what he was asking me to do. I fully believed the story he'd told me earlier. And it was hard to deny that there was something strong between us. I even thought that he was telling me the truth that he'd never intended to hurt me. If Samuel hadn't forced Asher to deceive me, I don't think he would have.

But there *was* the pesky matter of his sister being held captive by our mutual enemy. If Asher was given the choice between saving her and fighting alongside me to defeat Samuel, I couldn't be sure what he'd do. And under the circumstances, could I really blame him for choosing her? She was his family, and we'd only known each other for a week.

Sister trumps potential girlfriend. At least in this case.

I also had to remind myself that the Cleri was *my* family and their safety had to be my first priority. Still, it was hard for me to completely ignore the fact that I'd finally found my perfect match. But if Asher was never given the ultimatum, maybe I could save all of us. Asher and his sister included. So I ran back to Asher, threw my arms around his neck, and gave him a long kiss that, had we not been in the middle of a war, would have definitely been the start of something hot.

When I pulled away, his eyes stayed closed for a few beats before he opened them and studied my face dreamily. I ran my hand down his cheek, noting the perfect softness of his skin. Kissing him once more, I pulled back and looked at him.

"I love you too, Asher," I said, hoping he knew it was true.

He smiled at me in that lopsided, love-struck kind of way. It almost made me feel bad. Slowly, I stood up and took a step away from him, watching as his smile dropped in confusion.

"I love you, but it's safer for us both if I don't let you go," I said apologetically. "I hope you understand, Asher, and if we get out of this thing alive and you still feel the same way, I hope we can both find a way to make it up to each other."

Then, before I could change my mind, I jumped through the hole in the shed and out into the darkness of the night.

• • •

I'd been too preoccupied with what had been going on in the shed to realize what had been going on just outside. Once I'd stepped out, though, I was taken aback by what I saw.

People were running around in states of panic. Some of my friends were being chased by our enemies, while others were doing the chasing. Sparks were flying. So were fists. For a moment I just stood there, unable to believe what I was seeing.

I'd known that things would get ugly when we finally came face-to-face with Samuel and his coven, but I wasn't ready for the chaos that surrounded me. People were crying out in anger and pain and fear—it was hard to tell the difference.

A zap of magic narrowly missed my face as it zinged past me and hit the wall to my left. Pulled back into the moment, I found myself running for the middle of the fight before I knew what I was doing. I didn't have time to think about whether it was smart or the right thing to do, I just ran, feeling strongly that I had to get in there.

I pushed my way through the crowd as I tried to get a handle on what was going on. It was hard to tell who needed help and who was holding their own, but I tried to assess the danger levels as I ran by.

I passed Jasmine first, recognizing right away that she had things under control. The girl who was trying to hit her with a spell was beginning to waver as Jazzy dodged every one of her commands with ease. There was a grin on my friend's face that I recognized—she knew what she was doing and the girl was no match for her. A few seconds later, Jasmine yelled out the words to the spell that she'd shown the rest of us, letting out a satisfied whoop as a hanging plant exploded and the pieces fell down on the Parrishable in front of her.

Our eyes locked for a moment, but then we were both moving again, ready to take on the next Parrishable to cross our paths. Spying a lone shovel lying on the lawn, I stepped onto the flat part and the handle found its way into my hand. I tossed it lightly in the air, feeling its sturdiness.

A guy began to rush at me, arms raised menacingly. I didn't flinch as I swung the shovel around and knocked him out. Two more guys followed him and I didn't slow my step as I stopped them, too. Walking through a gazebo my parents had built many years before, I lifted the shovel up and over my head until it rested between the beams and created a bar. Swinging off the ground, my body picked up speed and I kicked a wild-haired woman square in the stomach as she attempted to block my way. I flipped off the bar, landing with ease lightly on my feet, and then followed the woman as she stumbled backward and onto the ground.

I guess my time as a cheerleader had taught me more than just how to boost school spirit.

The woman was older than me, probably around my parents' age, and it didn't seem right to hit her like the others. So as she began to raise her hand to cast a spell, I shouted out a sleeping spell that left her snoring on the ground.

Stepping over her body, I kept on toward the back of the house. The noise around me was deafening, between the crashes, explosions, and shouts. Thank God I'd insisted the Cleri be briefed on hand-to-hand, because no way could we have handled another trip to the hospital.

My eyes found Peter as soon as I rounded the corner. He was the smallest person in the fight by far, but I no longer saw him as the most fragile. Peter had taken his time at the cabin seriously, and to my growing admiration I could see that he had a mean-looking muscle head cornered.

Just as Roid Rage was about to lunge, Pete hit him with a stunning spell. The force of it made the guy's body stiffen, and his eyes went wide with surprise. He hadn't been expecting the move from Pete, who at first glance might have seemed unimpressive. Fallon, who had been on his way over to help Pete, slowed down as he saw the spell go flying. I shook my head at him to let him know to back off. He did, and we both stood there to watch what the youngest member of our coven would do next.

Unable to move now, the Parrishable watched as Peter walked calmly over to him, stopping only when he was close enough to stare at him nose to nose. Then, without hesitating, Peter pulled back his arm and punched the kid in the mouth.

"Small guys have power, too," Peter said as a trickle of blood ran down the guy's face and dripped onto his shoes.

Having done what he'd intended, Pete turned around, noticing me and Fallon for the first time. Within seconds, he was back to his old self, and waved excitedly before giving us a lopsided grin. When all was said and done, he was still the same Peter.

The three of us hurried over to each other and surveyed the damage being done around us.

"We have to round everyone up. It's not good that we're all separated," I said, looking for as many of our coven members as I could. A quick glance showed that although many of us had been managing to stay on top of the fight, a few had clearly not been ready for battle. Rushing to Penelope, who was lying unconscious on the ground just feet from me, I picked her up and hoisted her over my shoulder, then slowly made my way to the porch.

Peter and Fallon were doing the same, picking up the fallen and dragging them back to what we'd deemed home base.

"Cleri! Fall back!" I screamed, hoping everyone would hear me above the clamor. There were already more of the

Parrishables on the property than I'd anticipated, and we hadn't managed to disarm as many as we'd planned, leading up to our pièce de résistance. There were still over two dozen men and women running around, attacking my people with magic and by physical brute force. We may still have been standing, but I knew that would change the longer we let them pick us off one by one.

It was time to band together and use the power of the coven to end this once and for all.

I threw spells into the crowd as our enemies attempted to follow us onto the back porch. When we were practicing with the spell book earlier, we'd managed to recharm the house so the Parrishables wouldn't be able to get inside, so we were able to leave our wounded in the kitchen and stand our ground in front of its doors.

As my coven gathered on the porch behind me, I began to see exactly what we were up against. The Parrishables were coming in waves now. Some were wounded and clearly angry about it, while others looked like they had several rounds still left in them. But the hate and fury was obvious and I wondered how it had gotten to that point. Why did a group of people dislike us so much that they'd want us dead? Was the promise of power really so enticing that people would be willing to do anything to get it?

That's when I realized just how much damage Samuel Parris had done over the years, not only to our coven but to his own members. It was the worst kind of brainwashing, and it had to stop. And the only way that would happen was if he was taken out.

"Is everyone here?" I asked loudly without looking behind me. For the time being, the Parrishables were standing their ground in front of us, not daring to move into our territory. I knew the spell we'd done on the house wouldn't last much longer, since it took all our concentration to keep it up and what we planned to do next would require our total attention. And not just from some of us. From *all* of us.

"Yeah," Fallon said, as I felt his presence suddenly at my side. Oddly, this was comforting.

Before I could give this more thought, a booming voice seemed to come out of nowhere and echo through the night.

"And so we meet at the end, finally ready to start a new beginning." Samuel Parris's words reverberated across the yard, and I watched as his eerie form appeared at the back of the crowd. His coven parted in the middle as he made his way slowly toward us, his black eyes boring into mine. My insides started to turn to Jell-O, but I continued to stand tall, placing my hands firmly on my hips, planting my feet slightly apart. No way was he ever going to know the kind of effect he had on me.

"What are you gibbering about?" Jasmine asked him, suddenly appearing on my other side, forming the third tip of a triangle with our bodies.

I silently willed her to keep quiet. Samuel's power was radiating from him and sending waves of aftershock our way. Pissing him off now wouldn't be a good idea. Not before we put our plan into action at least.

"You let your underlings speak on your behalf like that?" he responded, with the slightest hint of a challenge in his voice.

I had no choice but to answer, now that he was addressing me directly. "She doesn't really take kindly to being told what to do," I said without sarcasm.

"Yet you are her leader. You are the one that runs this coven. Letting your subordinates step out of line and forgetting that you are in charge is what will be your downfall."

"Really? In my world, I don't control anyone. It's called free will and I recognize that we all have it. If I were you, I'd worry about your *own* coven. I bet they're a bit sick of following you around by now. Better be careful or you may just get a spell in the back."

"They wouldn't dare turn against me," he said, brushing my comment off like it was ludicrous. "And if they did, I would put them in their graves."

As he said this, a few among him began to look around at the others uncomfortably.

"At least I know how to dispense with those who choose to disobey me," he said, lifting his finger warningly. We all turned to watch a figure float up from the side of the yard, arms overhead and legs dangling oddly as if broken. As the body moved into view, I nearly gasped.

There, being pulled through the air unconscious, was Asher. He was pale except for the welts and bruises that were all over his face and arms. I immediately wished I'd undone his cuffs and urged him to leave this place.

"It seems that poor Asher here made the wrong decision," he said.

And with that, he let Asher's body drop more than ten feet to the ground in front of him.

Chapter Twenty - Nine

"I thought that perhaps his loyalty toward his family would encourage him to do the right thing," Samuel said, looking straight at me. "But I should have known that dealing with children can prove difficult at times. Getting my own niece to make up that story about Bridget all those years ago was nearly impossible. I had to use an encouragement spell just to pull it off. Still, I would have thought it easier to make this boy deceive you. After all, there was no allegiance to your coven when I sent him to you."

Samuel gestured at Asher, who was still lying in a heap on the ground. I wanted to run over to him to make sure he was all right, but I knew the moment I stepped off that porch and away from the safety of the house, all hell was going to break loose. So I had to stay where I was. It was obvious by now that what Asher had said was true. He'd been forced into my life and had been pulled in two different directions. Either betray me or lose what was left of his family. I didn't envy his choices.

"It is true—the boy *was* a disappointment, but this one proved worthy." He pointed off to the side. Suddenly Emory was walking out of the shadows toward Samuel. She had a big grin on her face and strutted around like she'd just been announced the next Miss America. "She ended up surprising even me. Once given the proper encouragement, Emory went forth and made me proud. Oh, and to hear about her talks with you regarding your dearly departed . . . it was *inspired*. Come here, dear, and take a bow."

I gritted my teeth and ignored the fact that my head was telling me to destroy the double-crosser. What Samuel was saying was true. Her deception was far worse than anything Asher had done, simply because she and her family had been members of the Cleri for as long as I could remember. We'd grown up together, trained together, even had family dinners together. The fact that she'd willingly set her sights on destroying us? Well, that was disloyalty that couldn't be forgiven.

"Thank you, Reverend," Emory said, taking her place at his side. There was no sign of the innocent girl she'd been with the coven while she was under our roof. The smile on her face now was devilish, which matched her all-black ensemble. Guess the flowery Emory was gone for good. "It's an honor to serve you."

"Why?" I startled myself as the question escaped my lips before I could stop it. I didn't want to show that I even cared to hear the answer, but I knew it was what everyone else was wondering as well. And after all we'd been through, I felt we deserved a response. So I let the question linger in the cool night air.

Emory looked up at Samuel as if waiting for his approval. When he nodded, she turned back to me with a sneer. "Why?" she asked. "You seriously have to ask? Okay, how about this: The Cleri was a dead end, Hadley—emphasis on *dead*. There was all this power but no one was using it. We were encouraged by our elders to keep our magic hidden from the world, stifled. That's no way for a witch to live."

"They weren't telling us *not* to use our magic. They were trying to teach us the right ways to use it. We can't just use our powers for our own selfish reasons. It leads to chaos and disrupts the order of things. It's not our purpose, not our way of living," I said.

"And I think it's time to do things differently," Emory said. "I was sick of being weak. So when Reverend Parris came to our family and offered us more, I knew I had to do it. It was my destiny."

"It was your destiny to be a traitor? Because that's what you are. You betrayed your own coven, the ones who loved you. . . ."

"*Loved* me? Are you kidding me with this? Hadley, the only person you care about is yourself. I mean, why else would you come back here when you know that the only person we're after is you? Do you even care that you're going to get all of them killed?" Emory asked, narrowing her eyes at me. "Because that's what's going to happen. We will win and they will die. And it will be all your fault."

I looked around at the rest of my coven, feeling momentarily guilty over the fact that she was right. There was no guarantee that any of us would live through the night. And this wasn't a secret to the rest of my coven. In fact, I'd told them they could leave before the Parrishables caught up to us, and there would be no hard feelings. Yet, here they were. My eyes reached Fallon's and then Jasmine's and moved on to Sascha's and Peter's. I could see a resolution there that made me stand up straight again. Letting them make their own choices to stay, instead of running away and taking that decision away from them, was the difference between how I ran my coven and how Samuel ran his. With the Parrishables, no one had a choice. Samuel told them what to do and they did it. No questions, no free will.

In the Cleri, we all had freedom. And freedom is power.

"The Cleri are the bravest group of people I know. And they have more heart and determination than you ever could. Go ahead and do your worst," I answered, placing my hands on my hips. "I'm going to have so much fun destroying you."

The sound of applause rang through the backyard. My eyes flew back to Samuel, who was clapping enthusiastically. "Bravo! Good show! But might I point out that you chastise us for our desire for power, yet you have existed on these same principles yourself for so long? You have no qualms about doing whatever you can to get ahead, and you would roll over anyone to get what you want. My dear girl, you are no different than I. You thrive on the power you have over others. You get drunk on it. Nothing feels better than knowing you hold dominance over those around you. Just talking about it makes me shiver with excitement."

His body trembled slightly as he said it. The sight of this made me want to gag, but I swallowed back the bile and then took a step toward him, almost stepping off the deck as I did so. The motion made Samuel's eyebrows rise.

I cleared my throat. "I am *nothing* like you," I said to him, my voice strong and steady. "You *are* right about one thing, though. I *am* powerful. Possibly even more powerful than you. But I would never seek out that power at the expense of those around me. You see, Sammy, there's a reason you've never been able to vanquish our line completely. It's because our focus is always on the greater *good*. No one witch among us is more important than another, and it's in our working together that we've become stronger than any army you could summon. So I suggest you leave my house now or you'll learn exactly what it means to go to war."

As I finished, the air around me grew silent with tension. The Parrishables were giving each other sideways glances, and a few even dared to look back at Samuel for his command. The Cleri stood behind me and by my side; Peter had stepped up on the other side of Jasmine, creating a powerful lineup. Part of me hoped the Parrishables would back down and I wouldn't have to put any more of my coven at risk, but I knew this was just wishful thinking.

Finally, when the silence was starting to get uncomfortable, Samuel took one step toward me and said, "Then we fight."

As if he'd given a *Braveheart*-style battle cry, the whole crowd of Parrishables came running at us at once. Seeing that right in front of me was much more terrifying than anything I'd ever experienced before. They might not have been brandishing weapons, waving them overhead and threatening to cut our limbs, but the scene was actually much worse. Because instead of holding weapons, they *were* the weapons. And when your imagination was all that stood between you and your enemy, that left for a lot of possibilities.

Luckily, we'd prepared for this exact moment.

"Now!" I yelled out.

In perfect unison, all the Cleri who were still left joined hands, creating a band of twitches all linked together, and we said the spell we'd rehearsed earlier that day.

"Sluggashim deliberum!"

The moment it was out, everyone who'd been rushing toward us seconds before stopped in their places, as if frozen. I couldn't help but smile as I saw that the spell had worked, and we'd managed to buy ourselves a little more time to take care of the next phase in our plan.

"Okay, guys, we don't have long before this wears off. Do you have this?" I asked, turning my head to the left and then the right to look each of them in the eyes. I didn't want to leave them, but I knew I was the only one who could do this next part and I needed them to hold the Parrishables back until I could get in place to do the next spell.

"We're fine. Just go do what you have to do," Fallon said, a smile playing across his lips. "We've got this."

"You sure?"

"Piece of cake," he answered.

Torn between wanting to stick around to help and knowing that I needed to go if we were going to have any chance of winning this thing, I gave my coven one last reassuring look and then ran back into the house, leaving them outside without me.

It wouldn't be for long, though. I sprinted through the kitchen, narrowly missing the table as I passed, and then around the corner and up the stairs. Busting through the door to my parents' room, I stopped in front of the window and threw it open. Climbing out onto the roof, I looked down at the crowd gathered on my lawn, hoping to see that they were still where I'd left them. Sighing with relief because they were still in place, I carefully made my way across the shingles and came to a stop at the edge of the roof, directly behind my coven.

Now standing ten feet above everyone else, I had a better view of what we were up against. And it wasn't pretty. The Parrishables outnumbered us two to one and they mostly consisted of adult witches. Though age didn't matter much in terms of how powerful a witch was, it did mean they had more experience under their belts. My only hope was that after what I was about to do, the odds would no longer be against us. In fact, I was pretty much banking on it working because it was all we had.

As I prepared myself for what I was about to do, I saw that the freeze-frame spell the others were casting was beginning to weaken. Their hands were shaking now and some of the Parrishables were starting to move as if they were in slow motion and not just frozen anymore. I had to move quickly if I was going to get this done.

Closing my eyes, I put all my concentration into the spell I was about to do. Finding a calm within myself I hadn't tapped in to in a while, I began to say the words:

> *Blood is thick and it runs through our veins.*
> *Let the ties it binds give way to our brains.*
> *The power passed on from lineage down line*
> *Will now come through us; what is yours is now mine.*
> *Let life bring back what death took away.*
> *We call upon family to make evil pay.*

I could feel the power building up, beginning to burn inside me as I said the words. This spell had been the last one written in the family book—it was the one I'd witnessed Christian scribbling down in my dream. I hadn't thought much of it until after my dream with Bridget, when she'd mentioned that the whole family was there for me and that all I needed to do was ask for help.

The burning feeling inside me was growing, and I looked down at my hands, half expecting them to be on fire. Instead, Christian's ring—which I assumed had at one time been Bridget's—was glowing like when Christian had worn it in my dream. The power radiated through my body even more intensely than the last time I'd performed one of my ancestor's spells, and I wondered if I might actually explode. Luckily, the universe had different ideas.

Suddenly I felt the energy leaving my body in spurts. It came from my hands, my sides, my head; it was spilling out of me every which way. It didn't hurt. In fact, it felt good, as if I were letting go of a pressure that had been building up inside me for a long time. As I watched, the bursts of energy started turning into outlines of light, and the concentrations of light were taking on shape. Before my eyes, they began to look more and more human, clearly taking on hands and legs and heads. It was hard to make out their features at first, but as I continued to stare, even those became more prominent.

The last of the tendrils of light burst from my body, and the force was intense enough to throw me off balance, but just as I was teetering precariously toward the edge of the roof, something pulled me back and steadied me.

Looking behind me for the answer, I nearly yelped out in shock. There, standing close enough to touch, was my mom.

"Mommy?" I asked in a tiny voice, unable to believe what I was seeing.

It was her, that much I could tell, but she was sort of hazy around the edges, and staring at her kind of hurt my eyes, almost like I was staring at the sun.

"Hello, Hadley," she answered back, making me nearly choke with happiness. The sound of her voice awakened feelings that I'd been trying to get a handle on ever since she was taken from me. I wanted to cry, but knew there wasn't time for that. I could feel the magic below me wavering and I knew the Parrishables were about to be freed from our spell and pick up their pace.

"I miss you." Stupid, I know. Of all the things I could possibly say to her, *I miss you* was what came out.

"I miss you, too, baby," she said, leaning her head to the side sadly. "And I'm so proud of you."

I smiled as a tear slipped down my cheek. "I've been trying really hard to do what you asked me to," I said.

Now it was her turn to smile. "And you have. Now you must finish it."

"I don't know if we're strong enough," I answered, biting my lip.

"You're not," she said, "if you're alone. But with all of you together and with our help, we will send Samuel to the place where he belongs."

"Your help?" And then it was as if a lightbulb had gone off in my head. I looked down at the Cleri below and saw that now, standing beside each of them, were their parents. Not quite as they'd been before, but shining brighter and just a little bit blurry so their features weren't entirely clear. By this point, Fallon, Jasmine, Sascha, Peter, and the others were barely holding on to the freezing spell and had turned most of their focus to the ones they'd thought were gone forever. They seemed as surprised to see their parents as I was, but no one moved from their spots.

Out of everything in the book, we'd chosen this particular spell as our last defense against the Parrishables because it was meant to invoke the power of our ancestors. Allow them to work their magic through us, so we could be a force much bigger than we actually were. There was nothing in the spell book that had said we'd actually be visited by our family members. That they would appear to us in person. This was a surprise.

Since we were all focusing on the spell to invoke our ancestors and their power, the magic we'd been doing to keep the Parrishables at bay began to dissipate, and as a group, the Parrishables began to gain use of their limbs again. But as soon as they saw the glowing outlines of the Cleri on the porch, they slowed to a stop on their own, confusion on their faces. Then their eyes moved up to the roof, where I was perched. They began to point in surprise and talk in hushed whispers as their gazes fell just behind me. I hesitantly looked back and saw that my mom and I had been joined by dozens of other figures. Each was radiating light and there was a wide range of time periods of dress. And then I recognized two faces.

Bridget and Christian.

"We're all here for you, honey," my mom said, as if reading my mind. Maybe she had. It didn't matter. What *did* matter was that every one of my relatives was standing behind me, ready to take down the enemy that had plagued us for centuries.

My mom reached out her hand and I took it, and then I let Bridget take my other hand. The current of electricity that flowed through our bodies was severe, but this time I knew what to do with it.

The Cleri members below me were all doing the same thing, and the gesture seemed to be intimidating the Parrishables. As I watched, they began to take steps backward, their interest in attacking us waning. Samuel's face had gone from smug to angry as soon as he'd seen who'd joined our fight.

"No!" he screamed, losing his composure for the first time since I'd met him. "I killed you! I killed all of you!"

"Haven't you ever heard of things coming back to bite you in the—" I began to ask. Only, I'd barely gotten the sentence out of my mouth before Samuel was hurling a spell my way.

"Hadley!"

Just as I was bracing myself for the blast of Samuel's spell, a figure threw itself out in front of me, taking the hit instead.

"Do it now." Bridget's words found their way to my ear and I knew I had to listen to her.

"Exterminus departo!" I screamed as loudly as I could, feeling the power rush through me and head straight for Samuel.

The spell hit him square in the chest and there was an explosion that looked like a pile of fireworks going off. Sparks rained down on us and left the air filled with smoke. Wait, not smoke. I reached my hand out to see what it was.

Ash.

I shuddered to think what that meant, but forced myself to look through the haze to see if it was possible. Could it really be over? Struggling to see through the dirty air, I realized it was true. Samuel was gone and there was a blackened spot on the ground where he'd been standing.

As the Parrishables began to come to the same realization, they started to back out of the yard, rushing to get as far away from us as possible. I thought about sending a few stunning spells their way but decided it would be wrong to hit them when they were retreating. Instead, I turned to my mom to exclaim over what had just happened.

But she was gone.

Looking around frantically, I saw that they were all gone. Vanishing at the same moment that Samuel had, it seemed. I was alone again, with no one left to watch after me.

Except that I wasn't. Because there was someone still lying at my feet. Someone who had jumped in front of me in order to save me from being hit with Samuel's spell.

And that someone was Asher.

Chapter Thirty

It took Sascha over twenty minutes to pump magical energy back into Asher after he'd been depleted of it by Samuel's spell. Luckily, it turned out that the magic had only grazed Asher's shoulder, and he hadn't received the full force of the hex. We guessed this was the only reason he wasn't dead right now. Once I'd seen that the Parrishables were leaving as quickly as they could, I had knelt down next to Asher and found that he wasn't breathing and performed CPR on him until the others could reach us.

Jasmine said that I was yelling the whole time, screaming for Asher to "wake the hell up!" Her words, not mine. I can't actually remember what I said out loud, but I know that in my head, I was pleading for the universe to give me more time with him. The thought of losing another person I cared about was too much to bear, and I knew that with the fight over, I'd have more time than I wanted to process all the loss I'd been through lately.

But as I watched, Sascha brought Asher back. I couldn't see anything physically happening, of course, since the magic was all internal, but his cheeks started to gain a little color and finally he opened his eyes and stared straight into mine.

"Did I ever tell you that you're *drop-dead* gorgeous?" were the first words out of his mouth. Then he flashed me that sideways smile of his and I nearly jumped him with joy.

But I restrained myself and rolled my eyes instead. "Boy, do you know how to sweet-talk a girl," I said sarcastically, but took his hand in mine. We both knew what the other had done. That we'd chosen to help our families over each other, but we also knew it was the right thing to do. Now the plan was to make him a part of that family by welcoming him and his sister into the Cleri as official members.

Not that this news went over well with everyone in the coven. True to form, Fallon complained for hours about it, threatening to leave if we invited traitors into the group. But then Asher showed Fallon a few spells in private, ones that they refused divulge to me, and suddenly Fallon was Asher's biggest fan. He began to follow Asher around like his minions did him, and I realized how much he was probably missing his dad. Not that his dad was unusually powerful, but he and Fallon had had a really great relationship. Now that Asher was the oldest male witch in our coven, Fallon seemed to need someone to look up to. And Asher was happy to oblige now that the immediate threat against his sister was gone.

Speaking of, we'd found Asher's sister, Abby, wandering around in the woods behind the cabin after having been abandoned by one of the Parrishables in his haste to flee. She'd barely said ten words to me. In all fairness, she hadn't said much to Asher either, but according to him, she was always on the quiet side. I could only imagine how being kidnapped and held by a magical lunatic who killed your parents would cause you to retreat even further into yourself. In fact, I admired her for even being able to function after all she'd been through.

Still, I hoped Abby would eventually let down her guard and take the time to get to know me. From what Asher said about her, I think we'd really get along. Things were likely to get better once there was a little distance between us and what had happened with the Parrishables.

There was no concrete evidence to show that Samuel and his coven were gone for good, of course, but we all believed that he was gone for now. The threat of war was over and we could go back to our regularly scheduled lives. Whatever that meant.

Most likely, the bulk of us would be sent to live with relatives—aunts, grandparents, family friends, not all of which were magically inclined—who would all happily take us in. I was nearly eighteen and figured I could probably duck the authorities until I was able to take care of myself. And with Asher and his sister right down the block, it wasn't like I was going to be alone. I could finish up my last year of high school, maybe apply for colleges, cheer. All my plans from before were sort of up in the air considering what I'd been through. The way I looked at the world was different now. I was going to need to do some serious soul searching now that I didn't have to look over my shoulder anymore.

"What's the first thing you're going to do when you get home?" Asher asked me on our drive back from the cabin.

"Take a bath, sleep for about a year, and then go to cheer practice," I said, not even having to think about my answer before saying it.

"You'd rather hang out with a bunch of cheerleaders than spend time with me?" he asked, in mock shock. Then he thought about it and shook his head. "Never mind. I'd choose cheerleaders over me too."

"Har-har," I said as we pulled into the driveway. Just being in close proximity to my house made my heart both quicken and ache at the same time. It was so weird to be back after all that had happened and doubly weird to come back to an empty house. The only thing that was different, though, was that I no longer felt *alone*. I'd talked to my mom in my dreams and then with the spell . . . well, just knowing it was possible to still be able to communicate was enough to make it all more bearable. Now I was just going to have to create a new normal.

I went to put my key in the door but paused when I noticed that it was already slightly open. Not much, just a crack. I looked back over my shoulder. Asher had already started to follow his sister as she walked over to their aunt's house, but he slowed down and called out to me.

"Everything okay?"

I listened for a noise that would alert me to someone being inside. But there was only silence. I let out the breath I'd been holding and told myself that not every weird thing that happened meant I was still being stalked by Samuel. In fact, the last time I'd been home, I'd left pretty abruptly and hadn't exactly stopped to lock up. The whole damn place was probably unlocked.

"Yeah. It's nothing," I said, my initial fear subsiding. "I'll see you in a few hours?"

"It takes you that long to destinkify yourself?" he asked, walking back toward his aunt's.

"Well, isn't that the pot calling the kettle smelly?" I answered, pushing the door open.

"Ha!" he said. "I'll see you soon."

"You too," I said, walking into my house.

A look around the living room showed that nothing had changed since the attack the night of the football game. The place looked like a tornado had swept through it, upturning furniture, breaking lamps and vases, and collapsing tables and chairs. Black char marks covered the walls, while mud and dirt appeared to be permanently etched into the carpet. I stood just inside the door for a minute and replayed the events of that night in my head, still amazed I'd gotten out of there alive.

If things had gone just a little bit differently, the house would be completely empty right now. The thought filled me with sadness and I trudged the rest of the way inside, kicking the door closed as I went.

Part of me knew that it was just a matter of time before I broke down, but in the meantime I was too exhausted to care. Dropping my bags in the entryway, I headed upstairs to take a bath and then lie down for a much-needed nap. At this point, though, I couldn't be positive I wouldn't just crash right away. Sleep sounded *very* good at the moment.

Arriving at the door to my bedroom, I pushed it open, longing to crawl under my covers and disappear for a while. But when I looked inside, I froze.

There, standing across the room and staring out the window, was a man. His back was to me, but I could tell he was strong and tall—both traits I wasn't so psyched to see in an intruder. He didn't turn around right away, even though I was sure he'd heard me. I resisted the urge to scream or run; I was too tired to fight anymore. Giving up, I surrendered to the fates and waited for him to make a move.

"I'm so sorry," he said.

Confusion washed over me as I recognized the man's voice. It couldn't be . . . could it?

Suddenly I was running toward him and before I could

think about what I was doing, I flung my arms around his body and hugged him as tightly as I could. I squeezed so hard I thought my arms might break and let loose the tears that had been building up for weeks now. As he turned around to face me, I collapsed, allowing him to catch me as I fell. Slipping to the floor, he held me in his arms and stroked my hair while shushing me quietly.

When I'd stopped sobbing, I dared to look up at him, fearing that I would find he'd disappeared. But he was still there, and that got me crying all over again. Finally I dried my eyes with the back of my hand, sniffled, and managed a wobbly smile.

"They ambushed me on my way to the hotel and took everything I had. I was told you and Mom were dead. They said there was nothing to come back to. Then they tried to get me to join the Parrishables. When I refused, they tried to kill me, too. Eventually I got away and headed straight here. I had to see if they'd been telling the truth. And then I saw the house," he said, his head dropping to touch the top of mine. Then, more quietly, he added, "I got your note. I'm so sorry I couldn't get to you sooner, Had."

"It's okay, Dad. You're here now," I said, cradling my head against his neck, enjoying the realness of the touch.

"Tell me what happened."

"Where do I start?" I asked absently, truly unsure how to describe all that had happened since he'd left.

"Why don't you start at the beginning."

Epilogue

I ran through the night as quickly as I could, branches hitting my face and arms as I raced against the clock. The crackle of something being broken put me on edge. I couldn't tell whether the noise was coming from me or something else lurking in the darkness. Either way, I wasn't scared. I'd learned by now that things that go bump in the night are nothing compared to real evil. And real evil? Well, I'd vanquished it.

For now.

I squinted and fought to see as I dodged trees while making my way to my destination. I knew that if I slowed down, even just a little bit, I wasn't going to make it there in time. And that wouldn't be good.

"Come on, come on," I whispered, propelling myself forward, trying to see what lay ahead.

When I caught sight of a glow of light in the near distance, I slowed my pace and chose my steps carefully, so they wouldn't hear me coming. Sneaking closer, I peered through a few branches into the clearing.

There they were. Six bodies, gathered around a roaring fire, with their heads covered by hoods. The light cast shadows around the clearing, making it look like the whole place was teeming with spirits. They were talking in low voices now, and I strained to hear what they were saying, almost expecting the worst.

As time passed I knew I had to act, so without hesitation I burst through the bushes, landing in a fighting stance just a few feet away from the group. Several of the figures jumped, turning around quickly to stare at me in surprise, while the others just looked on with murderous expressions as they tried to decide out what to do next.

"Okay, Had. The whole jumping-out-and-scaring-us thing was fun the first hundred times, but now it's just getting old," Jasmine said, crossing her arms over her chest. "You're lucky I haven't hit you with a stunning spell yet. And trust me, it wouldn't be pretty."

"Oh, come on, guys!" I said, standing up straight and placing my hands on my hips. "I'm only doing this for your own good. You need to be ready at all times. I'm just preparing you. . . ."

"Preparing us for what?" Fallon asked, pulling off his hood and leaning back until he was resting on his elbows. He seemed annoyed—which was no different from any other day really, except that ever since we'd fought the Parrishables, I'd felt as if we'd gotten past our differences, or at least taken a break from torturing each other. "Samuel's gone. You blasted him like a bug zapper, remember? He's toast. Extra crispy."

"We *think* he's gone," I said. "We don't know for sure. That's why we have to continue to meet. To keep watch in case he comes back."

I looked around the circle until I spotted Asher and flashed him a smile. He smiled back, patting the ground next to him. As I began closing the distance between us, my stomach filled with butterflies just like it always did when his eyes met mine. I loved that even though we'd been dating for about six months now, I still got excited every time I saw him.

Once I reached him, I sat down and his hand found its way into mine. I looked down at our intertwined fingers and felt my skin grow warm. It might have been the heat coming from the fire, but I doubted it.

"Hey," he said.

"Hey," I responded, a shy smile on my face.

"Do you really think he's going to come back?" Jinx asked nervously, breaking up our little moment. I forced my head to turn and focus on her.

Jinx had been released from the hospital a few weeks after we'd gotten rid of the Parrishables, but I quickly learned it was going to take her a lot longer to fully heal. When she mentioned Samuel and the Parrishables, she unconsciously touched her hand to the spot on her abdomen where she'd been stitched up. I was sure this wasn't a coincidence. Jinx may have physically healed already, but we all knew she was having a hard time dealing with the aftermath of our war. I felt badly for her, but that was sort of why I'd been insisting on us all meeting on a regular basis anyhow.

"I don't know, Jinx," I said softly. "I hope not. But that's why we're doing all of this. To make sure he never comes back. And that if he does, we'll be ready for him."

Everyone grew silent, my words hanging in the air as we thought about all the things we didn't want to actually say out loud. Finally, Sascha cleared her throat.

"Hey, at least this time you get to do magic with us," she

said, shrugging. "You sort of missed it all the first time around, you know?"

"Tell me about it," Jinx said slowly. "I can't believe I didn't get to see everyone. That must have been crazy cool."

I smiled as I thought back to the moment when I laid eyes on all our relatives standing behind us as we vanquished Samuel. The scene was pretty epic and I didn't want to admit it to Jinx, but I hadn't been able to get it out of my mind since.

"You're not the only one who missed it," Asher reminded her, a hint of jealousy in his voice. Asher still didn't remember much of anything that happened after the shed blew to bits that night. I think it had something to do with him taking the hit from Samuel—the blast must have scrambled his brain or something. Good thing, too, because almost dying could be a pretty traumatic experience.

"That's just because someone was busy being a hero and all," I said, leaning over and kissing him on the cheek in front of everyone. His scowl turned into a goofy grin and he leaned into me so our shoulders were touching. I caught Fallon rolling his eyes but ignored him.

The truth was, things between Asher and me had been amazing since everything had been brought out into the open. We'd fallen into the habit of spending most of our free time together, which was nice since we were still getting to know each other in a way. I'd begun to forgive him for lying to me, and he chose to ignore the fact that I'd left him locked up when Samuel attacked. Now that we were finally being honest with each other, our relationship was really starting to get good.

"That's sweet—and I'm bored," Jasmine said abruptly. "Can we talk about the fact that our families are trying to send us away for the summer? Has anyone else figured out where they're carting us off to?"

"No clue," Sascha answered as she inspected her nails. "But I highly doubt it's model boot camp like I requested. I've wanted to go there for years, you know? I was born to be on the catwalk."

"Catwalk, streetwalk, all the same if you ask me," Jasmine muttered, before flashing Sascha a grin to show she was just joking.

"You're hil-a-rious. Glad to see your humor wasn't beaten out of you during the fight."

"Nope. Still intact," Jasmine said, grinning deviously.

"My dad still won't talk," I interrupted, in an attempt to stop the bickering. "But since school just ended, I figure they've gotta tell us soon. And as long as we're all headed to the same place, we'll be fine."

When we'd arrived back home after the fight with Samuel, our group had been broken up for the first time in weeks. Some of us had family members or friends of our parents come to stay with us while we looked for more permanent places to stay, while others, like Peter, had been sent to live with nearby relatives. Not everyone went to live with a magicking family— but the civilians were close enough relatives that they could be trusted with our secret. Regardless, we were all still adjusting to our new living situations, but we always felt safer when we were together. Defeating an evil coven will do that to you.

But then about two weeks ago, the adults started hinting that they were sending us away for the summer, information most of us weren't too excited about. Besides the fact that it had taken so long for life to get back to normal, we'd grown rather resistant to surprises. I wonder why. At least it appeared like we'd be going away together. We just had no idea where or what we'd be doing. I, for one, hoped that wherever it was, there was electricity. I was not the kind of girl who liked to rough it.

"I can't believe you're all leaving and I have to stay here and go to summer school," Peter said, whining.

"It's not our fault you're not as quick as the rest of us," Fallon said snarkily. I frowned. It was true: Pete had been the only one of us who hadn't been able to get back on track once we'd eventually gone back to school. As time had wound down, his teachers decided he would be better off taking his classes over again than receiving such low grades for the year. His aunt and uncle had agreed and signed him up for the summer. Still, that was no reason to make fun of him.

"Can it, Fallon," I warned. Turning back to Peter, I gave him a sympathetic look. "Pete, I'm sure you'll have more fun here than wherever we're going."

"Yeah, right," he muttered miserably.

"Everything's going to be fine," I said, trying to convince both of us of this fact. I looked down at my cell phone to check the time. "It's getting late, why don't we start this thing?"

Everyone slowly got up from their places on the ground and stood together in a circle. I could tell a few of them were tired or possibly even bored. Then again, we'd been doing the same thing every week since we'd gotten back to town. We'd meet up late at night when the adults thought we were tucked away in bed, and that's when we'd do it.

From location spells to binding spells to ill-intention-detecting spells, we'd cast just about anything that might tell us that Samuel was alive. But so far, we'd come up empty. That didn't mean we were going to stop, though. No way was I letting anything sneak up on us again. Nope, next time we'd be ready—no matter what the evil was.

"Okay, gather hands and cast with me," I said, looking around at my coven members with a hint of magic in my eyes before starting the first incantation.

Acknowledgments

What started out as an experiment of sorts became the beginning of my dream come true. And so many people had a hand in making Life's a Witch the phenomenon it is today. Here's my attempt to say thank you to as many of you as possible:

To my lovely publishers, Simon & Schuster: you have completely changed my life. I can't think of a better publisher to help me create the Life's a Witch empire. Thank you. Alexandra Cooper, you're the Yoda to my Skywalker, the Miyagi to my Daniel-Son, the Dumbledore to my Harry Potter. You saw the potential in me and this story, and have helped make me a much better writer. Thank you so much for sharing your wisdom, creativity, and excellence with me. Justin Chanda, you remind me of Joss Whedon—which is the highest compliment I could pay a person, considering how intelligent, imaginative, and utterly amazing he is. Just like you! Bernadette Cruz, you rock my marketing world . . . thanks for all of your hard work and great ideas! Paul Crichton, publicist extraordinaire—you have the gift of spreading the word. Let's set the media world on fire! Lucy Cummins, you've created three absolutely spellacious covers, complete with magic, fabulosity, and fun! The lovely Amy Rosenbaum . . . besides being adorable, you brighten every visit to the office and feed my need for a good read. You're also the true queen of puns. And Siena Koncsol. You are my soul-sister. There's no one else I'd want to head into an apocalypse with, fight beside in the upcoming zombie war (you know it's coming), and sit next to in the dark as we watch scary things go bump in the night. We should totally be superheroes together. Everyone else at S&S who has contributed their talents and hard work to bringing this book to life: Thank you, all!

Behind every great author is an even more amazing team. Thanks so much to mine: Kevan Lyon, you are by far the greatest literary agent in the history of the world. Seriously. No one compares. Thanks for taking a chance on an unknown writer. Taryn Fagerness, I have so much gratitude that you've brought my books to Italy, Catalan, Spain, Brazil, and Romania. Next: the world! And the überfabulous Brandy Rivers . . . you're a total superstar to me and should have your own reality show. I can't wait to conquer Hollywood with you!

So many have believed in me and helped me to get LAW to where it is today. None of that would've happened without the generous help of Wattpad and its staff. You have been there with me every step of the way and have created a platform that makes dreams come true. And without all my twitches on the site who fell in love with Hadley and her crew, this story would still be unknown. My fans are simply the BEST and I love you ALL! Calvin Reid, you continue to be a driving force in my rise to success. Thank you for being one of the first to see something special in me. And lots of love to all the book bloggers out there who've helped get the word out about the LAW series. I'm so proud to be a part of your reading lives.

To all of those out there who are continuing to tell amazing stories, and inspire me on a daily basis to create bigger and better and more complicated characters. You are amazeballs: Joss Whedon, Ryan Murphy, Meg Cabot, Tina Fey, Ellen DeGeneres, Tori Spelling, and Judd Apatow. Thank you for letting me into your worlds.

And of course, I couldn't survive without my own "coven": Tammy West, I'll never again make the mistake of lumping you in with others . . . you're the inspiration for every sassy thing said in this book; Amanda Healy, you keep me calm when my life feels like chaos; Kate Chapman, you're always there for me and the first to cheer me on; Mary Eustace, you were the first person to read *WTS*, thanks for your encouragement and love; Darcey West, you're better than a publicist and such a great friend; Rebecca Schuman, you never told me I couldn't achieve this impossible dream; Jessica Grant, you might be the only one who fully understands the rejection and strength it takes to go on this journey—keep at it; Marisa Walker, my first six books wouldn't have been readable without your editing, guidance, and friendship; Morgan McMurrin, you are a bright, shining light on every dark day; Jessica Pribush, your support has never wavered; Courtney McCabe, there's no one more passionate about life and love; Stephanie Perricone, you're SO the president of my fan club; Toni Misthos, you are the reason people picked up my first six books in the first place; Sue Chouinard, thanks for always welcoming me into your family; Alicia Chouinard, you are the original Hadley and my biggest cheerleader; Denise Cummings and Pip's Place, thanks for plying me with gluten-free fuel so that I could write for *hours* every day.

My family, new and always—you're the ones who are there for me through every up and every down. Without your love and support, I wouldn't be where I am today. Mom, you're my rock, my best friend, and my biggest fan. Couldn't have done this without you. Dad, thanks for letting me pave the way and never telling me to dream smaller. Jacey, I wish I were half as cool as you are. Amy, you're one of the most determined people I know. Cody and Cash, you both rock my world. Andrea, Price, Katy, and Ryan, you've given me another family that loves me unconditionally and will always be there to cheer me on. Thank you for allowing me to be a Gielen.

ACKNOWLEDGMENTS

To The Powers That Be, I get now that I've just got to let things happen the way that they're supposed to. Your plan is much bigger—and so much better—than mine ever was. Thanks for letting me tell your stories.

Lastly, to my husband, Matty. Thank you for indulging in my grand ideas and for encouraging me to let my mind run wild. You're the funniest, smartest, and most driven person I know and I couldn't ask for a better guy to take over the world with. I love you like a kid with celiac disease loves gluten-free cake. (And that's a lot!)